GW00391334

The Lovers and the Loved

The Lovers
and the Loved

HARRIET CRAWLEY

HEINEMANN : LONDON

William Heinemann Ltd
Michelin House, 81 Fulham Road, London SW3 6RB
LONDON   MELBOURNE   AUCKLAND

First published 1990
Copyright © Harriet Crawley 1990

The lines of 'The Love Song of J. Alfred Prufrock' on page 110
are from *Collected Poems 1909–1962* by T. S. Eliot
and are published by permission of Faber and Faber Ltd

A CIP catalogue record for this book
is available from the British Library
ISBN 0 434 14322 7

Phototypeset by Input Typesetting Ltd, London

Printed and bound in Great Britain by
Mackays Plc, Chatham

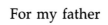

For my father

1 They were waiting: a newspaper photographer and a reporter on the doorstep of No. 10 Buckingham Row.

They were impatient, bored, and above all hot. A heatwave gripped the city, and along this typical London street of neat white houses the window panes hurled into the air the lurid reflection of a summer sun. Eleanor and Dominic noticed the two strangers and stopped.

'Vultures,' Dominic said. 'I shall frighten them away with my stick.'

He looked an extraordinary sight on this blazing day of July in his three-piece suit with his walking cane and his twenty-five-year-old face.

'No, no, it was bound to happen,' Eleanor said, and gripped the hand of her two-year-old son, who was pointing at a bird in the sky.

'We could go back to the park,' Dominic said, staring at the tourists who had gathered outside the railings of Buckingham Palace, and beyond to the soft green willows weeping into the ponds of St James's Park.

'I don't want to walk any more,' Eleanor said.

'But I won't have them pestering you. I won't!'

'They'll only come again – oh, Dominic, I don't care. I really don't. It's time for tea, isn't it, Orlando? Yes, my darling boy, it's time for tea . . .'

Orlando was talking to a dachshund as it fouled the pavement.

'All right then,' Dominic said, 'home it is!' and he stepped out swinging his cane. Immediately, they were spotted.

'Quick,' said the woman reporter, and the photographer, a middle-aged man, pressed the camera to his face and frantically took pictures. The woman stepped forward, a notebook and a pencil in her hand.

'Miss Wynn, we are from the *Sun*,' she said.

'Uninvited,' said Dominic.

The woman put her hand on Eleanor's arm.

'Assault,' Dominic warned.

'I only want to ask a few questions.'

'Yes?' said Eleanor.

'Miss Wynn, you were commissioned to paint a portrait of the Queen.'

'Indeed,' Dominic said.

'Miss Wynn, we understand the commission has been cancelled.'

'Rubbish! I am Dominic le Jeune – Miss Wynn's agent – '

'Painters don't have agents,' the reporter interrupted.

'My dear woman, I am in the Yellow Pages, under "AA", after Alcoholics Anonymous and before the Automobile Association. I am entirely responsible for the creation of a new profession. It is not the least of my achievements. Dear me, how exhausting. Where was I? Yes, now . . . as I was saying, I am Miss Wynn's agent and – yes, you may quote me – no one has ever cancelled a commission. People everywhere want to be painted by Miss Wynn. There is a queue a mile long.' Dominic threw out his arm and involuntarily the photographer followed the gesture and found himself staring down an empty street.

'So the painting is going ahead?' the reporter asked drily.

'As soon as – ' Eleanor began.

'As soon as what?'

'As soon as I've had my baby.'

'Your second illegitimate child,' the reporter said sourly.

'I believe the word "illegitimate" has been removed from English common law,' Eleanor replied.

'Tea-time, tea-time,' Orlando chanted.

'Yes, I know, my darling, you're hungry,' Eleanor said. 'Dominic, be an angel and take Orlando inside.'

Dominic hesitated. Then he gave the intruders his most disdainful look and took the child by the hand, saying, 'Come, infant.' They disappeared into the house.

'Miss Wynn, you didn't name the father of your first child.'

'No, I didn't.'

'Why not?'

'There was no need. It wasn't important.'

'To the child?'

'He'll know when the time comes.'

'It's commonly assumed – '

'Always a mistake,' Eleanor said softly.

'It's commonly assumed the father is Edward Verney.'

'Really?'

The woman reporter waited. Eleanor said nothing.

'I see, I see,' said the woman. 'Well, this time you have not been so discreet. This time,' and she nodded at Eleanor's large stomach, 'we know the father. It's Vincent Buonarotti.'

'You don't know anything.'

Eleanor smiled at the reporter, who waited and then, angry that she had not provoked a reaction, blurted out: 'Alexei Kinski!'

'Yes?'

'Ah ha!' said the woman, writing furiously. 'So you admit it!'

'Admit what?'

'That it's Alexei Kinski – that he's the father!'

'He will be surprised.'

The woman stopped writing. 'Do you deny it then?'

'Of course I deny it. It isn't true.'

The woman tightened her lips. 'Miss Wynn, why are you doing this? What have you got to hide? Are you protecting someone . . . or . . . are you ashamed?'

'Ashamed?' Eleanor said sharply. 'Did you say ashamed?'

Unnerved, the woman looked down at her notebook.

'I have one last question,' she said. 'Do you have any plans to marry?'

'No.'

'None?'

'None.'

The woman closed her notebook. 'Miss Wynn, are you setting an example for the modern woman?'

'I'm not setting an example for anyone. I'm trying to live my life, that's all. Now, if you'll excuse me, I must go and get tea for my son.'

Eleanor went into the house and closed the door. The journalist and the photographer lingered for a moment on the doorstep, then set off down the street.

'Well,' the photographer said, 'I got the picture all right. Her talking to the little lad, side view, so you can see her condition.

3

I mean, it's obvious there's a bun in the oven. I only hope the picture editor is satisfied. Crusty old bugger.'

'It doesn't make any sense,' the woman said.

'I think it's him. The agent. *He's* the father.'

'Don't be so stupid, Larry!'

'What do you mean?'

'Haven't you got eyes in your head? That man is gay.'

'Really? Do you think so? He seemed a nice sort of bloke.'

'It doesn't make sense. She's a beautiful woman – she could marry anyone.'

'Lovely hair,' said the photographer. 'I always look at a woman's hair.'

They walked on in silence. Then suddenly the woman reporter stopped in her tracks and, talking to no one in particular, said, 'What does she think she's doing?'

Later Eleanor stood in her studio by an open window and considered the violent colours of the evening sky: vermilion and cadmium red and French ultramarine and cobalt violet mixed together in hectic streaks. Orlando was asleep in his cot at the foot of the unmade bed. The studio smelt as it always did of paint and white spirit. This was her sanctuary, her home. Canvases large and small leant unevenly against the walls; newspapers and books stood on the floor in disorderly piles, and on every table and chair were scattered unfinished sketches, catalogues, electricity bills and dry cleaning tickets. In the centre of the room, on an easel, stood the painting of the moment: a few bold strokes, the outline of a face, and an eye looking out at the world with caution.

Eleanor leant out of the window; black birds swept across the darkening sky. 'Where are you, Vincent?' she said to the first pale stars. 'In the opera, at the back of the auditorium, listening to a new production, shaking your head at the conductor because he is going too fast? And Edward, where are you? In Peking at a theatre, or eating soft-shell crabs in Shanghai? Or standing on the Great Wall, staring at the barren mountains of Mongolia, feeling the sharp wind prick your face?'

Alexei would be reading; Alexei was always reading or getting drunk.

Eleanor closed the window. There had been choices. It could have been otherwise.

It all began with a birthday, four years ago.

2 'Wake up! It's twelve o'clock!'
'Go away.'

Eleanor pulled the bedcovers over her head. At the foot of the bed stood Dominic, a dark silhouette against the bright sunlight which flooded the studio.

Undeterred he went on, 'Have you forgotten? It's your birthday! Look! I've brought the champagne. We must celebrate!'

'There's nothing to celebrate. Go away, Dominic. I feel ill.'

'You don't feel ill. You feel old. It's a common complaint among the middle-aged.'

Eleanor sat up.

'I am *not* middle-aged!' she protested, and then, after a moment's thought she threw herself back against the pillows. 'Oh, perhaps I am. Perhaps that is the whole problem!'

'How old are you?'

'Don't ask.'

'No . . . no, I'm interested.'

'I'm thirty-six. I can remember when I was six. I had a doll called Martha. I used to tell Martha everything. She was my friend. She and I made so many plans together . . . I was so full of hope. I can remember exactly how I felt. I can! I swear it! When I was six years old I had a vision of life that was so glowing and so glorious!'

Dominic, who was not listening, said, 'I'm twenty-one, but of course I don't look it. I pass for seventeen . . . that's what I was told the other day. It's a disadvantage to look so absurdly young. People are reluctant to do business with a boy.'

'I don't want to hear about your eternal youth. Go away!'

Dominic stood in that arrogant, elegant way of his, his head thrown back, his hair redder than ever in the shifting beams of midday sun which poured through the studio skylight. His pale skin was peppered with freckles and his flame-coloured hair was shoulder length and tied at the back with a black velvet bow. He wore his usual extravagant clothes: voluminous

6

Turkish trousers and a raw silk Indian shirt with a jewel at the neck. In his right hand he swung a black and gold cane.

Eleanor got out of bed, wrapped herself in a green silk dressing gown and took her mass of dark hair and pinned it to her head with a comb. She stretched out on her favourite piece of furniture, a battered chaise-longue in faded red velvet, and said, 'It's all right for you, Dominic. You're young. All life is ahead of you. There's plenty of time for . . . everything! But for me it's different. I am thirty-six. Time is running out.'

'Running out for what?'

'For children! I must have children!' She said the words with a frantic fierceness. 'I only have a few more childbearing years left. I think about it all the time. Waves of terror sweep over me – it's terrible! You have no idea! I can't work, I can't sleep. The other day I was walking down a street and I stopped – I couldn't take another step. I was frozen in . . . in . . . panic!'

Dominic, who had been uncorking the champagne, looked at Eleanor with disdain.

'I've read about this. It's hormonal. This crude urge to breed has something to do with a genetic imbalance. It will pass,' he said.

'It won't pass. It's with me day and night. And you want me to celebrate another birthday. Why should I? What's ahead? One more year of my life that will be just the same – no different from the last – and at the end of it I will be just as I am now – alone and childless . . .'

Dominic handed Eleanor a glass of champagne. She took it but was too distressed to drink.

'I can't go on like this,' she said.

'I don't see why not.'

'I wish I could make you understand,' Eleanor said urgently. She hesitated and then, in a quiet, tense tone, she said, 'I am so *alone*.'

'You are *not* alone,' Dominic replied scornfully. 'You are only alone in your mind.'

'That's it. I am alone in my mind and I don't like it.'

'This is bourgeois nonsense. There are millions of women who get married and have children because they are not fit for anything else. You are not one of them. You are a painter. That is your life. I drink to you, Eleanor Wynn, the artist!' He threw back his head and drained the glass, and immediately poured himself another. 'And now I shall drink to myself. I discovered you. I made you what you are!'

'You did,' Eleanor agreed. 'You changed my life.'

He came out of nowhere, this extraordinary young man with carrot-red hair and dimples and blackbird-like eyes which darted from one object to another. Eleanor, who earned her living teaching at the Camberwell School of Art, had placed an advertisement in the local newspaper for a lodger and Dominic was the first to reply. He did not bother to telephone; instead he appeared on her doorstop and introduced himself with a slight bow.

'Dominic le Jeune,' he said.

Eleanor held out her hand; he kissed it. Dominic had acquired these foreign habits at an expensive Swiss school which he had been forced to quit when his father, half Turkish, half French, declared bankruptcy. In part this was due to bad business, in part to a divorce greedily conducted by Dominic's mother, a beautiful, irrational Irishwoman. That explains the incongruous face, Eleanor thought: red hair from County Clare, currant-black eyes from the Bosphorus and the elegant hands from France.

First bankrupt then dead, such was the fate of Dominic's father. His mother lived in comfortable boredom on the edge of Lake Geneva, resolutely and notwithstanding the most extravagant pleading from her son keeping her alimony to herself. The bright light in the firmament was a Chinese 'father', a Hong Kong millionaire who in a moment of drunken camaraderie had adopted Dominic as his 'son'. So far it had been a most lucrative association. Li Ho Shan was a passionate gambler and Dominic was his constant companion from Las Vegas to Macao. In victory Li Ho Shan was munificent, tossing hundred-dollar bills across the table into Dominic's greedy hands. In defeat the Chinese was given to uncontrollable rages, and it was in the wake of his latest outburst (for two days and nights he had lost at roulette) that Dominic had fled.

'It's only a tantrum. It'll pass. It always does. He needs someone to gamble with. But, for the moment, I'm very short of readies – I can't afford an hotel. I can barely afford this,' he said.

He inspected the room with calm superiority.

'It's not very luxurious,' Eleanor said apologetically.

8

'Beggers can't be choosers. It's clean, but is it quiet? I'm working on a poem about the Chinese Emperor who built the Great Wall. I shall dedicate it to my adopted father, who, hopefully, will show his appreciation in hard cash. You live alone?'

'Not exactly.'

'A boyfriend?'

'Well . . . yes . . .'

'Unemployed?'

'No, he's not unemployed. He's in the Foreign Office.'

Dominic stared at Eleanor and seemed about to say something but then changed his mind.

'I'll take the room. And if you don't mind, I'll stay. Right now,' he said.

Before Eleanor could say anything Dominic had stretched out on the bed.

'Don't you have any luggage?' she asked.

'It got lost in Atlantic City. Bloody Pan Am. But I've got my poem,' he said, pointing to the Turkish saddlebag on the floor. In the same offhand manner he went on, 'Why doesn't he marry you – this boyfriend?'

'You do ask personal questions!'

'Well?'

'I don't know. I don't think he wants to get married . . . people don't.'

'The man's a fool.'

Eleanor smiled. The compliment was attractive from someone so young. She asked, 'Do you have a girlfriend?'

'Certainly not.'

'I see.'

'No you don't. But I can't go into that now. I'm too tired.'

Eleanor was about to leave the room when she turned back and said, 'May I ask you a question?'

'By all means.'

'How old are you?'

'Nineteen.'

'You were nineteen, Dominic. Do you remember?'

'Of course I remember. What bathos. What bad melodrama. There you were, teaching all day, painting all night, selling nothing, earning nothing, impoverished, bad-tempered, ugly

9

– well, if not ugly, drawn, wan, utterly undesirable! You drank undrinkable plonk and filled your coffee with that abhorrent powdered milk. I don't remember one single bottle of fresh milk in your fridge. The whole thing was a lamentable pastiche on the popular concept of the struggling artist.'

Dominic, evidently pleased with his powers of recollection, took a long sip of champagne and continued, 'I don't know what you would have done without me, I really don't. I came, I saw, I conquered; that's how it went, more or less. I brought those Dark Ages to a speedy end, didn't I? And replaced them with a glorious new dawn. When you think of it, Eleanor, your life divides into two separate eras: BD and AD, Before Dominic and After Dominic. Either way, you are the planet and I am the sun. Therefore, once again I must toast myself – here's to my own genius!'

Perhaps 'genius' was the right word for Dominic, Eleanor thought. He had not been a lodger for more than a few weeks when one afternoon he knocked politely on the studio door and said, 'When I came here as a lodger you said, "Will you answer the telephone during the day, while I am out at work?" '

'Only if it's not too much trouble.'

'It's no trouble at all. The telephone doesn't ring.'

'I know. It's so depressing. But I've got a painting on show at the Cadogan Gallery and I keep hoping someone will notice and ring me up and give me a commission.'

'You need an agent.'

'Artists don't have agents.'

'Then I shall be the first.'

Within a few days Dominic had printed five hundred gold-embossed cards which read:

Dominic le Jeune
Artists' Agent

He asked for Eleanor's address book and interrogated her on the background of her friends, waving his hand impatiently when she digressed into details about their characters, interested only in their bank accounts. He drew up his list of prey and then, sitting for hours in front of the telephone, he worked with a manic intensity, cajoling and persuading. Within a few months there were clients, many of them foreign, all of them rich and eager. The price of Eleanor's paintings trebled. She became fashionable; she became famous. She won the National Portrait Competition and her face appeared on the front page of *The Times* and she was invited to dinner by people she had never met and paid lavish compliments by complete strangers.

The Chinese 'father' relented, as Dominic knew he would, and reconciliation was sweet and came in the form of a lump sum. Dominic bought an art gallery in Motcomb Street and in the front window he placed a portrait by the award-winning artist Eleanor Wynn.

'Do you remember those early triumphs, do you?' Dominic said.

'Of course I remember.'

'And we've only just begun. The world hasn't seen anything yet!'

Dominic put down his glass and came forward and sat on the edge of the chaise-longue, his eyes bright with excitement. He spoke feverishly.

'We are on the verge of glory! In a few weeks the Dominic le Jeune gallery opens with the first solo exhibition of your work. This is your big moment, Eleanor! This show will cause a stir of dazzling dimensions, you wait and see. Thanks to my superb planning and foresight you are about to become an international star. I've decided to launch you on the American market. I shan't go into detail now – all will be revealed in time. But I can tell you this – be prepared for a new life!'

'A new life,' Eleanor said. 'I should like that.'

For a while, drinking champagne with Dominic and listening to his Gothic visions of the world, Eleanor forgot her birthday, but as Dominic got up to leave, adjusting the jewel at his throat and inspecting his long fingernails, the panic returned.

'Don't leave me, please. I don't want to be alone – not today,' she said.

'I'm a busy man. I have other commitments.'

'Please stay . . . I must talk to you! I must explain. I know it's all exciting . . . but I am so troubled . . . Oh, Dominic, please help me – I'm not happy!'

'Oh, for God's sake!'

'We have a right to be happy. It's in the American Declaration of Independence!'

11

'This isn't America. And I can't stand any more of your neurotic meanderings.'

'You don't know what I feel inside.'

'And I don't *want* to know,' Dominic said, pulling on his beige kid gloves. 'But I would like to know when you are going to finish *that*!' With his cane he pointed to the huge canvas leaning against the far wall of the studio. 'In a week from now I shall send for that picture – it's to be the centrepiece of the exhibition. Let's hope the paint is dry.'

'I should have finished *weeks* ago,' Eleanor said anxiously. 'I don't know why I'm having such trouble. It's so nearly there . . . and yet I can't find a face. One face – that's all I need.'

'What about darling Edward?'

Eleanor turned sharply to Dominic; her eyes were angry.

'I don't think I have ever heard you say one nice word about Edward,' she said.

'What sort of word did you have in mind?'

'Well . . .' For a moment her mind went blank. 'Charming.'

'Don't be absurd.'

'All right then . . . handsome. Even you cannot dispute that.'

'Looks are entirely subjective.'

'Dominic, will you please stop this. I love Edward.'

'Rot.'

'I do. I'm devoted to him.'

'Exactly. The sort of relationship we read about between old age pensioners.'

'Go away, Dominic. Leave me alone.'

'One minute you beg me to stay, the next you throw me out. I wish you would make up your mind. It's all so tiring.'

Merrily he strode towards the door, tapping the ground with his cane. He was on the point of leaving when he turned back and said, 'You don't *need* a husband. You don't *need* children. That's for . . .' he waved his hand vaguely, 'other people.'

Dominic shut the door firmly as if the subject were closed, leaving Eleanor sitting on the edge of her crumpled bed staring at a thousand particles of dust floating through the shifting beams of sunlight, wondering if white lead mixed with titanium and barium yellow would give the sort of hazy gleam which shimmered before her eyes; and all the time in the background of her mind, like a Buddhist prayer, she could hear the chanting of a phrase: 'Time is running out . . . Time is running out . . .'

The studio reeked of paint and white spirit. Eleanor needed air. She went out for a walk in St James's Park and was drawn, inevitably, to the children's playground. She stood by the swings and the climbing frames and watched the children swing and slide and romp in the sandpit. This journey to the sandpit had become her daily torment. The world seemed filled with small, vulnerable, infinitely lovable children, all belonging to other women.

She walked along the edge of the lake and noticed nothing but children: chasing ducks, pointing with small fat fingers at the sturdy pelicans, marvelling at the elegant drift of a black swan. She became fascinated by a small girl of two or three who held out an unsteady palm with breadcrumbs and trembled with delight as a bird pecked away at the food. The girl could not stand the excitement and suddenly shook her hand. The crumbs fell to the ground, the bird flew away, and startled she cried out, 'Mama!' A woman nearby stepped forward and picked up the little girl and held her close with immense tenderness, and together the mother and the child seemed whole; and the joy Eleanor had felt turned to pain as she considered: 'There are millions and millions of children in this world and not one belongs to me!'

Slowly and miserably she turned away from the impressive symmetry of the Horseguards and walked along the edge of the lake towards Buckingham Palace. A little boy of three or four dashed forward chasing a dog and fell at her feet. He burst into tears. Eleanor picked him up and rubbed the gravel from his hands. His eyes were brown and trusting. All at once she longed to take him home, and all at once she understood those women who snatch babies out of prams. The boy stared at Eleanor with great solemnity and then ran to a woman sitting on a nearby bench; she took his head between her hands and kissed his forehead. Eleanor stood and watched, silent and defeated.

That afternoon she lay on her bed, and she cried with the vehemence of a child. She could not check the stream of hot tears; her head pounded; she felt sick. She kept telling herself, 'The pain will pass . . . sooner or later it must pass. After all, you are not immortal. One day you will die, and then you will have peace.'

She stood beneath the studio skylight, under a darkening sky, in the vortex of her despair. Was there no way forward? No solution? What about Edward? He had been her lover for five years, but he had never spoken of marriage, except in the most deprecating terms. He was quoted in a gossip column as saying, 'Eleanor and I are confirmed bachelors.' It was no use building up hopes; Edward was not the marrying kind. 'What can I do?' Eleanor cried out loud. 'I am powerless to change my life.'

She slept, and in her dream she saw white Buddhist prayer flags fluttering on a mountainside in the Himalayas, and half hidden in cloud she saw the roof of a wooden temple; in the courtyard the rows of prayer wheels were turning in the wind, filling the air with their haunting tinkling noise. The tinkling grew louder; Eleanor woke and realized that the telephone was ringing.

'Eleanor, is that you?'

'Yes . . . yes . . . where are you?'

'You know where I am,' Edward said. 'I'm in Sheffield, brushing up my Japanese.'

'Why aren't you here? It's my birthday and I'm all alone.'

'I know it's your birthday. Happy birthday, darling. I rang you last night but there was no answer.'

'I went to a party with Dominic. We came home incredibly late. The dawn was breaking and the sky was the colour of a ripe peach – '

'I wish you wouldn't go out with Dominic,' Edward interrupted.

'But he's my agent!'

'You didn't take drugs, did you?'

'Edward, what is this? I don't take drugs – you know that. Why are you being so unkind? It's my birthday. Please be nice.'

The voice softened. 'I am always nice to you.'

'Do you love me?'

'Of course I love you. I've told you, I shall always love you.'

'That's nice,' Eleanor said gloomily.

'I must go or I shall miss my train. You haven't forgotten that we're having dinner tonight? You're so unreliable, one never knows. That was a joke, my darling, in case you start to cry. Joke, yes?'

'Terribly funny.'

'I thought we'd eat at home, unless you want to go out. I don't really like restaurants. They're so noisy.'

'And expensive,' Eleanor thought. She had never got used to Edward's frugality; he was allergic to spending money, just as some people were allergic to shellfish.

'As you like,' Eleanor said.

'If you want to go out, then we will. Whatever you like. You're the birthday girl.'

'No, no, let's stay at home.'

'I think it is best. Especially tonight. We've got a lot to talk about.'

'We do?'

'We certainly do. These last few days have been eventful, to put it mildly. Take a deep breath, Eleanor. I've been posted to Peking.'

'Edward, that's wonderful! You must be so pleased . . . it's what you've always wanted. Well done, my love. I'm delighted for you.'

'It is good news. I shall be one of the youngest ministers in the Foreign Office. It's the perfect move at this stage of my career.'

'That's that,' Eleanor thought. 'He's going to Peking. I won't see him again. I shall be without a lover. Alone. Once again.'

'There's one minor problem,' Edward said.

'Oh?'

'They're very clever in the Foreign Office. It's the carrot and stick technique. First the carrot, in my case Peking, the posting I have always wanted. And then the stick. The Head of my Department wants to send a married man. Of course I've tried to talk him out of it, but he's adamant. So eventually I caved in.'

'Oh?'

'Of course I did! I'm not going to pass up Peking on a technicality, for God's sake. I told him that I was engaged.'

'But you're not engaged, are you?'

'I told him I was engaged to you.'

3 It was raining in Wandsworth. Eleanor stopped for a moment on the crest of a hill, and through the rain-spotted windscreen she studied the mysterious, murky scene, composing a picture in her mind. Most of the narrow houses were dirty and run-down, but now and then a house had been newly painted and was gleaming white. Edward lived in one of these. This was an up-and-coming area. Frail young trees were struggling to grow in protected circles cut into the grey pavement; there was a pub with a vulgar green façade out of which staggered a drunk, unsteady and oblivious to the wet evening. On the opposite side of the street was a Chinese restaurant and above the entrance a faulty neon light shuddered; it was a sickly shade of yellow.

Instinctively Eleanor translated the colour into paint: deep cadmium yellow mixed with white lead – and if that wouldn't do, then try cadmium orange alongside barium yellow, and a flash of violet or green. In front of the black railings stood black polythene refuse bags, glistening in the rain. The atmosphere was dismal and wet until Eleanor looked beyond the rooftops and the church spire, to the purple storm clouds, pulling across the September sky releasing shafts of brilliant light (she was reminded of those golden beams from Heaven in fifteenth-century Flemish paintings of the Nativity). The golden light was dazzling. 'It's not to be believed,' she told herself. 'If I painted what I see now, people would say, "It's impossible, the sky doesn't look like that" . . . and yet it does . . . now, this minute . . . there must be a way of making what is true seem real . . .'

Slowly the golden light mellowed; and slowly, growing stronger with every second, a vast, all-encompassing rainbow vaulted Wandsworth and the world. Eleanor had never seen such a rainbow. She got out of her car and stood in wonder. She even reached out with her hand in the hope she might touch the shimmering semi-circle. The bands of light were trembling, making it almost impossible to define what colour they really were: before her eyes blues were changing into greens, and yellows into oranges, and whites were turning blue. A second rainbow appeared, fainter than the first, but just as perfect in shape, like a ghost. Suddenly her attention was caught by something new. A front door opened and a man in a trilby hat stepped into the rain holding in his hand an umbrella which he was opening. Eleanor watched him through the misty veil of drizzle, his sharp silhouette black against the light. The painting was complete, Eleanor thought. It even had a title: 'Rainbow over Wandsworth'.

Edward Verney was brilliant; at times Eleanor thought he was too brilliant. He was one of the finest Oriental scholars in the Foreign Office. Not only did he speak fluent Chinese, both Mandarin and Cantonese, but he wrote the language with a certain poetic flair (Tang poetry was his first love), and now he was perfecting his Japanese. He did not even count European languages among his accomplishments. To say that you spoke French, German and Italian was like saying that you could read.

In the Foreign Office he was a rising star. Unlike most young diplomats Edward had never been posted to a backwater; he had always been at the heart of things. In Brussels he had worked for the Commission calculating subsidies to hill farmers; in Washington he studied arms control; in Tokyo he analysed Japanese trade barriers; but his speciality was Hong Kong. Edward nurtured one supreme ambition: to be the last Governor of the Colony, the man who would mastermind the transfer of power from Britain to China in 1997. Of course he would be knighted, most probably be given a peerage, and in later life he would make witty speeches in the House of Lords peppered with quotations from Confucius. All this seemed well within Edward's grasp, and the new appointment to Peking was definitely a step in the right direction.

Edward knew exactly what he wanted. He always had. At the age of twelve he had decided to become a diplomat. His father was a professional soldier but Edward considered himself too clever for the army. And anyway, as he told his father, there will never be another war, and without a war what is the point of the army? He took a first in Chinese at London

University (at Oxford they did not teach Oriental languages) and went on to sit the Foreign Office examinations, which he passed with distinction. He made quite an impression, this beautiful young man with the austere expression of a priest. When he was asked why he wanted to join the Foreign Office he said, 'To serve my country.' Several of the examiners smiled. Edward sat straight-backed and impassive until the smiling stopped and said, 'I do not look on this as a career but as a vocation.'

Eleanor would tease Edward about his high-minded approach, and yet at the same time she was drawn to this man who, at all times, was so decisive. Living as she did in a chaos of doubt, she felt sheltered by his certainty. Also, Eleanor hated to live alone; only cats were born to solitude. Long ago she had decided that any lover was better than no lover, and year after year there was always a man. Edward was the male presence in her life.

It was an attraction of opposites, everyone said so. (Dominic called them the 'B and B' – the Bohemian and the Bore.) Eleanor had many friends, Edward had few. She was gregarious, he was solitary. She was an optimist, he was a pessimist. But it was in their pasts that the contrasts were most stark. For Eleanor, childhood had been a time of rich discovery and intense joy. Edward, on the other hand, looked back on his boyhood, especially his adolescence, with loathing.

He was thirteen, in his first term at public school, when his world fell apart. His father, Edwin Verney, was about to leave for Hong Kong, where he had been appointed Second-in-Command of British Forces, when his mother, Rachel, ran off with a Spanish sculptor. Edward was taken out of Winchester and brought to Hong Kong, where he lived with his father for the next five years. His mother made him, his mother ruined him; this was the irony of it all, he would say. In Hong Kong he received an extraordinary education, far more interesting than the predictably classical routine of Winchester, and he mastered Chinese. At the same time his mother vanished from his life. All letters and postcards sent to him from Salamanca were confiscated by his father before he could read them. He was eighteen before he saw his mother again, and when he did, she looked beautiful and she was smiling. He never forgave her. It was his duty as a son to show his mother respect; this he did, but he could not like her. He never would.

Edward was a proud pessimist. For him life was to be endured rather than to be enjoyed; but it was to be endured with dignity. All inner pain was to be hidden. The most intelligent philosopher, to his mind (even more shrewd than the great Confucius), was Buddha. How wise to teach that through detachment and the crushing of human desire came true peace of mind! Without hope there could be no disappointment. It was obvious! Every morning for half an hour Edward meditated; his aim was to distance himself from life.

'Say it again,' Edward said.

'I don't want to say it again,' Eleanor protested.

'Go on. Just once more.'

'All right then. Yes, I'll marry you.'

He kissed her slowly and softly and held her to him, kissing her hair.

'Edward, you are crying!' she said.

'I'm happy, that's all . . . I've been awfully worried. I wasn't sure you'd say yes . . . I wasn't sure at all!'

He kissed her eyelids and her forehead, and his hand closed over her breast.

'What about my birthday present?' she asked.

'Later.'

'And my dinner?'

'Later, later . . .'

He made love to her that evening with tenderness and passion, kissing her everywhere, holding her, devouring her. Eleanor tried to respond but failed. Her mind kept wandering back to the huge unfinished canvas that was leaning against her studio wall and to the headless man in the foreground whose face was still a blank, and all the while Edward was sucking at her nipple. 'How can I be so distracted?' she thought to herself. 'I must concentrate!' She shut her eyes and tried to lose herself in Edward's lovemaking, but all her senses seemed to resist, and from somewhere in her memory came the recollection of a Norwegian theology student who had made love to her with Nordic intensity and revealed to her, for the first time, a world of uninhibited physical expression. They spent mornings, afternoons and evenings in bed and for months she had delighted in his passion. All the same he became a priest; women, he said, were not that important.

'Darling,' Edward said, 'are you all right?'

'Oh yes, my love, yes.'

At last she gave Edward her love, in the hand she laid so gently on his cheek, in her kiss so light that he sensed only the edges of her lips until she kissed him again and again and their kisses met and grew passionate. Eleanor could feel the rough hair of his chest against her soft breasts, and the taut muscles of his thighs against her own smooth skin, and she could smell the maleness of his body, and she felt warm and close, protected and possessed and not alone. He was inside her; they were part of each other.

She cried out, 'Edward, let's have a baby.'

Edward let out a strange sound and shuddered and sank back on to the pillows. Later, in the stillness, he said, 'I'm sorry, darling . . . I wanted you too much.'

'It was lovely.'

'No . . . no . . . I didn't wait for you . . .'

'It doesn't matter. It was lovely.'

'No . . . no, it wasn't. But most of the time it is, isn't it?'

'It's wonderful, darling. Just wonderful.'

Eleanor stretched her naked body against his and burrowed her head beneath his arm.

'I'll make you pregnant,' he said. 'I promise.'

In the five years that Eleanor had known Edward his sitting room had not changed. It was a room without colour: the curtains were oatmeal and the carpet was brown, and the walls were beige. The bookshelves were filled with even more books on the Orient; but above the fireplace hung the same portrait of a Verney ancestor, and at the other end of the room was the familiar monochrome Chinese painting, inscribed with Edward's favourite proverb: 'There are many birds in the sky but that is no reason to let them make a nest in your hair.' Eleanor shuddered even though it was a warm evening: these were gloomy surroundings. Edward had opened a bottle of wine and lit his cigar; he was humming a tune. She had never heard him hum before.

She stood beside him and said, 'Let's get married right away . . . Tomorrow! We only need two witnesses. Anyone will do! I don't care – do you? Look at that man down there, he'll do. Shall I go and ask him? There's always Dominic . . . and my friend Rosie . . .'

'Eleanor, please be *sensible*! We can't just rush off and get married. We must follow the correct procedure. First, we have to become engaged, officially.'

'You're joking.'

'I'm not joking at all. We must put an announcement in the *The Times* and the *Telegraph*, and perhaps in the *Independent*. I don't know. I'll think about it. We can do that in a few weeks.'

'A few *weeks*?'

'These things take time, Eleanor. There are people I must write to – my godmother in Chile, for a start. And there's my father and the various members of my Department.'

'But you all work in the same building! Can't you put your head round the door and tell everyone the glad tidings?'

'Darling, I've told you. In the Foreign Office we put everything on paper.'

'Even engagements?'

'Even engagements. There's no great hurry. I won't be going to China until the New Year. We'll be married by Christmas.'

'Christmas,' Eleanor whispered. 'But that's so far away.'

'I love you, Eleanor. I love you more than I have ever loved anyone. Do you realize that? There are times when you infuriate me . . . there are times when I don't *like* you, but I love you. I shall always love you.'

He spoke solemnly, almost sadly. Eleanor was touched. She said, 'I shall make you so happy! I shall be a model wife, so polite and charming. I'll have tea with all those other wives. I won't let you down, I promise!'

'Of course you won't let me down. Anyway, diplomatic life isn't that bad. We shall have plenty of time for ourselves.'

'And I can paint.'

'And you can paint. Painting is perfect for the Foreign Office.'

Eleanor looked at Edward uneasily, but she continued in the same lighthearted vein: 'I always think of the Chinese as either very young or very old. My paintings will be full of Mongolian babies with bare bottoms – did you know the Chinese children don't wear nappies? And those inscrutable old men and women with invisible eyes and a thousand wrinkles, and blue

21

skin. Every time I think of an old person I see Rembrandt's painting of his mother. Do you know the picture?'

Edward was not listening.

'When people get married,' he said, inhaling on his cigar, 'things change.'

'What do you mean?'

'Things change. It's obvious. Of course I want you to paint. I think it's important that you should be busy. But . . . I'm sure you'll agree if you think about it, my love . . . I don't think you should take it too seriously.'

'I have to paint seriously. It's the only way I know how to paint.'

'Now don't get all worked up . . . darling. You know I'm so proud of your painting. You're so good and you work so hard.'

'You never come to my studio. You never look at my work.'

'I do . . . and I think your painting is marvellous. But you might have to slow down a bit . . . that's all . . . When you get married there are other priorities.'

'Such as?'

'Well, me, for example!'

'You?'

'Yes, me! Husbands need looking after, my darling. And there'll be children. You want children, don't you?'

'Yes. Very much.'

'Exactly. When people get married – I'm afraid it's one of those things – there are sacrifices to be made. Marriage is hard work, Eleanor.'

'Have you been reading some sort of manual?'

'I'm serious.'

'I know.'

Edward sucked once more on his cigar and blew the smoke towards the ceiling. His face was stern; his jaw set. Eleanor paced the room nervously and finally she said, 'Why are you so gloomy? Really, Edward! We're talking about the blissful state of matrimony, not the Last Judgement.'

In her mind's eye she could see the crouched figure in Michelangelo's fresco, a soul in torment, hand over his face, terror in his eyes, being dragged into Hell. It made her uneasy that such a desperate image should come so readily to mind.

The conciliatory tone went out of Edward's voice. He spoke with authority: 'It would be wrong if I let you think that your life will go on as before. It won't. It can't. You'll have to adapt. You'll be entering a new world. My world. We *must* pull in the same direction. Of course you can paint. You must paint. But . . . you should look on it as . . . well . . . as your hobby.'

'Painting isn't my hobby. It's my profession.'

'Not any more! You will have a new role, my darling.'

'As what?'

'My wife.'

Eleanor turned away; Edward took her hand and stroked it.

'I can see that you are getting upset, but it's best to discuss these things openly. We'll both have to make big adjustments. I'm quite nervous about the whole thing.'

'Oh?'

'Of course I am . . . I've been a bachelor for years . . . and a very contented one. As you know I like being alone. Every evening after work I read for an hour or so, here, by the fire. It won't be easy – living with someone. I shall need to have time to myself after we are married. You do understand that, don't you? I must have my own time . . . my own space. I find that after a day in the office, dealing with all these slow-witted people who bother me with such stupid questions, I'm drained. All I want is to sit in silence with my book! You know my idea of Hell is a room full of chattering women. Men don't chatter, they talk. But women babble. It's interesting that the Japanese character for noise is a composite character made up of three symbols – all women. Very appropriate, I always think! But this is where your painting will come in handy. You can do your thing, and I can do mine. Of course there's the grim prospect of a screaming infant keeping one awake at night, but at least that's your department!' Edward smiled stoically and said, 'Marriage is hard work.'

'You've said that before.'

'My mother was never ready to make the effort.'

Suddenly Eleanor said fiercely, 'Your mother is a – '

'Yes?'

'Nice woman. I like your mother.'

'You don't know her. I don't want to argue with you, my darling. Not tonight! But my mother has a lot to answer for. She's the one person I shall not be inviting to our wedding.'

'But you *must* invite your mother!'

'Please don't tell me what to do. She's *my* mother and it's *my* wedding. She's not welcome. Don't make me angry, Eleanor.'

Eleanor stared at Edward; she was silent and grave. Her eyes filled with tears and one by one they rolled down her cheeks. Edward took her in his arms.

'I know, my darling, it's wonderful. We're going to get married,' he said.

4   'I always thought I would fall in love,' Eleanor thought. 'This is so disappointing.' She tried to calm herself. Everyone married once; it was hardly an original step, and if it turned out well or badly, that was not original either. It was something to be done, a decision to be taken, a step to be made. 'Yes . . . yes,' her inner voice interrupted, 'but your heart should be singing. Instead the air is thick with dread.' 'Everyone gets nervous,' Eleanor countered. 'Edward is the obvious choice. We have known each other for years. Don't you understand? We are friends. I am going to marry a friend.'

She began to cry; abruptly she stopped herself and straightened her back and told herself to stop all this and think of the children that she would have with Edward. 'They will bring me joy . . . they will make everything seem worthwhile,' she told herself. 'I am too greedy . . . I want too much. I cannot have everything. No one can. Except for Marcia.'

Marcia was Eleanor's sister, a beautiful woman for whom everything always seemed to go right. Nine years ago she had married Ralph Penrose, a Scottish landowner. He was a rich and devoted husband and they had three beautiful children, whose joyfulness and sweetness were a perpetual reminder to Eleanor of all that she was missing.

It was, by all accounts, a dull, rich and contented marriage. They went away at weekends to stay with relations; the household was dominated by a young, efficient nanny; no one seemed to have much to do at weekends, except in Scotland, where Ralph was planting forests. He was writing a history of Scotland which never seemed to get finished and Marcia was writing a book on how to cook game, which never seemed to get finished either; and yet they seemed perfectly happy, living an affluent, idle life, talking about nothing in particular and doting on their children.

Eleanor called on Marcia a few days after her birthday. She found her in the nursery on the top floor of her large house in Cheyne Walk feeding Clare, her baby daughter. Marcia held the child to her breast and smiled down at the tiny form. The baby was suckling intently, staring up at her mother with huge brown eyes. It was so intimate and so touching that for a moment Eleanor stood quite still and watched. She told herself that before long she too would have a child to hold and to feed and to love, and for the first time she felt no pain.

Eventually when the feeding was over, Marcia said, 'Here, you take her.'

Eleanor felt the small weight against her own body; she looked into the unseeing brown eyes, half closed, and watched the tiny fingers feel the vibrations of the air. Eventually the eyelids fluttered and closed and still Eleanor was staring down at the newborn child, listening to the soft sounds of life that came from the tiny creature.

'You should have a child, Eleanor. There is something so sad about a woman without a child,' Marcia said.

Eleanor sat in dumb helplessness, controlling the muscles of her face to hide her pain, and at the same time remembering the many, many times that her sister had chosen to wound, from her own impregnable happiness.

Marcia continued, 'Marry anyone with a bit of money. Money helps. And have children. That's my advice to you!'

Eleanor smiled at her sister and said, 'It always seems odd to me that people who are perfectly happy are always advising the rest of us to settle for so much less.'

'Who are these people who are perfectly happy?'

'Well . . . you! You and Ralph!'

Marcia gave Eleanor a look that was hesitant, as if she were about to say something. Suddenly she burst out laughing.

'Is that what you think? That's really funny!'

'Have I got it wrong?' Eleanor asked herself.

A telephone rang. Marcia left the room; moments later the nanny came and took away the baby.

Eleanor wandered slowly down the stairs of the large house. She could hear the older children in the nursery, fighting. A door burst open. Beatrice, aged three, ran from the room screaming, chased by her brother, Rowley, who was brandishing a plastic sword. Beatrice saw Eleanor and clasped her legs.

'And what's all this about?' Eleanor asked.

'She won't play the game,' Rowley said indignantly.

'And what is the game?'

'It's called Darkest Africa! I invented it. I'm Dr Livingstone, and Beatrice, well, she's always something different, but this time she is somebody's wife who is boiled alive and eaten by cannibals.'

'I don't want to play your game!' Beatrice screamed.

Eleanor was about to make peace between the two when, inevitably, the nanny appeared and the children were marched off to their bath.

Eleanor found herself in the drawing room. It was a pretty room, and on the side tables stood photographs, landmarks in the Penrose family life: the wedding; Rowley's christening; Beatrice's christening; Ralph and the children amid the heather, and in the background the pink stone of Kirkenny, the Penrose castle. There was as yet no picture of Clare. Eleanor thought of her huge brown eyes; the other children had blue eyes, so did Marcia and Ralph. Only Eleanor's mother had brown eyes. 'They must come from her,' Eleanor thought. The door to Ralph's study was open. Eleanor picked up a few magazines aimlessly and wandered closer to the open door, through which she could see her sister speaking on the telephone. Her voice was just audible.

'No . . . No . . . You come here on Sunday afternoon. Ralph is in Scotland this weekend and I'll send the children to the park with the nanny. I must see you . . . I miss you so much . . . I think of you all the time . . .'

Marcia turned round suddenly and through the open door saw her sister staring at her.

'I must go,' she said hurriedly and put down the receiver. She walked slowly into the drawing room. Eventually she said, 'You weren't meant to hear that.'

'I didn't hear anything.'

Marcia looked at her sister coolly and remarked, 'It's a pity we aren't better friends, you and I. I admire you, did you know that? You should hear the way I talk of you when you are not around. I am very proud of you. You have done something with your life.'

'So have you.'

'And what have I done?'

'You have brought three beautiful children into this world. You have built a home for . . .'

'Please!' Marcia said sharply. 'Don't patronize me, Eleanor.'

'I'm not. I would give anything to have a nice husband and three children.'

'Would you really?' Marcia laughed. 'I suppose Ralph is nice, but, God, he's dull! Dull as ditchwater. You cannot imagine how bored I have been these last years . . . bored out of my mind. But not any more! Not since I met Matthew! Now everything is wonderful . . . wonderful . . . Oh, don't worry, I am very careful and very correct.'

Marcia walked over to the drinks tray and poured Eleanor and herself a glass of wine. She continued, 'You've always had clever friends . . . I never have. I'm not used to men who know things . . . Matthew knows everything . . . he knows how the world began, how the seas and mountains were formed. He knows about ancient Egyptians and Early Irish monasteries. There's nothing he doesn't know! But imagine! He sits there and asks me what I think! At first I had nothing to say . . . I told him, don't ask me, I never read a newspaper. And he said, "Why not? You've got a brain – use it." And so now I read . . . I even read the *Economist* – well, bits of it anyway. And I've joined Friends of the Earth – that's his big interest – and we go to meetings about the Greenhouse Effect. I don't know how to explain . . . but he's opened so many doors . . . he's introduced me to so many ideas . . . My mind is reeling from it all . . . He makes me feel worth something in myself. To Ralph I am a wife and a mother. To Matthew I am a woman. Oh, I can't explain . . . It's as if I've been set free from the sort of Sloane Ranger prison I've been living in. Ralph's friends are mostly from the Hooray Henry brigade . . . they're always calling their wives "the old bag" or "the old girl", and they never talk to them about serious subjects, only the children, and that sort of thing.'

'I know.'

'The Greenhouse Effect is happening . . . did you know? It's not a myth . . . it's really happening, now! By the year 2030 the sea level will rise one foot at least, and East Anglia and Bangladesh will be flooded. And the world climate will change. There'll be more hurricanes and more rain. Only no one knows where it will rain. Perhaps in England. Or the Sahara. No one knows. Matthew made a speech about it all at a conference on the environment. It's funny how all of a sudden everyone is talking about the environment. For years no one paid any attention, and now the idea has caught fire. Matthew spoke beautifully. Without a note. I was so proud of him.'

'How long have you been seeing each other?'

'Three years.'

'I had no idea.'

'Of course not. I'm very discreet.'

'What are you going to do?'

'Do?' Marcia asked in surprise. 'Nothing of course. There is no need to do anything. Ralph doesn't know . . . no one knows . . . it's all fine.'

'Don't you want to live with this man?' Eleanor asked.

'Don't be so stupid!' Marcia snapped. 'I've got three children. I'm not that selfish!' She sat on the sofa twisting her fingers, staring down at her hands. Eventually she conceded, 'Of course I want to live with him. But it's out of the question. It's a little easier now that Clare is born. Every time I look into her face I see Matthew. You look surprised! Didn't you notice the colour of her eyes – brown and beautiful, just like her father! Now you're looking shocked – oh, I don't care what you think. I wanted to have a child with my lover, and I did. And I am so pleased that I did. I haven't slept with Ralph for years. Does that surprise you? You seem to have such absurd ideas about marriage. It's not what you think. Not at all. What was I saying? Oh yes, I don't sleep with Ralph. I can't bear him to touch me. Of course when I found out I was pregnant, I forced myself to make love again. And then of course I had to pretend the child was premature. It was quiet easy to deceive Ralph. He's so trusting. Oh, don't look so shocked. This is real life, Eleanor, not a Pre-Raphaelite painting.'

'I always thought you and Ralph were so happy.'

'No one is happy. You've always got that wrong.'

'Have I?' Eleanor thought as she turned away. 'Is everyone's life like this? Half-hearted? Mediocre? Messy?' She was dismayed at the pretence of it all which had fooled her, but even more dismayed that a happiness which had appeared so solid, so enduring, did not exist; it had been her own invention, destroyed in a few sentences.

It seemed to Eleanor the room itself had changed; the

warmth of family love had gone and the atmosphere was still and cold. Even the family photographs looked different; behind the smiling faces Eleanor read sorrow. She decided to leave.

In the hall as she stood beside the half-opened door she said, 'Edward wants to get married.'

'And you?'

'I don't love him.'

Marcia stared at her sister, her blue eyes bright with tears. In a voice filled with dejection she said, 'It doesn't matter.'

5   Eleanor threw open the studio windows and took deep breaths of the early morning air. It was half past six, the streets were still empty; the sky was opaque, reluctant to take on the blue of the day. All night Eleanor had stood in front of her painting, trying this face and that, an eye and a nose, but each time it was no good and impatiently she would take first a knife and then an oil cloth and obliterate these tentative signs of life. Edward's face did not fit; the stern, beautiful features were all wrong. She was searching for a man who lived by impulse, not in the measured paragraphs of a Foreign Office dispatch.

It was her most ambitious painting, over forty figures spaced on the canvas. The scene was straightforward enough: a summer's day in the new Covent Garden. The glass and iron buildings of the old flower market glinted in the sunshine. On the right-hand side of the painting a clown with a bulbous red nose was doing a handstand, while a fire-eater with orange hair and red striped trousers threw out his arms and blew spluttering flames into the air to an audience of enchanted children. A dog sniffed at a pillar box; a pigeon sat on a lamppost; meths drinkers were slumped on the ground beneath the columns of St Paul's church.

All this activity was incidental to the main event. In the foreground of the painting were two figures, a man and a woman who had just passed each other in the street. At exactly the same moment they had both looked back. Perhaps they knew each other, or perhaps it was a moment of delayed attraction in which each had been impressed by the face of the other and wanted to look again. Whatever the reason, for both people it was a moment of irresistible curiosity. The girl was Eleanor, head tilted back, green eyes laughing, her blue-black hair falling untidily; it was Eleanor at her most confident, ready to take on the world. The man was in a hurry; his hands were in his pockets; there was an urgency in his step. Almost

31

reluctantly he had turned around. Who was this man? Was he young or old? Surprised or indifferent? She did not know. His body was there but his face was a blank.

'I should paint in Edward and be done with it!' Eleanor muttered, exasperated at herself. 'But I can't . . . I can't . . . he doesn't belong!'

There was a part for everyone else. Eleanor's mother was sitting at a table drinking coffee and reading a newspaper, looking calm and elegant and wearing a hat. Eleanor's father was selling a red balloon to Rowley, the grandson he had never met; while Marcia was among the crowd, outstanding in her beauty and holding the hand of her daughter Beatrice, who was licking an ice cream and staring with fascination at the fire-eater. The waitress was Eleanor's friend Rosie, a pale, shabby figure, looking thin and much older then her years, in a crumpled white apron.

'My past, my present . . . it's all here,' Eleanor thought, 'except for Edward. Oh God . . . he doesn't belong to my world and I don't belong to his.' And suddenly a fierce sense of dejection and defeat was raging within her. She took deep breaths and reined in her thoughts. Sternly she told herself, 'There is no turning back.'

It was a melancholy time, the prelude to their engagement. They built no castles in the air; there were no flowers and no celebration dinners; instead they spent long and silent evenings together in Edward's house (he would not come to her studio; he said the white spirit made him sick). It was all so calm and sensible and infinitely dispiriting that Eleanor found it hard to believe that once he had been moved to tears.

One evening Eleanor arrived to find Edward deep in conversation with Mr Chen, the owner of the Chinese restaurant at the far end of the street. Mr Chen, a short, wiry Chinese with a missing front tooth, was waving his arms around in agitation.

'I'll do what I can, Mr Chen, I promise, but it's very difficult,' Edward was saying. 'The British Government is not giving citizenship to the people of Hong Kong.'

'My mother is British,' Mr Chen said, waving the black passport in his hand.

'Hong Kong British,' Edward corrected.

Mr Chen's eyes narrowed. 'How come Chinese not good

enough for Britain? African good enough. London is chock-a-block with large and unruly Africans who rob old ladies and rape young girls in dead of night. London is full of such people.'

'It's very difficult, Mr Chen. We are a small country. We cannot take any more immigrants.'

'When African man come to London, he get citizenship. And then he send for wife and children, and brothers and sisters . . . and one hundred members of family arrive. For African people it is easy. For Chinese impossible. I am British citizen. I ask only for my mother. One person. My mother.'

'I will do what I can, Mr Chen. I've told you. But for the moment your mother's visa has expired and she must go back to Hong Kong.'

'She no go back. Never. She no wait for Communists to come and kill her second time round. They kill her family before, in Shanghai, in 1949. My auntie and two uncles, and their children, everybody murdered by Communist Chinese. Now British Government is pushing off, abandoning people of Hong Kong to the same Communist Chinese. My mother say, she no hang around to be murdered second time round.'

'Communism is changing, Mr Chen. China is opening up.'

'Don't you believe it.'

'Mr Chen, you mother cannot stay in London without a visa.'

'You no tell police? No, please!'

'Of course I won't tell the police. But she must go back. If she stays here as an illegal immigrant I can't help her.'

Mr Chen turned away, dejected, his hands falling by his side, the passport dangling in one hand. Eleanor stepped forward.

'Mr Chen, Edward will do everything he can. I promise. We'll try to help your mother, I promise!' she said.

Mr Chen's face brightened. 'Thank you, lady, thank you very much.'

'That was foolish,' Edward said as they went inside.

'Why?'

'I can't help him. This government has said repeatedly it will not give the Hong Kong Chinese British passports. How can we, Eleanor? There's no room.'

'There's always room for a few special cases. And it seems

33

to me we have an obligation to the people of Hong Kong, whatever you say. After all, it is a colony, and British companies have got rich on the backs of the Chinese.'

'I'm tired, Eleanor. I don't want to get into this. You don't understand. We have signed an agreement with Peking. They have promised to give Hong Kong special status – to let it operate more or less as it does today. The British government has done its best. I can't get involved in individual cases . . . I'm sorry.'

'Please help Mr Chen's mother.'

'There's nothing I can do.'

'Please . . . he's only a child . . . he wants his mother to come and live with him. That's more than most British people!'

'Eleanor, don't annoy me.'

'His mother, for God's sake.'

'Eleanor!' Edward was almost shouting. He left the room, and when he came back he was carrying an armful of papers, and without speaking he sat down at his desk and set to work.

'Why am I here?' Eleanor asked herself as she sat in the colourless sitting room, a book open on her lap, staring at Edward, his beautiful head bent over his work. 'I could be painting. I *should* be painting!' Edward looked up from his desk, and smiled absently. 'He's nervous,' Eleanor thought, 'we're both nervous.'

'There's something I want to ask you,' Edward said.

'Yes?'

'Do you want an engagement ring?'

For a moment Eleanor said nothing. An engagement ring had not featured in her thoughts. Did other people have engagement rings? Marcia did, a blue sapphire set in diamonds, but then Marcia would. Her mother wore an engagement ring until she lost it on a trek in Nepal. But today, did people still have engagement rings? Surely not. Eleanor never wore rings. She could not paint with a ring round her finger.

'I haven't thought about it . . . I don't know. I don't have any jewellery,' she said.

'Exactly!'

'I'm sorry?'

'You don't have any jewellery – which means you don't like it!'

'Does it?'

'Of course it does, my darling. Of course, if you *want* a ring, that's different. There is this family brooch – my mother used to wear it, but it doesn't belong to her. It's a Verney brooch. I could sell it and buy you a ring.'

'No . . . no . . . Don't sell anything. I don't want a ring.'

Edward put down his sheath of papers, got up from his chair and kissed Eleanor on the forehead. 'I knew that's what you would say. You see how well I know you!'

They were making love when the doorbell rang.

'I'm not expecting anyone, are you?' Edward said. He got out of bed and walked to the window. 'Oh God! It's my mother!'

By the time Eleanor came down to the sitting room Rachel Verney was standing in front of the fire with a drink in her hand.

'If it isn't the beautiful Eleanor! How very nice to see you,' Rachel said. 'I'm so sorry to barge in like this, but as I was explaining to Edward – don't look so grim, Edward darling, I'm only staying for a moment – as I was explaining to Edward, we've had a puncture and darling Humphrey has taken the car to a garage round the corner. When I realized where we were – in your street, imagine! – I said to myself, I must come and see my dear boy. How are you, Edward?'

Rachel Verney was still a beautiful woman. Eleanor tried to strip the face of age and paint this woman in her prime, with high cheekbones and a flawless skin and bright, flirtatious blue eyes. All this had survived, but not the figure. Rachel Verney was large in every part, bosom, waist and hips.

'I am fine, Mother,' Edward said.

'This room could be so pretty if only you would introduce a little colour. I never understand why bachelors always choose brown.'

'The house is always let,' Edward said. 'There's no point doing it up.'

'My dear Eleanor – how long is it? A year at least. I'm always saying to Edward, come down for a weekend and bring that lovely Eleanor. But he never does. You see, Edward doesn't really like me.'

'Now, Mother, please . . .'

'It's true, it's absolutely true, and there's nothing I can do about it!'

Rachel Verney stepped back to look at a portrait that hung over the fireplace.

'That is Edward's great-grandfather – do you think there's a family likeness? Of course in those days the Verneys were rich. Today they have nothing.'

'We have brains,' Edward said.

'And virtue,' Rachel Verney added, 'we mustn't forget virtue!'

'Mother!' Edward warned.

'I am just telling Eleanor about our family. You see, my dear, the Verneys pride themselves on virtue.'

'Mother . . . what nonsense!'

'You do! All of you . . . and especially your father!'

'Mother, please stop this . . .'

'Don't you think your father is virtuous?'

'He's no worse and no better than anyone else.'

'No worse! Indeed not. He's better than anyone else. Mightily better! Or so he kept telling me. That's the trouble with the army, it makes everyone so superior. Oh, don't worry, Edward, I won't embarrass you in front of Eleanor. Get me another drink, dear. Why don't you two get married?'

Eleanor looked at Edward and waited for him to tell his mother they were indeed getting married. But Edward said nothing.

Rachel Verney went on, 'You would make such a handsome couple. I like good looks. Now Edward's father is good-looking, but let me warn you, my dear Eleanor, it's not enough. We women, we need attention. And flattery. Oh, I do like a lavish compliment! It puts me in a good mood for the entire day! I used to be pretty, really very pretty. But Edward's father never noticed that sort of thing. He was above it all. It took another man to tell me that I was beautiful, and I ran away with him. He was Spanish. Spanish men are very passionate. We never married. He was too jealous. But we loved each other – oh, how we loved each other!'

Rachel Verney looked at her son, as if she expected some comment, but he said nothing.

'Edward thinks I was monstrously selfish. He thinks that I destroyed the family – don't you?'

Still Edward said nothing.

'Of course you're right. I did. But I would do it all again. I couldn't live with your father a moment longer. To stay married for your sake – no, I couldn't do it. Even if I had never met Paulo, I still would have left your father. We only have one life. You can't throw it away in the name of duty, at least I couldn't. But you don't understand that, do you?'

'Mother, I have nothing to say. I am your son, I have no right to criticize you.'

'Listen to him! It's all out of a book – thoughts of Confucius, or Mencius, or one of those Chinese sages. I wish for once you'd say what you really think, but you won't, I know. Well, let me tell you something. I ran off with another man – yes. But I was never going to leave you. I planned to bring you to Spain to live with me, but your father was too quick for me. He just took you out of school and sent you to Hong Kong. I rang, but he put the telephone down. I wrote – do you know that I wrote every week? But he never showed you the letters. Finally I got on an aeroplane and came to Hong Kong but you weren't there – you were in Shanghai. I waited around for weeks – oh, it was so terrible – and then I went home without seeing you. I left you letters and presents . . . I suppose your father destroyed them all.'

'No he didn't. He kept your letters, and when I was older he gave them to me. And your presents. Books and clothes. Cotton shirts from Marks and Spencer. Of course by then the shirts were too small.'

'You read my letters?' Rachel said, and the defiance drained from her face.

'Yes, I did.'

'But then you must know how I missed you! How I longed to be with you – '

'Father said I could join you in Spain if I wanted to. But I didn't.'

Edward turned away from his mother and stared grimly at the window. A great sadness came into Rachel Verney's eyes.

'See?' she said to Eleanor. 'He won't even look at me! I am never to be forgiven. I abandoned my son and I am forever condemned. You're a hard man, Edward . . . like your father. Verneys don't forgive. Be careful, Eleanor.'

Edward turned around and faced his mother. He said, 'I have never reproached you . . .'

With a voice that was suddenly hard, Rachel Verney said, 'Don't you think silence is a reproach?'

No one spoke. Eventually Rachel said in an anguished voice, 'I've tried so hard to make it up to you, Edward darling.'

'I'm not your "Edward darling",' said her son.

The doorbell rang. Rachel Verney smiled and sipped her drink.

'Dear Humphrey, he's always so punctual. Humphrey is my lover. Do you think I am too old for a lover?' she said, directing her question to Eleanor.

Edward gave his mother a furious look and left the room.

'Of course you're not too old,' Eleanor said.

'I know I'm fat. But men don't really mind. Anyway, Humphrey can't talk – he's pretty large himself! He's a wonderful cook. We plan to open a restaurant and I shall get even fatter. I must go – Edward doesn't like Humphrey. Edward doesn't like anything about me. Is there anything I can do to repair the damage? What do you think?'

'I don't think so. He doesn't want to forgive you – he wants to hate you. I've tried to dilute this hate but Edward clings to it. Your son is a strange man, Mrs Verney.'

'I wish you'd marry him. You are far and away the nicest girl he's ever been out with. And I must say, I do like your painting. I was in Motcomb Street the other day and I passed a gallery and in the front window was one of your portraits. It was magnificent!'

They were interrupted by Edward, who came back into the room with a large-faced man in his sixties, balding and with a black moustache. Humphrey was wet and cold, but even so Edward did not offer him a drink.

Eleanor said, 'Would you like a whisky? You look so cold.'

'Beastly British weather. Thank you. I would love a whisky. Has Rachel told you? We are opening a restaurant in the South of France. We're going to specialize in the best of British cooking. People think we're mad, but you know, it's rather original. And if the best of British doesn't work, then we'll move on to the best of something else. Either way we can live in the sun. That's what we want, isn't it, my poppet? A sunny old age!'

Eleanor kept the conversation genial. Edward left the room to return only as the visitors were leaving. As they said good-bye, Rachel Verney pressed Eleanor's hand and whispered,

'Edward's a good man underneath. I think you could be very happy. Think about it!'

In the sitting room against the background of a crackling fire, Eleanor said, 'You could have told your mother we're getting married. She would have been so pleased.'

'I shall write to her.'

6   The wounds of childhood that never heal, of these Eleanor knew nothing. She had grown up in a cocoon of love. At times she wondered if it was almost a disadvantage to have quite such a happy childhood; the difficulties and disappointments of later life seemed all the more severe because they came hard on years of secure affection.

It was not a banal childhood. Eleanor's father, Wensley Wynn, was an extraordinary man, one of the last genuine explorers. He felt at home in the deserts and rainforests and remote mountains of this world and was forever uneasy in the conurbations of the twentieth century. They lived in a pink stone house in Somerset, and before each journey Wensley would spread out a map of the world on the drawing room floor and show his small daughters where he was going, pointing out oceans and deserts and mountain ranges along the way. During his long absences he sent postcards of wild animals and waterfalls, and exotic stamps with tropical flowers, and on his return the house would be filled with boxes of strange objects: wood carvings from Alaska, spears from Nagaland, feathered headdresses from the Amazon, and twisting pink shells and smooth white stones, and stuffed birds and mountain butterflies.

In those early years her father was always leaving or coming home; he would stay just long enough to tell the children about rogue elephants and bush fires and the treacherous sands of the Gobi Desert and the murderous bandits on the shores of Lake Van; and then he would be gone.

The centre of Eleanor's early life was her mother, Anne Wynn. She was devoted, unsentimental and beautiful. She had a lovely voice and the softest laugh and she always seemed to be laughing; life amused her. Eleanor could not remember a time when she had not adored her mother. At night Anne Wynn would kiss her girls goodnight and Eleanor would clasp her mother about the neck and refuse to let her go, and laugh as her mother protested, 'My hair . . . don't muss my hair.'

The Wynn marriage was legendary, ending only in death. Anne was more than a wife to Wensley, she was his partner and his companion. With the two girls in boarding school, she joined her husband on his expeditions to the rainforests of the Amazon with their astonishing richness of vegetation, to the lost cities of the Taklamakhan desert buried in centuries of sand. They went to the tips of the world, north and south, and stood on Cape Comorin and on Tierra del Fuego; on Annapurna and Machapuchere. Anne took the photographs, and kept notes, and the passports and the medicine chest. Wensley dedicated each of his widely read travel books: 'For my wife Anne', 'For Anne', 'For A'.

Eventually Marcia and Eleanor were allowed to join these expeditions, and for several weeks at the start of each autumn term they were the centre of attention. Other girls had been to Athens or Rome, but Eleanor and Marcia had seen the elephant fair of Patna, and listened to a thousand prayer wheels in the dzongs of Bhutan, and eaten raw baby squid in Hokkaido and chrysanthemums in Kyoto, and been stung by sea urchins on the Australian barrier reef. Eleanor was especially proud when, at the age of seventeen, her passport was full and she needed a new one.

Wensley Wynn was killed in a helicopter crash on the Everest landing strip as Eleanor and her mother looked on. He was buried on a Himalayan mountainside where the grass provided rich grazing for yaks. He left nothing but debts and an attic full of relics from all over the world (an impossible jumble of tribal feathers and loincloths, of phallic drinking vases and whalebones). There was nothing to do but sell the family home in Somerset. Anne moved into a cottage on the edge of an Oxfordshire village. She never complained, and even at her husband's memorial service there was no public grieving. No one, not even Eleanor, saw her cry.

There was no question of retirement. On the contrary, Anne Wynn announced to her friends that at the age of sixty she was turning professional. For years she had been the official photographer for her husband's travels; now she would market her skills. She decided to concentrate on flowers and animals, and within a year she was official photographer for Oxfordshire nurseries, Whipsnade Zoo and Windsor Safari Park. Proudly she told everyone, 'I am a working widow.'

She was not elegant enough, Eleanor thought as she scrutinized the figure of her mother in her unfinished painting. There must be pearls around her neck and more lace at the cuffs, and her hat should have a wider brim. Anne Wynn dressed as if she lived in another century; in the painting she must stand out in her beautiful eccentricity.

Eleanor dipped her brush into titanium white and barium yellow and almost lost heart; in her mind's eye she could see Vermeer's portrait of the woman in a yellow cape edged with fur, wearing a pearl earring, and as the pearl caught the light it became in some magical way the focus of the whole painting. There was genius in the painting of a pearl. 'I must not be put off,' she told herself. 'I am not Vermeer, I am only Eleanor Wynn, but I must always be Eleanor Wynn at her best!' There must be pearls and lace and the fringes should be longer, and the hair must be piled a little higher on the head; and there must be more of a smile; her mother was always smiling at her own thoughts.

'Darling, is that me?'

Eleanor spun round to find her mother standing in the middle of the studio, wearing the same hat as in the painting. She flung her arms around her mother and said, 'What do you think? It's not finished, of course. That man needs a face. But apart from that, and a little more vermilion in the fire-eater's fire, and a touch more purple in the sky, apart from all of that it's nearly ready. What do you think?'

'Don't rush me! Don't rush me! Let me have a proper look.'

For several minutes Anne stood silently in front of the canvas, and as she stood there Eleanor examined her slender form and thought to herself, 'How elegant she looks. So utterly distinguished. I haven't captured her slender grace, but then in my painting she's sitting down. She should be standing. Oh dear. I can't change it now.'

'What a bold idea . . . Oh, Eleanor, this is very fine! I do congratulate you! You know, I was thinking the other day, it's the women in our family who are creative. They always have been. My grandmother was a beautiful pianist – today she almost certainly would have been a concert pianist. And

42

Mother was a fine watercolourist. Those flower drawings of hers – you know, the roses and lilies – they are beautiful. And now there's you – the most gifted of us all.'

Anne pulled the edges of her gloves until they slipped from her hands, and asked, 'Do I really look that old? I suppose I do . . .'

'I haven't painted you old. I've just painted you . . . well, you!'

Anne smiled. 'You're not given to flattery, and I like that. People go around saying you're as old as you feel, which is of course nonsense. You're as old as you look.'

'Sixty-three isn't old.'

'I don't need comforting, thank you, darling.'

'I've something to tell you,' Eleanor said.

'You're getting married to Edward. I know all about it. Marcia rang me.'

The women stared at each other in silence.

'Why don't you say something?' Eleanor said impatiently. 'You're supposed to be pleased and delighted and all of that.'

'Darling, your happiness is more important to me than anything in this world. If this is what you want . . .'

'I am thirty-six. I can't wait any longer.'

Anne put her long thin hand on Eleanor's cheek, and smiled into her eyes and said, 'I think you're absolutely right to marry Edward. He's perfectly nice. And in time you will grow very fond of him.'

'Fond!' Eleanor said desperately. 'I don't want to grow fond!'

She began to cry and her tears fell on to her mother's hand. Anne did not take her hand away but stared with absolute concern into her daughter's weeping eyes. 'My child, my child,' she whispered.

Eleanor stumbled to her bed and sat on the edge, her head in her hands, sobbing, with her mother by her side stroking her hair and whispering words of comfort. In sudden bursts between the tears Eleanor said, 'I have never been in love! I have never felt the Grand Passion that is supposed to mark every artistic life. I have never really loved a man – not totally – not completely – not in the way I want to – not "even to the edge of doom". And now . . . now I am to marry Edward.'

'I don't think you should marry anyone in this state.'

'You don't understand,' Eleanor said fiercely. 'I must! I must!'

'I do understand, and I still say to you that you don't have to marry Edward.'

'I must have a child. I shall go mad if I don't have a child.'

'You don't have to marry to have a child.'

Eleanor looked up through her tears.

'What do you mean?' she asked.

'I mean what I say . . . you don't have to marry to have a child.'

'No, I'm not strong enough to have a child on my own. I couldn't cope . . . I'd be lost . . . Oh, why is it so difficult for me, my darling mother, why? Look at you . . . you married the man you loved.'

'Who told you that?'

'No one . . . I just assumed . . . you seemed so happy together.'

'When I married your father I was in love with someone else.'

Eleanor looked astonished.

'I thought Daddy was the love of your life,' she said.

'Did you? I wonder why.'

Suddenly Eleanor got up and paced the room; she was angry.

'This is ridiculous. Everywhere I look, on close inspection, absolute love disintegrates! But it does exist! I refused to accept that it is a fiction. Men and women have loved each other unconditionally, and those same men and women have married. It is not all compromise!'

'I don't feel that I compromised by marrying your father,' Anne said quietly.

'But you weren't in love with him, you said so! You will tell me that he was your friend, your companion. But that's not enough, and it shouldn't have been enough for you. I wish you had never told me. I am disappointed . . . terribly disappointed . . . it seems so second best.'

Anne laid her hand gently on her daughter's arm.

'It was not second best – that is where you are wrong. I had a wonderful life with your father and I was touched, deeply touched, by his devotion.'

'Devotion,' Eleanor conceded, 'I forgot about devotion.'

44

'Don't imagine I did not love your father. I did, I loved him dearly. He was so helpless, so badly organized – he needed someone to look after him. And he was interesting. In all our married life there was never a dull moment. He gave me a lovely life. When I think of all the beautiful places he took me to, all that I saw – the tribes, the wildlife, the jungles, the flowers – what a rich time we had! I was very lucky. But then I knew what I wanted.'

'And what was that?'

'I wanted something out of the ordinary. Something unpredictable. So I married an explorer.'

'And the man you left behind . . . what happened to him? Who was he? Tell me about your love!'

'Don't pry. I like to keep my secrets to myself.'

Eleanor stepped forward and hugged her mother and laid her head on her shoulder. She said, 'Don't ever die, will you? I don't think I could stand this earth if you were not on it.'

'My darling,' Anne said softly. 'My darling, of course I shall die.'

Eleanor pulled away.

'You're not ill, are you? There's nothing wrong, is there?' she asked.

'Don't fuss. You know I hate fuss. I'm fine.'

'You would never say, even if you were at death's door.'

'Well, I'm not. Now you must work. It's a magnificent painting, but I want to meet the man – the central character. He is all there, in body but not in soul. Eleanor – to your canvas!'

Anne Wynn took her daughter's hand, and the touch of those long, feline fingers, of the soft, ageing skin, of the frailty of her thin being, brought back a vivid memory: cool hands on a burning forehead. Whenever Eleanor was ill in bed with chickenpox or flu, her mother would place a cool hand on her burning forehead and Eleanor felt cured. It was the coolness of the hand that healed, a beautiful, fragrant coolness that drove away all worry and all pain.

Eleanor took her mother's hand and kissed it.

'How quaint,' Anne said, laughing. But all the same she was touched; her eyes were tender with love. She hesitated and then said, 'Yes, you must have children. Marry Edward. It's the right decision.' Anne drew her daughter to her and held her for a long time. She kissed Eleanor on the forehead and whispered, 'Happiness.'

Abruptly Eleanor said, 'Edward asked me if I wanted an engagement ring.'

'He *asked* you?'

'Don't,' Eleanor interrupted quickly, 'say anything.'

Dominic was the last to know. One afternoon he came into the studio and found Eleanor standing by the window. She said to him, 'I've got bad news for you. I'm getting married to Edward. We're going to live in China.'

Dominic stood quite still. His hand tightened around the handle of his cane. For several minutes he said nothing, and then abruptly he banged the cane sharply on the floor.

'That's it!' he exploded. 'That's the end of you as a painter! As a serious painter, I mean. Of course you will think you can go on. But you can't. Not living with him. Not in that environment. Let's have no illusions – painting is total or it is nothing. You will disintegrate as an artist, do you understand that? I can just picture your degenerate efforts five years from now – ghastly chocolate box scenes of women in paddyfields which you will expect me to exhibit in London. Well, I won't, I'm telling you now. You are a fool, Eleanor. You have a gift and you are about to throw it away. As a painter you are finished. Dead. Buried.'

Dominic stalked about the studio like a caged animal, banging his cane on the floor, and now and then using it to knock over a book.

'Why isn't Edward in your epic painting? Eh? Have you thought of that? I'll tell you why – '

'No you won't! Leave me alone! Leave Edward alone!'

'I'll tell you why he is not in your painting – because you don't like Edward. He may be in your mind but he is not in your heart. If he were, then he would be here, in the picture, alongside all of us!'

'Leave me alone! I must finish my painting!'

'You'll never finish it. Not now.'

He was right. She never did finish the painting; but she tried. For the next three days Eleanor did not leave the studio. She did not go to bed; she would bath at strange hours, in the afternoon or the middle of the night, and the change of clothes, and the freshness of warm water gave her energy. Twenty, perhaps thirty times she outlined the basic features of a mythical man, only to destroy them almost at once; by the end of the week the surrealist creature with a body and no face was tormenting her with his defiant nothingness. She began to hate her own creation, especially since in every other part of the canvas there were people she knew and loved. The singular stance of Rosie, as a waitress holding a tray, stood out. Rosie had been the model in the life class at the art school where Eleanor first taught. There had always been something derelict about her, and yet she had beautiful eyes, huge and solemn and slightly protruding. She would keep religiously still while the class drew her thin legs and small bosom; now and then she would shiver in front of the two-bar fire, and when it was time for a break, one or other of the painters would step forward with a warm coat and put it round Rosie's shoulders, and the class would sit on the elevated stage where she sat, and talk, as if they were all trying to make her feel at home and unashamed. What had happened to Rosie?

The sullen cockney voice startled Eleanor.

'That's me, innit? The girl with the tray?'

'Rosie, how extraordinary, I was just thinking about you!' Eleanor said, hugging her. 'I'm very glad to see you.'

It was the same scrawny face, and the same enormous eyes, but they seemed more dejected than usual.

'It's me, innit?' she said, nodding towards the canvas.

'Yes, it's you.'

'On my own, always on my own.'

Slowly she walked over to Eleanor's large bed and sat on the crumpled sheets, where she heaved a miserable sigh and looked at Eleanor with eyes of blank despair.

'I don't have to go on, do I?'

'No one has to go on. But death is a dull alternative to life. If you don't believe in Heaven and Hell, that is.'

'I dunno. I fancy the peace and quiet.'

'Rosie how old are you?'

'Twenty-four.'

'You're so young!'

'I'm a thousand years old.'

'You look tired and thin – you never did eat enough – and that's enough to make anyone depressed. Why don't you let me get you something to eat, and you can sleep here tonight. You can sleep in my bed, and you'll feel better and stronger. What do you say? I can make you spaghetti with meat sauce!'

'Nah.'

'I'm so glad to see you. Stay a while.'

'Nah.'

'Have you got a job?'

Rosie shook her head.

Eleanor said, 'Are you looking for work, because if so you have come to the right place. This studio is a dreadful mess and I don't have time to tidy up. Can you help me?'

'That's what they said at the centre. Do something useful.'

'I'll give you £10.'

Rosie was sure to accept. Ten pounds was not much, but it would buy more of the powder and the pills that brought all the colours of the rainbow into her grey life.

'Cash on the table?'

'Sure.'

Eleanor handed over a £10 note, and slowly but methodically Rosie cleaned the studio. Later they drank tea together, and Rosie kept staring at the bed with her bloodshot eyes; the temptation to sleep was strong.

'One day you will be happy, Rosie. One day we shall all be happy. It's in the American Declaration of Independence,' Eleanor said.

'This ain't America.'

'I know, but it's a message for all mankind: life, liberty and the pursuit of happiness.'

'Don't you read the papers? There ain't no happiness in America. It's all rape and murder.'

Wearily Rosie got to her feet and arched her back, and Eleanor thought of the Degas drawings of the ironing women, yawning and arching their backs.

'I'll be on my way. Thanks for the money. And the chat. See you.'

Suddenly exhausted, Eleanor threw herself on her bed and slept. She did not wake until the next morning. In her half-consciousness she became aware of a figure standing in the middle of the studio. Gradually the outline grew sharper and she recognized Dominic, tapping his cane on the wooden floor.

'That's it. The picture comes with me,' he said.

'You can't take it!' Eleanor said, throwing off the covers. 'I'll finish it today. I promise!'

'Too late. Your time is up.'

7 'Are they any good?' Eleanor asked herself as she looked from one painting to another. In a few hours her first solo exhibition would open. Dominic and his assistant Theodore were carefully positioning the neatly typed out labels alongside each canvas. The massive, unfinished painting with its blank face had been entitled 'Pilgrim' by Dominic.

'We go on to the attack,' he said to Eleanor. 'We tell everyone that the painting *is* finished. It's quite finished. The blank face is intentional. It's full of meaning. We can leave the intellectual art critics to tell us *what* meaning. They love to write rubbish, so let's give them a golden opportunity!'

'Isn't he devious?' Theodore giggled, pulling on his gold earring. He was a young and beautiful boy of eighteen, impeccably dressed in a white suit and a spotted bow tie, and through his round spectacles he gazed adoringly at Dominic, as he enthused, 'He's so frightfully far sighted. Always a step ahead. Brilliant, absolutely brilliant.'

'Pilgrim' was a good title, Eleanor decided. It reminded her of her favourite poem by Yeats:

> One man loved the pilgrim soul in you
> And loved the sorrows of your changing face . . .

Eleanor had never seen so many of her own paintings assembled in one room. The terracotta walls of Dominic's gallery set the pictures off, strengthening the darker tones, heightening the paler shades. At first glance, each painting spoke to Eleanor in a personal language, reminding her of when and how that particular canvas had come into being; she remembered the sitter and how he or she sat; and she remembered how she herself had felt at the time. But on second sight the pictures assumed an existence of their own. They were no longer 'hers'; they were independent of their creator.

'But do they speak to people? Do they say, "Here's the pity

of it all, we dream out our lives, and those dreams remain unfulfilled. We are doomed to disappointment, it is part of the human condition!" Do my paintings explain all of this? The madman revolts against his fate; the wise man accepts his destiny, and those who are happy are those who laugh. Do my paintings tell this tale?'

Life had brought Eleanor moments of great joy, but the moments that came to mind as she surveyed the last few years of work were joys of the mind; they did not involve people. Eleanor's pleasures were cerebral: a passage of music, a book, a sculpture, a painting. Next to art, life had been dull. Eleanor had formed passionate friendships with the dead, and just to hear the names of Mozart, Crivelli and Hemingway brought a smile to her lips.

'I have become an intellectual,' she thought to herself sadly.

Dominic was anxious. He darted about the gallery instructing the women from the catering agency who were preparing trays of delicacies, and the barmen with their buckets of ice. Theodore followed.

'No prices,' Dominic said. 'It's too vulgar. We'll have the price lists on this table and our guests can take one – or a sausage roll – it doesn't matter. We're not after sales this evening, but impact. As always I have a master plan. This entire exhibition is designed to impress one person and one person only. She is one of the richest women in the world: Mrs Ethel B. Wingate.'

Breathlessly Theodore announced, 'Mrs Wingate has just telephoned – well, no, she didn't ring herself – it was her driver. Like the Archangel Gabriel he was heralding her arrival. He telephoned from the car. They are currently circling Belgrave Square.'

'Eleanor,' Dominic said, 'pay attention. The woman who is about to walk into my gallery is the most sensational patron of the arts since Cosimo de Medici. You name it, she pays for it – opera, ballet, theatre. Recently she has conceived the most charming idea – to build a National Portrait Gallery for the American nation. You see, there isn't one. Naturally she wants all her friends to be painted. So generous! She has come to England with the express purpose of recruiting British portrait painters – she thinks we're the best! Oh happy woman! During her first week in this country she met Dominic le Jeune – artists agent *extraordinaire*. I am the latest in a long line of acolytes. The devoted admirer. My new role in life is to guide the footsteps of Mrs Ethel B. Wingate. This Sunday I accompanied her to Communion – an essential duty as the dear lady is a born-again Christian. We talk about Jesus all the time. He is my friend too.'

All conversation stopped as a large black Rolls-Royce drew up outside and the visitor entered the gallery. Mrs Ethel B. Wingate smiled perpetually, showing off gleaming white teeth. Her hair was stiff with lacquer, and her long fingernails were painted bright red. She wore an enormous amount of expensive jewellery: gold bracelets encrusted with diamonds, bright emerald earrings, a huge diamond ring. But the face was intelligent and she had a direct way of looking at people which appealed to Eleanor. Also she had a firm handshake. Unlike so many rich patrons that Eleanor had met, Mrs Wingate really looked at paintings. She did not carry on a continuous stream of pointless chatter; in fact most of the time she stood in front of the picture and said nothing. It was only when she came to the unfinished painting of Covent Garden that her expression changed. The calmness left her face and anxiously she asked for a chair. Out of her handbag she pulled a handkerchief and wiped her forehead.

'Are you all right?' Dominic asked, mildly annoyed.

'It's nothing,' she said breathlessly. 'But you see, I wasn't expecting this. Oh ye of little faith!'

'Indeed,' Dominic said solicitously.

'What is she talking about?' Theodore whispered to Eleanor.

'I've no idea.'

'Mrs Wingate. Let me share this moment with you,' Dominic said soothingly.

'But it's so obvious. Don't you see?'

'See what?'

'That man – without a face – it's Jesus!'

Theodore gasped.

'Where is the artist? Let me see her. Eleanor, isn't it? My dear child, I want to thank you from the bottom of my heart for this deeply moving experience. Of course I realize that most probably you did not set out to paint him. But the Lord moves in mysterious ways. What exactly did you have in mind?'

52

'Nothing. I couldn't find a face.'

'And why not? The world is full of faces.'

'I know the world is full of faces, but somehow none of them were right for my painting. Given a little more time I am sure – '

'Child, child,' Mrs Wingate said, taking Eleanor by the arm, 'do not turn away from the Lord. When He speaks you *must* listen. Now come with me. It is time you and I had a little talk.' And she led Eleanor away to a corner of the gallery, where she held forth.

'I looked at your painting and suddenly I was overcome with the most profound sense of His presence. He is in our daily lives, only we do not see Him. But in your painting the girl understands. She turns to look again. Of course you have used yourself as the model. That is quite natural. But it's clear to me that the girl is Mary Magdalene. She has recognized Him. Oh, Eleanor, I can't tell you how excited I am! I should like to buy this painting for a church that I have built in San Antonio in memory of my late husband, Edgar Wingate III. He loved England. We spent our honeymoon in London. I shall hang the painting above the altar. Would you consider making one or two minor additions?'

'What sort of additions?'

'I don't mean to be indelicate. I can sense your concern and I would not tamper with your artistic integrity. But perhaps you could see your way to adding a few symbols. Like a dove perching on the lamppost? And the traffic warden, could he possibly carry a lily? And around His head – might there be a halo? Very faint, but just visible.'

'Mrs Wingate, I don't want to disappoint you, but my painting is not for sale – it isn't finished.'

'Oh . . . pride! The worst of all human sins! Don't smile. Please don't smile . . . the spirit of the Lord is in this picture. And I must have it!'

Mrs Wingate gave one of her most dazzling smiles, and then she went on, as if the matter were decided, 'You and I are going to be friends. I can tell. But first let's talk business. I have a proposal to put before you. I should like to commission you to paint a friend of mine. I think his name may be known to you . . . he's rather a star in the opera firmament.' She paused for effect and then said, 'I'm referring to Vincent Buonarotti.'

'We've all heard of Vincent Buonarotti,' Eleanor said.

'Yes, indeed, although I must say I do not altogether approve of all the publicity he seems to generate. One day it will go to his head. But for the time being he enjoys a cult status in the United States and it is high time he had his portrait painted. It's long overdue, and you, my dear girl, are the right person for the job. Of course if the painting is a success, as I am sure it will be, there could be other commissions. I have formed a foundation to build a National Portrait Gallery in memory of my late husband, poor lamb. I shall be needing many contemporary portraits. You . . . you don't seem very enthusiastic, Eleanor – what's the matter?'

'No . . . No, I am enthusiastic . . . It's only that it may be difficult for me to travel.'

Mrs Wingate brushed the remark aside. 'Are you afraid of flying? I have the most marvellous pills. Now, let's discuss your fee and the deal is done.'

'Dominic deals with all of that.'

'Very well then,' and she called for Dominic, who flew to her side. 'My dear boy, we have business to discuss. Oh, I am so excited. The Lord has sent me to you. Praise be to Him. We are each other's destiny. Dominic, Dominic, where are you?'

Dominic took Mrs Wingate into his office, where they remained for ten minutes. They were both smiling when they emerged, and Dominic escorted his visitor to her large black limousine and waved her off with his shocking pink silk handkerchief.

Once the car was out of sight he leapt into the air and danced around the gallery shouting, 'We've done it! We've done it! This is the break we needed. Eleanor, you are made! She loves your work – she loves you – and she loves me! Our worries are over. I've always said you only need one patron, that's all. Well, Mrs Wingate is it! As an enormous favour I've sold her your unfinished masterpiece. Don't look so surprised! Who says it's not finished? Everything is finished – at a price! But that's only the start. You won't believe the deal I have pulled off! Oh, what a skilled negotiator I am! So controlled, so cool. I didn't show a thing – no eagerness, no excitement. I considered everything slowly, as if I were doing *her* the favour. It worked a treat! You are to go to New York next week and for the princely sum of £20,000 – yes, let me say that again – £20,000 – *that*, my dear girl, is double the fee of artists twice as famous as you – for £20,000 you paint Vincent Buonarotti. Oh, by the way, you stay at the Hotel Pierre in a suite. Free, of course. For a month.'

'I don't believe it!'

'It's true. I swear it.'

'Twenty thousand pounds! New York! Vincent Buonarotti! I don't believe it!'

'Champagne – Theodore, bring the champagne!'

'You are brilliant, Dominic. Absolutely brilliant!' Theodore gushed.

'Of course I'm brilliant. There's only one Dominic le Jeune. Don't just stand there, Theodore – bring the champagne!'

'I'm sure Edward will be very pleased,' Eleanor said.

'Who cares about Edward?'

'I care!' Eleanor said sharply.

Dominic shrugged his shoulders. 'Well . . . Anyway, Edward will keep. He's like that Long Life milk – he won't go off. He's too bland to decay . . .'

'Dominic!' Eleanor said.

'Sorry, sorry. I promise to be good. Oh, I'm so thrilled! Now, let's get ready for the rush of visitors. All the art world will be here tonight, all those gluttonous critics. Theodore, have we enough smoked salmon sandwiches? And what about the asparagus tips, you haven't forgotten those? No . . . no . . . everything must be laid out on white napkins, not placed on the tray *tout nu* – does no one around here know anything about civilized living?'

'I do!'

Dominic turned to face a short man with a black moustache and dark, seductive eyes. Dominic's manner changed. He became flirtatious.

'Hugo! You're early,' he said.

'I'm always early. It's a cliché to be late.'

'You're not to distract me. I'm very busy.'

'I didn't come to see you. I came to see the lovely Eleanor and her paintings.'

Hugo Kyle was the art critic for the *Independent*. Dominic

was aroused by his presence. Now and then they exchanged a glance or a secret smile. 'They are lovers,' Eleanor told herself, and suddenly she longed for the conspiracy of love.

The gallery was crowded with people, talking, and the talk and the tinkle of glasses merged into one discordant sound punctuated by shrieks of laughter; people seemed to be embracing endlessly and drinking and eating.

Eleanor, who had greeted people for over an hour, moved away to a quiet corner of the gallery and observed the scene. Marcia had brought with her a man, not someone that Eleanor knew, and there was no doubt in Eleanor's mind that this man was Matthew, Marcia's lover. Marcia was smiling at him, her eyes intoxicated with love. He touched her cheek; they both laughed; they moved from one painting to another, together.

'She is not discreet,' Eleanor thought. 'She must be careful.' And all at once, in the middle of the celebration, Eleanor felt a weight of sadness descend. Her eyes followed Marcia. She thought, 'You always hear that people in love look different. Well, they do. Look at Dominic. Look at Marcia – look at her eyes, bright and shining – she's more beautiful than she's ever been – and she's so happy! Look at her – take note – she's a woman in love.' Eleanor thought to herself, 'I have never felt like that.'

Eventually Edward arrived. Eleanor watched him from her corner. He looked uncomfortable; he knew no one and he was not a man to make an effort with strangers. Without looking at the paintings he crossed the room to Eleanor.

'Darling, this is awful. Such a lot of people, I can't breathe. Do you have to stay long?' he said.

Before Eleanor could answer, a man in glasses floated past, saying, 'Fabulous, darling, just fabulous, especially the nude. The nude is terrific.'

'Do you know all these people?' Edward asked.

'Darling,' a Greek woman with a thick accent said, kissing Eleanor. 'It's a triumph – that's all I can say. Your portraits – a new Rembrandt, that's what you are.'

'No, no. I'm not a new Rembrandt.'

'Let me be the judge . . . Oh, look, there's Georgie! How ill he looks! Georgie! Yoo-hoo!'

'I must show you this,' Edward said. 'I keep forgetting. I

56

got my secretary to type it out.' He handed Eleanor a sheet of
white paper. She read:

The engagement is announced
between Edward Verney, the only son of
Mrs Rachel Verney and Brigadier General Edwin Verney,
and Miss Eleanor Wynn,

daughter of Mrs Wesley Wynn and the late Wesley Wynn . . .

Eleanor stopped reading and pleaded, 'Can we go through
this another time?'

'I want to send it off tomorrow. Please have a look.'

'Super exhibition,' said an anorexic creature, blowing Eleanor a kiss.

She studied the typed sentences and said, 'My father's name
is spelt wrong – it's Wensley, not Wesley.'

'I wrote Wensley. The stupid girl typed it wrong.'

'I've just had rather an exciting hour.'

'I can see you are enjoying yourself. You are the centre of
attention, my love.'

'That's not what I meant . . . Before the exhibition opened,
we gave a private showing to Mrs Ethel Wingate. She liked
my work and she has commissioned me to paint a portrait of
Vincent Buonarotti in New York. The fee is £20,000. It's so
much money I can hardly believe it! Just think, darling, we'll
be rich. We can buy all sorts of things – a compact disc player
– I've always wanted a compact disc player!'

'Have you accepted?'

'Of course I've accepted. It's only a month. I'll be staying at
the Pierre – imagine! Oh, I wish you could come too, but it's
only a month and then I am paid – just think, Edward –
£20,000!'

Edward said nothing. He was looking at Eleanor with anger
and hurt in his eyes.

Eleanor put a hand on his arm and asked, 'Aren't you
pleased for me?'

'You decided – just like that?'

'Of course I decided. It's a wonderful offer. What should I
have done?'

'You should have asked me.'

Edward turned his back on Eleanor and pushed his way
through the crowd past the red lipstick smiles and gloved

hands holding glasses and disappeared into the street. A bearded elderly man took Eleanor by the arm.

'Miss Wynn, at last I am finding you. Ze painting of Covent Garden – is your most interesting work, I am thinking. Ze man with no face . . . to me his identity is no secret – he is a symbol of original sin – the evil in man which follows us wherever we go . . . the evil that in this century alone has produced Auschwitz and Cambodia . . .'

Eleanor was sitting on a bulging suitcase in the stillness of her studio holding a letter. It was from Edward and it read:

Darling,
   I've gone back to Sheffield to finish my course in Japanese. I think it's best if we postpone the announcement of our engagement until you are back from America. Painting seems to be uppermost in your mind these days.
   Love, Edward

Eleanor read and reread the letter until her vision was flooded by hot tears. She remembered his hurt and angry eyes, and the way he had walked out of the gallery without looking at one of her paintings, and in her mind she accused Edward: 'You don't care! My work, my painting, is of no consequence to you!'

She opened the windows of her studio and inhaled the warm air of summer. She must train herself not to mind. 'There's no turning back,' she reminded herself.

She found a pen and a piece of paper and began to write a conciliatory letter. She begged him to understand that it was important for her to go to America and to establish herself as an international portrait painter. Eventually she tore up the letter. She felt ridiculous, imploring her lover to understand that she wanted to succeed, that she wanted to practise her art. She would not beg. She would go to America, paint a fine picture, return and marry Edward.

That night she could not sleep. She dreamt that she was in a house with Edward and someone was pulling curtains across the windows shutting out the light. She was sitting at one end of an enormous table, Edward was at the other; they sat in complete darkness with one candle burning; Edward was reading a newspaper. On her plate a fish had grown cold. She looked down at her plate. It was filled with tears.

It was early morning when she was woken by a timid knock at her door.

'Who is it?' she asked.

'Me Rosie.'

'Rosie! Come in.'

'I ain't alone.'

'Come in!' Eleanor said, pulling on her dressing gown.

Rosie came in. She looked quite different. She wore blobs of red rouge on either cheek, heavy eye make-up and red lipstick. Beside her stood a man in his early twenties in a black leather jacket sprinkled with badges. His head was shaved except for a central brush of red hair that stood out stiffly. He wore gold earrings and his hands were covered with tattoos.

'This is Rick. We're together,' Rosie said.

'Nothing permanent,' he said.

'No, just for now.'

'Like today.'

'Yeah, today.'

'Rosie, I'm off to America. If you like you can stay here. As long as you promise to keep it tidy. And please, no parties. You can have a few friends but not hundreds.'

'Really?'

'Really.'

'Great. I ain't got nowhere of my own. We won't make no mess.' Rosie smiled, showing her uneven teeth. 'Innit great?' she said to Rick. Rick nodded.

Later Rosie helped Eleanor into the taxi with her suitcase.

'He's not as bad as he looks. With them punks it's all bark and no bite. He goes home to his mum for Sunday dinner.'

Eleanor got into the taxi and Rosie stood on the pavement watching the taxi draw away, waving and smiling. Eleanor waved back and hoped for Rosie's sake that Rick would stay for this day and the next and the one after that.

8 In Central Park the leaves were falling, brown and brittle, on to the ground baked hard after a long New York summer. Above the tops of trees rose the skyscrapers of Manhattan, and the thousand panes of glass hurled back the reflection of a bright autumn sun. Eleanor sat on a park bench by the entrance to the zoo staring at a maple tree in full flame. The colour – red oxide and raw sienna and cobalt violet – was outrageous. This was no sane autumn colour on the brown or amber scale; it was an outburst of pure joy, a tree on fire. In the park men and women jogged on regardless (how could they pass this tree and not stop and marvel?) and children with earphones clamped to their heads performed their skateboard acrobatics.

Eleanor had come to New York to paint, but for the first two weeks the sitter refused to sit. In vain Ethel Wingate pleaded with Vincent Buonarotti, but he stood there, his head thrown back, laughing, and saying over and over, 'Impossible, Ethel my dear! When? How? I am working twenty hours a day! There is no time . . . unless she can paint me asleep. Yes? Eyes shut?'

'I don't want a picture of you asleep,' Ethel said firmly.

It was Dasha, Vincent's Russian wife, who persuaded him, in the entrance hall of the Metropolitan Opera House, under the Chagal paintings.

'It would please Ethel,' Dasha said in her soft Slavic accent.

'It would, my dear, it would,' Ethel said. 'And it would please Eleanor – the poor girl has come all the way from England.'

'We owe so much to Ethel,' Dasha said.

At last it was settled. Each morning before rehearsals Vincent sat for Eleanor in his office. He sat, but he did not sit still. From the moment he arrived he summoned his secretary, Sally Anne, who spoke in a languid Southern drawl, which seemed out of place with Vincent Buonarotti's frantic pace.

'G'mornin', Vincent . . . an' what a beautiful day it surely is out there – '

'Messages, Sally Anne, let's have the messages.'

Into his hand Sally Anne pressed faxes and memo sheets, which Vincent read at high speed, and as he tossed the pages to the floor a torrent of instructions were issued: 'Get me Richard in Sydney. He wants to do *Rigoletto* in modern dress. I've told him it's old hat. Jonathan Miller has beaten him to it, so why does he insist? Now where was I? Oh yes . . . I want to talk to Henry. What time is it in London? Two o'clock in the afternoon? Call him, call him right now! Are we standing in an open drain? What *is* that smell?'

'White spirit. Please don't move your head, Mr Buonarotti. You change position all the time and you are always talking. It is difficult to paint a mouth when it's always moving.'

Vincent looked up from the papers in front of him.

'*Parlo . . . si . . . è vero . . . purtroppo per niente . . .* They're all idiots! Giuseppe has scheduled *Traviata* at La Scala in the same month that I'm doing it here at the Met . . .'

'I love *Traviata*,' Eleanor said.

'He wants Caballe. I have got Caballe. And I shall keep her. For a start I can pay her twice what they can in Italy. But it's all so tiring . . . Dio mio! I am getting old and fat before my time . . . grey hair, I suppose you have noticed my grey hair?'

'Of course.'

'And I suppose you are going to include it in your painting?'

'I like grey hair. I think it's very attractive in a man.'

'You do? Ah. Well, that is nice to hear. You are a very pretty girl. Let me have a proper look. Yes. Indeed, you are *bellissima*. Why haven't I noticed you before?'

'Please keep your head still, Mr Buonarotti . . .'

'Vincent – call me Vincent.'

'Vincent, please keep you head still.'

'Giuseppe will have to cancel his *Traviata* – or else find someone else. That Scottish girl who was so good as Suzanna – she would do it – and she would do it very well. Give the young ones a chance and they can make the old stars tremble. Sally Anne – get Giuseppe on the line!'

It was the fifth sitting.

'Too early for California,' Vincent was saying, 'and too late for Japan. But Italy – la mia bella Italia – is wide awake. Sally Anne, get me Guido in Rome. I want to stage *Aida* in the Colosseum. We shall need to build a floor. Otherwise the set is perfect. And the lighting – I shall take charge of the lighting myself. We can make the most delicious, ghostly effects. From those ancient stones I shall evoke two thousand years of history! I shall have not one, not five – but seventeen elephants. The *polizia* will go crazy . . . Last time we had elephants they escaped and ran all over the Corso. This time I shall suggest that we turn the Caracalla baths into elephant stables. Now the Minister of the Interior – that humourless bigot – won't like that at all. I can hear him now: "Who do you think you are, Buonarotti? You want to invade the shrines of Italian culture, for what? Opera!" And I shall tell him that I wish to honour one of the great citizens of Italy – Giuseppe Verdi! That nothing is too fine for Verdi – and we shall have a glorious, pompous, rhetorical argument and . . . in the end . . . as always – I shall win!'

Eleanor, who was standing holding her palette in one hand and a long paintbrush in the other, and wearing an old overall spattered with paint of all colours, said, 'You sound like Dominic.'

'Who is Dominic?'

'He's my agent. Mr Buonarotti, I must ask you – '

'Vincent. That is my name.'

'Vincent – your chin. Hold it up, please.'

'And now what? I can't telephone. I can't read.'

'Look at me, that's right – straight at me. This painting is all in the eyes. If I don't get the eyes I have no painting.'

Eleanor held the palette tightly and with a long brush she stabbed at the canvas in fast, short brushstrokes. Leaning back against his seat, in a slow detached voice, Vincent said, 'What about my eyes?'

Eleanor spoke slowly and deliberately; 'You have the most unfaithful eyes I have ever seen.'

'Really?'

'Yes.'

'Don't tell Ethel Wingate. She's a born-again Christian. Ethel would call it adultery.'

'And what do you call it?'

'I call it *divertimento*.'

'And your wife? What does she say?'

Vincent threw out his arms.

'She adores me! I am her life!' he said.

Eleanor was not listening. She had stopped painting and was standing back from her canvas frowning. Suddenly she took a palette knife and furiously she began to scrape off the wet paint. She cried out, 'It's no good! It has no life, no heart! It's a likeness . . . nothing more!'

Vincent did not move from his chair. He leant back and watched.

'No good!' Eleanor repeated fiercely. 'I can do better than this, I really can!'

'What are you doing?'

'It's no good. It won't do!'

'It won't do? You take up hours of my time and then tell me it won't do?'

'I have *not* taken up hours of your time. And anyway you won't sit still. You're impossible.'

'Impossible!' He threw back his head and laughed. 'She says I'm impossible. No, my dear girl, you're wrong. Everyone loves me, didn't you know?'

'My boyfriend doesn't love you. We were about to get engaged when I told him I was off to New York to paint you. He is very, very angry. I can feel his fury across the Atlantic. He hasn't written. Not one letter. He hasn't telephoned either. Not once. Perhaps I was wrong to come to New York, I don't know. But I am sure that my boyfriend doesn't love you!'

'*Carissima*. I am always sympathetic to love stories. After all, I am Italian. You are upset. You cannot paint. I understand. Lasciamo stare! In a few months you will be calm. We can start again. Soon I start work on my film of *Bohème* . . . afterwards we meet again . . . next year.'

'We meet again next week! I promised Ethel Wingate to paint your portrait. But I can't paint you here – in this office! There's no atmosphere, no life! I need to see you on the stage with your singers, in *your* world, not surrounded by telexes and the telephone. Please, Vincent – let me come with you to your rehearsals. I won't speak, I promise! Let me watch you, and then I can compose a good painting! Please!'

Vincent did not answer at once; he rocked himself in the black leather armchair and said, 'I like you. I will help you.

But now we start at the beginning. What do you know about me?'

'Only what I have read in the press. There was an article, or rather a hagiography, in *Time* not long ago. It was pretty informative.'

'Hagiography? Really?' He smiled broadly. 'Really?'

'That's not quite fair. Beneath the lavish compliments were a few bare facts.'

'Such as?'

'Well . . . you are related to Michelangelo! So the article says. But I wonder – Buonarotti is a very common name in Italy, like Shakespeare in England . . .'

'We have the family tree . . . there is no doubt!'

'I'd like to see that family tree.'

'Go on! Go on . . .'

'Your father, Carlo Buonarotti, was from Piemonte – not exactly Michelangelo territory, but I suppose we have to allow the possibility of migration in four hundred years.'

'That is very generous of you.'

'As I say, your father came from Piemonte – he was a conductor – a good one by all accounts. Your mother was British – I think her name was Teresa, am I right? Yes, I thought so! I associated her with Bernini's statue of the ecstasy of St Teresa in Santa Maria della Vittoria in Rome. Was she a passionate woman? For some reason I imagine that she was. Anyway, your mother was an actress – not a very successful one – and she met your father in Italy when she was playing Juliet and they eloped. I like that. They married and lived all over the place – London, Rome, Milan, Vienna. But what about you? I seem to know more about your parents than I do about you. Let me see . . . Oh dear, I don't know anything about you except that you are the most famous opera producer in the world. You have made three films – *Carmen*, *Tosca*, and *The Marriage of Figaro*. You have produced everywhere in the world – now and then your direct, and now and then you design the set. Some people think you have too many fingers in too many pies – that you dissipate your talents.'

'The world is full of jealous mediocrities,' Vincent said, smiling. 'Go on, go on, I am enjoying this!'

'What else do I know? Oh yes – you are a major shareholder in the Classical Record company and people say you're very rich. On the personal front you have a wife and two teenage children, Marina and Nicholas. You wife, Dasha, is Russian. She was a dancer with the Bolshoi, until she came to America on a tour and met you. You fell in love. Dasha asked for political asylum and you married. It was romantic and wonderful!'

'It was, it was,' Vincent said, smiling and clapping. 'Well done. Those are indeed my essentials. Although I must assure you that I am directly descended from Michelangelo's brother . . . Michelangelo himself had no children. But this was not enough for my mother. She adored the paintings of Van Gogh so she called me Vincent. Imagine! I carry the name of two geniuses. Alas I am not in their mould – don't look like that – I know my limitations – I am competent and dedicated. *Basta!*'

'In that case you must charm all the journalists. They have never described you as "competent and dedicated" – they eulogize . . .'

'Of course I charm the journalists! I charm everyone! You are delightful, have I told you that? It's those green eyes and that black hair that is so unusual. When I was a boy, I knew some gipsies in the Roman Campagna who looked just like you, with black hair and green eyes. My English miss, you belong to another time and place – look at the shape of your face! It's pure eighteenth century! That's where you belong, in a Gainsborough painting!'

'My mother has a Gainsborough face.'

'Who are you, Eleanor Wynn? You must tell me all about yourself. And who is this fiancé? He should ring you once, twice – even five times a day. Is he not madly in love? Does your absence not cause him the acutest pain? Don't tell me he's a banker?'

'No. A diplomat.'

'That's worse. They are full of superficial charm.'

'And you?'

'I'm a man of passion. It may last a day – or a year – or a lifetime – but it is hot. *Capisci?* If I am not in love I don't feel well, I don't direct well, I don't sleep well. Love is essential to my work.'

'And your wife, how does she feel about all of this?'

'She's Russian. They learn from the very start that life is

miserable, sad, *eccetera*, *eccetera* . . . They suffer. A Russian feels alive through suffering. Dasha and I have a tremendous marriage. Indestructible. Also, one important point – she's the most noble woman I know. Nobilissima, I bow to her.' Vincent rose to his feet and bowed low to the wall, where he had hung a photograph of his wife. He turned to Eleanor. 'You want to see my world? Andiamo . . . You shall see Buonarotti direct!'

Vincent led the way and Eleanor followed, along the clean corridors of the fourth floor, past efficient secretaries in their executive offices; down, floor by floor, through the vast building of opera, past rehearsal rooms where musical directors were rehearsing arias; past the half-open doors of dressing rooms from where Eleanor could hear the sound of piano and violin; through the wardrobe room with a thousand costumes hung on racks, past dresses and breeches and jackets in gold and velvet and silver lamé, festooned with pearls and lace. Eleanor noticed that many of the clothes were labelled with the name of the singer for whom they had been made: 'Domingo'; 'Price'; 'Pavarotti'; 'Van Os'.

Eventually Vincent and Eleanor arrived at the back of the stage, which resembled a great warehouse filled with stage sets and props. Eleanor recognized the boat from *Tristan*, a minaret from the *Seraglio*, the grey rooftops of Paris from *Bohème*, and battlements from *Macbeth* and a giant crucifix on the altar from *Tosca*. Suddenly she found herself on the stage itself, dimly lit – staring out at the vast and empty theatre, at row upon row of empty red velvet seats, and layer upon layer of gilded balconies rising up to an ornate ceiling that was sprinkled with chandeliers. The vastness of the auditorium was impressive. To Eleanor it seemed beyond human capability that one voice could reach every corner of this monumental hall; and yet she knew that it could and did, night after night.

Vincent said, 'Tonight and every night 3,800 people fill this hall – not one seat is empty.' With his hand he reached out and his fingers gave shape to his words: 'I am the magician. I hold these people in the palm of my hand. It is my task to bewitch . . . to enchant!'

Those near Vincent were listening; and as he moved away, others watched. Whatever Vincent did or said was noticed; he was the centre of attention, automatically. People wished to be aware of his presence, just as they wished to hear fragments of his conversation. He was admired; he was adored. 'He's a man of charm and I must paint that charm,' Eleanor told herself. Vincent went on speaking, unaware (or so he pretended) that others were watching and listening.

'Now and then – not often, thank God – the opera is a disaster. Years ago, when I was in my twenties, I put on *Così Fan Tutte* in Manaus in the north of Brazil. We had a plague of mosquitoes. It was not the season for mosquitoes, but for once they deviated from their natural cycle and came in their trillions. We had no air conditioning, and while Dorabella and Fiordiligi were singing '*Sento O Dio*', these little monsters were buzzing about. Calestra was Dorabella – it was her first *Così* – I knew at once that she would become a great diva, but that night, poor girl she nearly gave up her career. There she was, opening her lovely mouth, and in flew a mosquito – '

At this point, Vincent began to sing loudly, 'Adioooo,' and everyone drew near as he continued, 'The poor girl coughed and spluttered and clutched her throat, and then, a moment later, she began again, *Adiooo*, and this time she slapped her own face and muttered, *Managgia* – which is Portuguese for damn, and tried to go on – Fiordiligi was laughing – it was grotesque – and by this time Ferrando was in trouble – the mosquitoes had got into his trousers and he was wriggling like this . . .'

Vincent imitated the singers, itching and slapping and swearing; stagehands stopped to look and laugh, and so did Eleanor. Eventually Vincent called the company to attention.

'*Finita la commedia*,' he said wiping tears from his own eyes. 'My friends, it's ten o'clock. *Andiamo adesso . . . forza!*' From all sides men and women in jeans and loose sweaters invaded the stage; some carried props; others stared up to the vault of the auditorium and shouted to the lighting men; while in the orchestra pit musicians were arriving, carrying their violins and cellos, double basses and bassoons. They spread out their scores on the music stands, each one lit by its own light, and began to tune their instruments. Against this discordant mix of tones, a vast double bed was wheeled on to the stage, and from all sides there were shouts: 'Further over, Jake! Pull the bed further over – and more to the left! – to the left – not the right! Wake up, Jake!' Behind the bed a wall was lowered with a high round window through which shone a full moon; from somewhere the top of a palm could be seen, blowing in the night. In the vastness of empty seats two groups had gathered, one at the front of the theatre, one at the back. Near the front two young men had spread out score sheets and were deep in conversation.

'Those two men are assistants to the conductor,' Vincent explained. 'They act as an extra pair of ears – just in case he misses something. Now and then a conductor will use them to judge the balance of the orchestra . . . you know, is the clarinet too weak, are the violins too strong? But their main job is to take preliminary rehearsals – that's what they enjoy. Those young men are full of ambition – already they see themselves as maestros!'

Suddenly Vincent turned to Eleanor and asked, 'What sign are you? Let me guess. I think you are a Virgo like me. Am I right?'

'Yes.'

'I knew it! We are ruthless perfectionists, but also, and this is what makes Virgos interesting, we are romantics.'

From the conductor's box a low, authoritative voice rang out: *'Meine Damen und Herren, bitte, Ruhe! Es ist Zeit . . . meine liebe Freunde* . . . Please . . . please . . . we must begin!'

The conductor stood, baton in hand, his head high, and his face taut with concentration. He was a man in his seventies with an elegant grey beard, and brilliant blue eyes. His nose was broken, giving him the air of a patrician. Vincent said, 'Is he not magnificent? How aristocratic he looks . . . how superior! You recognize him, of course? It is Karl Henkel. A great man. Come, let us greet the Maestro!'

Vincent took Eleanor by the hand (a gesture that caught her completely by surprise and made her feel rather foolish) and led her to the conductor, who was pondering the score while he stroked his beard with his long fingers. The two men embraced.

'Maestro, let me introduce Eleanor Wynn. She is a painter.'

'And what are you painting, my dear?' the conductor asked.

'She is painting me!' Vincent said, and threw back his head and laughed. 'She's a Virgo, and like all Virgos she is never satisfied. You know, Maestro, she has already destroyed one picture!'

'That is very good,' the conductor said seriously. 'I wish everyone would destroy bad work!'

They were interrupted by one of the young assistants, who whispered into the Maestro's ear. Karl Henkel answered in German, pointing to the score and tapping his finger vehemently on certain bars then he shook his head and said, *'Aber nein, nein!'*

Again Vincent took Eleanor by the hand and led her to the back of the hall. He relinquished her hand and sat in a seat in the stalls.

'Karl is a wonderful man . . . He has retired, except when I direct an opera. Then he comes out of hiding,' he said.

The platinum light from the full moon shone through the window and one shaft of white light fell on to Desdemona's bed.

'Do you like the set?' Vincent asked in a whisper, 'and the double bed? and the red damask? Look! Here comes Emilia with two candles, one she leaves behind, so! And the other she carries away. She will never see Desdemona again. Otello is such a fool! *Che cretino!* I am never jealous. Never! Do you like the opera? Are you enthusiastic?'

'I like the themes of opera.'

'Explain! Explain!'

'Opera is about passion.'

'Passion . . . yes, perhaps . . . but passion that destroys.'

'I don't care.'

'You talk like a Russian.'

Eleanor was staring at the stage; she could feel Vincent's stare upon her. Suddenly he called out to one of his assistants, 'Where is Regina? *Che passa?*'

A young man came over to Vincent and spoke conspiratorially into his ear. Vincent threw up his hands and said, 'Tell her to stop crying and come on stage and sing!'

He turned to Eleanor. 'Regina Bruce, have you heard of her? Of course! She cannot stop crying. At forty-one she became pregnant by her lover – he's on the board of the Met – a man without interest – I don't know what she sees in him – anyway, Regina was pregnant by her lover, who told her to have an abortion, which she did, to please him, and what does he do? He leaves her. And now she cannot stop crying.'

'What a terrible story!'

69

'Yes, it is a terrible story, but her tears are expensive. The orchestra is waiting. Ah! *Eccola!*'

The soprano appeared, the lights dimmed and the orchestra began to play. On the half-lit stage Desdemona knelt in front of the great bed and sang the 'Ave Maria', which rose and filled the theatre with its pitiful innocence. Violins reinforced the infinite sadness with their high A flat, which suddenly gave way to a bottom E flat five octaves lower from ominous bassoons. 'From Heaven to Hell,' Eleanor thought. Now Desdemona was asleep and Otello was approaching to give his kiss of death. Quietly Eleanor said:

> 'Ah, balmy breath, that dost almost persuade
> Justice to break her sword! One more, one more,
> Be thus when thou art dead, and I will kill thee,
> And love thee after.'

Vincent was staring at her.

'*Brava!*' he said. 'You know your Shakespeare!'

During the rehearsal that morning Eleanor wandered freely about the auditorium. She studied Vincent from many angles until quite suddenly the composition of the painting became evident: Vincent would be seated in the stalls, just as he was at that moment, his head tilted back, alert to every note from the orchestra and every movement on stage; his eyes were excited; his face was lit from below by a reading lamp which beamed its light on to the score in front of him.

'Lit from below,' Eleanor thought, 'just like Degas. Well, never mind. That's the painting.'

Eleanor began work the next day, not in Vincent's office but in the auditorium itself. The stage manager provided a board and a reading lamp, and with this simple equipment Eleanor sat unobtrusively to the side of the stalls from where she made detailed sketches of Vincent 'at work'. Above all she sketched the various positions of the head, and noted shades of light and dark. A few days later she was ready to start the oil painting. This had to be done in Vincent's office, where there was light. The pattern was the same: every morning Vincent would give Eleanor an hour of his time, only this time he was asked to sit as if he were downstairs in the stalls. A board was set up in front of a makeshift chair, and on this board Eleanor spread the score sheets. Vincent could not telephone; he could not talk; he was in a bad temper, especially when Eleanor asked him to look enthralled.

'*Ma che* "enthralled"? If you don't hurry up I shall miss my call to Japan.'

'Please don't frown. It distorts the eyebrows. You are making things very difficult. Please, Vincent! Let me have the other face, the face of irresistible charm.'

'You are very insolent.'

'And you are very spoilt.'

'I shall kill Ethel Wingate.'

'Not before she's paid me, please! I'm being paid a fortune to paint you, and the money is very welcome. It's my dowry.'

Vincent abandoned his pose and sat up.

'This boyfriend of yours – where is he?' he asked.

'In London.'

'Does he call you every day?'

'I've told you, he doesn't call me at all. It's too expensive.'

'Does he write?'

'No.'

Vincent sat back in his chair and mused. 'I never write to women.' After a moment he asked, 'Are you really going to marry this man?'

'Yes.'

'What for?'

'Children.'

Vincent sat up again and stared at Eleanor with interest. His eyes laughing, he said, 'Let me give you a child! My sperm count is enormously high.'

'I appreciate the offer, but . . . no, thank you. Now, if you wouldn't mind holding your head still. Quite still. Thank you.'

Eleanor noticed that her hand was trembling; she pressed the brush into the canvas until her wrist was steady.

Eleanor painted only from life. At the end of each sitting the canvas was not touched until the next morning, when she started again. She spent her days in the auditorium watching the rehearsals. She listened to Karl Henkel as he smiled like a father at the orchestra before him and begged the violins to be careful with the crotchets, which should be nice and clear and not too rushed. She listened to Vincent on stage as he asked the director of lighting to light the deathbed of Desdemona from below so that the pillars of the four-poster would cast shadows like giant columns against the wall behind. Vincent showed Otello how to fashion his hands for murder. Eleanor sketched this scene and many others. Wherever she went she had her sketch pad in hand and she drew portraits of the singers, and stagehands, the conductor and his orchestra, and Vincent in all his moods. When she had filled one sketch book she began another, sometimes using pencil or charcoal, and now and then pastels. All the time she warned herself, 'Not too much of the green pastel, and not too many horizontal strokes. You are not Degas and you never will be, so let's find out who you are.'

And all the time in her mind swam the beautiful music, and the pure and haunting voice of Desdemona. It reminded her of her mother's voice, of perfect pitch.

In this closed arena Eleanor felt perfectly content. She wanted nothing and no one. She liked to think of the 'real' world outside, New York choking with traffic and people, while she sat in a half-lit auditorium with people in fancy dress singing, shutting out not only the real world but daylight itself. 'How well I feel among these people,' Eleanor thought. 'I am creating. My soul is at peace.'

It was time to stop; her back ached. It was time to wander through the corridors and watch the wigmakers curling hair, and the seamstresses sewing pearls on to velvet. It was easy to get lost. There were sounds coming from every direction: the banging of a hammer, the lush cascade of a harp, the uneven roll of a tea trolley; and the soft sound of crying. Someone was crying. A door to a dressing room stood half open. Eleanor approached and recognized Desdemona sitting in the cold white room facing a mirror, her face buried in her hands. Eleanor stood quite still and waited. The face looked up. The eyes were red and swollen, the tears were streaming down the pale cheeks.

'Go away!' she shouted. 'Leave me alone!'

Eleanor left.

One morning Eleanor came into Vincent's office to find him looking through her sketch pad.

'You have been busy,' he said.

Eleanor waited, longing for his approval.

72

'I like your technique,' he said. 'Some of these drawings are good – very good. Ethel was quite right. Ethel is often right . . .' As Vincent spoke he turned the pages. 'Your passion for exactitude is cruel – look at me . . . my neck is so thick I look like a bull! Ah, this one is better, my wife would like this one – I look thinner!'

'Take it, please! It's yours . . . You've been very kind to me and I should like to give you a present.'

Carefully Eleanor pulled the drawing away from the sketch pad and handed it to Vincent, who asked, 'How's the boyfriend?'

'I haven't heard.'

'Still the same *commedia*? You don't speak to each other?'

'For the moment.'

'What a passionate relationship!'

Eleanor smiled. 'I'm happy in New York. I like what I am doing. I haven't felt so . . . so exhilarated in many years.'

'Come to our house tomorrow night. I'm giving a party for the cast of *Otello*.'

'Thank you. I would love to come.'

'Have you seen all the museums . . . all the art galleries?'

'Most of them.'

'What's your favourite painting in New York?'

Eleanor thought for a moment and then said, 'Chinese. Eleventh century. At Asia House. It's on loan from Taiwan. By Kuo Hsi. Called *Travellers though mountains and streams*. Monochrome black ink on paper. Perfectly beautiful.'

'I'd like to see it. Will you take me . . . sometime?'

'Of course.'

'Until tomorrow.'

9 The Buonarottis lived on the West Side overlooking Central Park. The style of their apartment was French with red lacquered walls, a *trompe-l'œil* painting in the dining room, and large satin bows looped above the interesting mixture of paintings: a Modigliani nude, a Dutch still life, a Japanese screen of one-legged cranes, Warhol's Chairman Mao.

Eleanor was nervous. She looked around the room and knew no one, except for Vincent who came forward to greet her. He told everyone that she was a fine painter. She met Iago and Otello, the lighting manager and the stage manager; she met the conductor's assistant and the set designer; and she met Dasha, Vincent's wife. 'She is beautiful,' Eleanor thought. 'Beautiful but sad.' Dasha was dressed in black and her hair was scraped back, like the dancer that she used to be, and the melancholy in her eyes was entrenched. The Russian accent was still there, guttural but mellow after so many years abroad:

'Thank you for your drawing of Vincent,' she said to Eleanor. 'I shall frame it. It is a drawing full of affection.'

'He is a charming man.'

Dasha smiled, but there was a world-weariness in her smile as if to say, 'So, you are his latest girl. And after you there will be another and another . . .'

Eleanor wanted to say, 'I have nothing to hide, and you – you have nothing to fear.' But her inner voice asked, 'Is that really true? You know that he likes you. Yes . . . yes, but he likes everyone . . . look at him laughing and talking to everyone . . .' Eleanor was so concentrated on this inner dialogue that all of a sudden she realized that Dasha had asked a question, and was waiting for an answer.

'I am so sorry . . . what did you say?' Eleanor said.

'I said,' Dasha said, laughing slightly, 'would you like some champagne?'

'Yes, thank you. That's very kind of you.'

74

Suddenly, an immense sadness settled like a cloud of dust on Eleanor's mind. She foresaw it all: she would become Vincent's lover, Dasha would know or guess; it would bring – what? . . . brief hours of happiness – and then she would be alone once again.

'This is ridiculous, and illogical,' the inner voice protested. 'You are in charge of your life, you don't have to follow this path. And what about Edward? Have you forgotten that you are going to marry Edward?'

'Yes,' Eleanor said out loud, 'I had forgotten.'

'Talking to yourself,' Vincent said from behind her, 'is eccentric. Let me introduce you to Regina Bruce.'

Eleanor found herself face to face with Desdemona. She remembered the same woman, her head bowed in painful weeping in the neon-lighted dressing room. Tonight Regina Bruce was once again the glamorous opera star, ostrich feathers draped around her neck. If she remembered the meeting she said nothing, but greeted Eleanor as a stranger and passed on, making a royal progress from one admirer to another.

Ethel Wingate entered the room noisily, greeting people with her blazing smile. Immediately she came up to Eleanor.

'My dear girl . . . I hear such good things about the picture. Sally Anne – you know Sally Anne, a perfectly charming girl – she's Vincent's secretary – well, Sally Anne says the picture is quite outstanding. And Vincent has been telling me about your drawings. It seems that you have done several hundred drawings. Now I have an idea. We are looking for a new theme for the Met calendar next year. Your drawings sound perfect. Of course, they must be seen by our committee, but I am in no doubt that the reception will be favourable. The Met calendar is most prestigious. If you are chosen as the artist, you would follow a distinguished line – Jackson Pollock, Sydney Nolan, David Hockney. Be a dear and send those drawings to my office.'

Ethel Wingate moved on. Eleanor found herself alone with Dasha and felt inhibited by her severe beauty. She also felt guilty. 'That's absurd. I have done nothing wrong!' she told herself, and she ventured, 'Your husband told me that you started an organization to help Russian refugees. What can you do for them?'

'For a Soviet man or woman – I am talking of course of

dissidents – it is not easy to live in the West. There – in Russia – you spend all your energies fighting for a cause that seems just and right. You are fighting for freedom and human dignity. You are fighting the system, and of course, most important of all, the KGB. Gorbachev hasn't changed that – not yet. After such a life of struggle, it's not easy to come to the West, where everyone talks about the stock market and the price of houses!'

Dasha took Eleanor by the arm.

'Come,' she said, 'there is someone you must meet,' and she led Eleanor across the room to a man slumped on a sofa. He was smoking and his fingers were dark from nicotine. He had a puffy, nondescript face and he was overweight, but his eyes were bright and intense.

'This is Alexei Kinski, a friend of ours from Russia, recently arrived. Alexei – this is Eleanor Wynn. She's the girl I told you about – she's painting Vincent.'

Dasha said something in Russian. Alexei began to laugh, heaving his shoulders. He held out his hand but made no attempt to get up, and then turned back to Dasha and continued his conversation in Russian.

'You must speak English, Alexei. His English is quite good but he's shy. Now I shall leave you together. Eleanor, make him speak English.'

Eleanor waited for Alexei to begin but he remained silent, inhaling deeply on his cigarette and blowing the white smoke into the air. It was quite clear to Eleanor that he was not going to start the conversation, so she said, 'Do you like painting?'

He looked at her and once again began to laugh, heaving his shoulders.

'*Do* you?' she insisted.

Still laughing, he said, 'In prison, no paintings!'

'No. Of course. But I thought perhaps here in New York you had been to the museums.'

'No.'

'I'd be very happy to show you some pictures . . . if you like?'

'No.'

'But if you've never been – '

'Painting is not important.'

'Why do you say that?'

'Painting is a bourgeois luxury!' And once again he began to laugh, this time throwing back his head and opening his mouth so that Eleanor could see his brown, decaying teeth.

Vincent, joined them, holding a bottle.

'More vodka for Alexei,' he said. 'You have to make up for eleven years, Alexei . . .' Vincent turned to Eleanor. 'Eleven years . . . that's how long he was locked up!'

Alexei held out his glass, which Vincent filled, and said, 'Everyone in Soviet Union is drinking vodka. Even guards in prison.'

Eleanor searched for the right words. 'Painting is a part of life . . . an expression of the human condition . . . I wish I could make you understand . . . it is so beautiful – '

'Beautiful! You know what is beautiful. To survive . . . that is beautiful! Everyone lives with eyes shut . . . painting pictures . . . singing opera . . . making so much noise you cannot hear the screaming men when the tube is forced down the nose . . . everyone lives with eyes shut . . .' At this moment Dasha walked past. 'Dasha is different . . . she understands. Dasha is great woman.'

A Russian pianist came over to talk to Alexei and they laughed and talked in Russian. Eleanor moved away and was drawn once again to Dasha, who stood by the window smoking a cigarette. Was her interest in this woman vicarious, she wondered? Was she trying to get closer to Vincent by talking to his wife?

Clumsily, or so it felt, Eleanor asked Dasha about herself. She phrased her questions cautiously, afraid to trespass on the privacy of this impressive woman, but Dasha answered her without hesitation, with an openness that took Eleanor by surprise; and her soft Slavic accent was beautiful to hear.

Dasha was the daughter of a famous choreographer; ballet was in her blood. By the age of eighteen she was the prima ballerina of the Bolshoi. She had a half-brother, Nicolai, with a different surname; it was not generally known that they were related. Nicolai was a poet. He distributed his verse in Red Square and was arrested and sent to a labour camp where, far from recanting, he organized strikes. Eventually he was interned in a psychiatric hospital and injected with drugs that made his legs and arms swell to grotesque proportions. In the end they flooded his veins with a poison that damaged his brain and polluted his imagination with horrific nightmares, destroying his memory and his creativity. Dasha saw him once before he died. He did not speak to her, but in his eyes she saw the agony of all mankind. When she heard that he had died she rejoiced: her beloved Nicolai was out of suffering. For a few long months she kept dancing and smiling at the KGB officials who brought the distinguished visitors from abroad to the Bolshoi. Graciously she was told, 'We do not blame you for the crimes of your half-brother – every family has a black sheep.' The Bolshoi went on tour to the United States. Dasha met Vincent, and applied for political asylum. It was granted and they married. 'In those days,' she said, 'I was beautiful.'

There was an eruption of laughter at the other end of the room. Vincent was telling a story and everyone was laughing. He was not only the centre of attention, he was also the centre of admiration; eyes glowed with hero worship; even Ethel Wingate was paying homage. Dasha did not seem to notice and continued with her conversation.

'In Soviet Union you can choose to know or not to know. If you choose to know, then you have no life. You are full of hate. Even your sleep is filled with nightmares. But this is no talk for a party! It is late! I must go to the kitchen and see what has happened to our dinner!'

'Can I help you?' Eleanor asked.

Dasha looked at her as if to say, 'Why are you being so solicitous?' Shrugging her shoulders she said, 'If you like.'

In the kitchen, behind a cloud of steam, the Chinese cook called out, 'Ten minutes, Mrs Buonarotti . . . I shall be ready in ten minutes!'

Dasha went back into the crowded drawing room. Eleanor stayed behind. She wanted to be alone; to breathe quiet. She walked the length of a corridor lined with posters from films and theatre productions by Vincent Buonarotti. Eventually she came to a bedroom door half open. She entered and found a young girl sitting at a dressing table staring at herself in the mirror. At once Eleanor recognized the girl from a photograph in Vincent's office; that was his daughter Marina, the star pupil at the American ballet theatre school. Marina had inherited Dasha's sorrowful face. Her auburn hair was tied back with a red ribbon, she looked liked a Degas statue except . . . except she was too thin. Her arms hung like sticks.

'Hello,' Eleanor said.

'Hi!'

'You're missing all the fun.'

'Is Daddy playing the piano? Sometimes he plays the piano and I dance.'

'Come and dance for us now.'

'Have they had dinner yet?'

'Not yet.'

'I'll come after dinner.'

'You don't want dinner?'

The girl shook her head.

The dinner was dominated by Vincent, who effortlessly held the attention of his guests. They were his captive audience as he spoke about the film he planned to make of *Bohème*.

'It is not easy, the mixing of two art forms, cinema and opera . . . Without a stage opera loses some of its intensity – that is inevitable – and film does not like the constraints of opera. The camera strains to be let free. Up to now the marriage has never really worked – *Carmen, Traviata, Don Giovanni*, each was good in its way, and bad in its way. My film will be quite different . . . because both film and opera are in my blood . . . I can fuse the two . . . *Bohème* will be a masterpiece!'

Suddenly, Gary, a stage designer, could contain his admiration no longer. He jumped to his feet and in his piping voice said, 'Vincent is a genius . . . It's true! I should know . . . I have worked with him on three films. There is no one like Buonarotti . . . no one!'

Eleanor watched the expression on Vincent's face. He was not embarrassed by the adulation, far from it, he was pleased, accepting the lavish compliments as if they were no more than his due.

Karl Henkel, the 'Maestro', arrived for coffee. He wore his dinner jacket as if it were his most comfortable suit, and within minutes he was telling the table that he had been to a party given for the Grand Duke of Liechtenstein.

'It was so boring,' he said, 'that I poured salt instead of sugar all over my strawberries!'

Vincent made a great fuss of Karl Henkel. First he gave the old man coffee and then Armagnac, and eventually, when he had taken his place at the head of the table, he held his glass high and cried out,

'Here's to you, Maestro!'

'Dear boy! Dear boy!'

'Here's to the finest conductor in the world!'

'I am the oldest conductor in world . . . and if Vincent has his way he will kill me before my time. He wants me to start from the beginning and conduct all the great operas once more for compact disc – imagine! At my age!'

'Mozart this year,' Vincent said, 'Verdi next year, and the year after Wagner.'

'You think I can conduct from the grave?'

'You are immortal, Karl, we all know that!'

Once again Gary the set designer jumped to his feet.

'I wish to drink a toast to our host. We are all honoured to be here at your table, and I drink to you, Vincent Buonarotti, a legend in your time!'

After dinner Vincent sat at the grand piano and played, and Desdemona and Otello sang, and Vincent's daughter Marina danced, and Alexei smoked, and Eleanor found herself on a sofa next to Karl Henkel.

'Where were you born?' Eleanor asked.

'In Austria – like Mozart and Hitler. I still live in Vienna . . . I like the atmosphere of gentle decay . . . And for music it is still the finest city in the world! Of course I am hopelessly prejudiced, you see I first made my name conducting the Wiener Philharmoniker – our love affair has lasted all my life! They still ask me to come back, every year they ask me, even though I have retired. Well, I am trying to retire, but am not succeeding!'

'Tell me about the orchestras,' Eleanor said. 'Which are the best?'

'Today? Let me see . . . For symphonic music the Berliner Philharmoniker has no rival. It is quite superb! But if you are talking about an orchestra that can play both symphonic *and* operatic music, then I would say to you my beloved Wiener Philharmoniker is the best . . . when it tries . . . but now and then it does not try! What else? Let me see . . . The Chicago Symphony is world class! Like everything in America it is bright and brassy but good – oh yes! It is very, very good. And now they have Barenboim – I feel sorry for the Orchestre de Paris. Without him they are nothing! What else? The London Philharmonic had its moments under the great Karajan, and Giulini, and for a while Muti worked miracles, but since those days it has deteriorated, I am sorry to say. But my dear child, that is enough about orchestras! Tell me about yourself. You are English and a painter. What else? Married? Divorced? In love?'

'I don't think I am any of those things.'

'Not married? Not divorced and not in love? Das ist nicht möglich! Such a beautiful girl! Are they blind in England? Years and years and years ago I had the most beautiful English girlfriend. Her name was Anne Cuthbert. You know her?'

Eleanor smiled. 'Anne Cuthbert is my mother.'

He hugged and kissed her and called for champagne and told everyone that this was the daughter of his lovely Anna – *'meine liebe, liebe Anna'* – and Eleanor and Karl Henkel sat together for the rest of the evening as Eleanor tried to describe her mother's life over the last forty years. Eventually Karl got up to leave.

'I give you lunch very soon!' he said to Eleanor. 'Your story is not finished. I want to know more. When I met your mother I was married. Ah! If I had not been married, perhaps you would not be on this earth, and that would be very sad for all of us!'

Vincent took Karl Henkel by the arm and led him downstairs to a taxi. Eleanor was putting on her coat while Dasha talked to Alexei.

'You look very tired . . .' Dasha was saying to the Russian. 'Go to bed, you need to sleep.'

'In bed I don't sleep,' Alexei said.

'Try. You cannot sit up every night until four o'clock!'

Alexei said nothing. Eleanor took her leave.

'Thank you so much,' she said to Dasha, 'and will you thank your husband for me? I had a wonderful time.'

Eleanor took a lift to the ground floor and walked through the marble lobby with yellow silk flowers in a grey urn, past the weary doorman on to the street, where a cold wave of autumn air stung her face and she came upon Karl and Vincent still waiting for a taxi.

'I'll take you home,' Karl said.

'It's the opposite direction,' Vincent interrupted, and at that moment a taxi drew up and Vincent helped Karl to climb in and waved to him as he rode off, bumping over the uneven New York street.

'Where does he live?' Eleanor said.

'Fifth Avenue and Sixty-seventh – '

'But I'm just next door!' Eleanor protested.

Vincent took her arm.

'Let's walk,' he said. 'I need a walk after all that music and all that wine.'

'And all those compliments,' Eleanor added.

Vincent stopped and looked at Eleanor.

'Too many?'

'I thought it was a little embarrassing!'

'I see, I see,' Vincent said, smiling. 'You found it all a little – what's your favourite word? Hagiographic!'

'I have to go,' Eleanor said, breaking away and hailing a taxi. 'I must get home. It's very late.'

'Karl adores you,' Vincent said.

'He's an extraordinary man.'

'You have conquered us all.'

Eleanor got into the taxi and sank back against the cheap plastic seat. She breathed deeply. The danger was passed.

10 'This is the operator speaking. We have a collect call from Mr Edward Verney in Sheffield, England. Will you pay for the call?'

Eleanor sat up in bed, marshalling her senses.

'Yes I will. Edward?'

'Eleanor?'

'Oh, darling, how lovely to hear you!'

'You haven't telephoned.'

'Nor have you.'

'You haven't written.'

'Nor have you.'

'For all I know you've got a new boyfriend.'

'Edward, what is all this?'

'Have you? Got a new boyfriend?'

'No, Edward, I haven't got a new boyfriend.'

There was a long, expensive silence, then Eleanor said, 'Edward. I miss you. I wish you were here.'

'Do you?'

'Yes I do.'

There was another silence.

'Edward . . . Edward. What is the matter? Please don't be angry. I shall be home soon. We're going to make a life together, my darling. If you still love me. Do you? Do you still love me?'

'I've told you. I shall always love you.'

'That's what you always say. But your voice is so cold. Oh, Edward, please say something kind.'

Another expensive silence crackled down the line. Eleanor burst out. 'This is ridiculous. I don't understand why you bothered to ring.'

'I wanted to hear the sound of your voice.'

The line went dead. Slowly Eleanor replaced the receiver.

It was the dress rehearsal. The sets were finished, so were the

83

wigs and costumes, and the fifteenth-century brocades. Karl Henkel took his place in the conductor's box and the full orchestra in evening dress played *Otello* at ten o'clock in the morning. Eleanor sat with her sketch pad on her knee, but for once she did not draw. Her eyes never left the stage; the outside world did not exist; the only life that mattered was here in the auditorium. She did not even notice Karl or Vincent; Verdi and his sweet music filled her whole being.

In the first interval she went backstage to find Regina Bruce. The diva was leaning back in the chair as a make-up artist reinforced the contours of her eyes; her hairdresser was adjusting the wig; the wardrobe mistress was sewing on a button.

'Eleanor! Come in! My wig almost fell off, did you notice? I'm not comfortable in these clothes – this bodice presses so hard on my bosom. I'm so glad that I wasn't alive in the fifteenth century. Of course, Desdemona is a young woman, early twenties I imagine. And here am I, all of forty-two. I mustn't complain. It's one of the great mysteries of this life that a soprano's voice gets better as she gets older. There are very few first-class sopranos in their twenties; the late thirties to middle forties, that is our golden era. I'm in my prime! It's quite funny, isn't it? Sit down. Have a cup of coffee.'

'You are singing beautifully. Everyone says so.'

'A little shaky here and there. I went to bed early but I could not sleep. I don't know why . . .'

Suddenly Regina stopped speaking. She stared into the mirror in front of her at the man who was standing in the entrance of her dressing room.

'What is this man doing here?' she said to her wardrobe mistress.

'But Mr Loder is on the board.'

'I don't care if Mr Loder is on the board. No one comes into my dressing room without my permission. The gentleman is leaving. See him out.'

The man left as suddenly as he came, like an apparition. The singer ordered everyone to leave.

'Not you,' she said to Eleanor. 'You can stay.'

Regina walked up and down the room, pulling nervously at her fingers.

'Look at my hands. I am trembling! He's trying to upset me in the middle of the dress rehearsal.'

84

She put her hand to her mouth to stop herself from crying.

'How can I help?' Eleanor asked. 'Brandy?'

'Are you mad?' Regina exclaimed. 'Brandy will set my throat on fire – no, thank you! Oh my God. Why did he have to come? He wants to upset me, I know!'

'Who is he?'

'Stephen Loder. He was my lover. The father of my child. My dead child. I had an abortion.'

'Yes. I heard.'

'Who from?'

'Vincent.'

'He would tell you! Never mind. Everyone knows. I had an abortion because Stephen didn't want children. I had the abortion and a few months later he left me.'

'Yes, I know.'

'We keep meeting. He's on the board. It's torture for me. Every time I see him I think of the clinic, and the day I spent recovering from the general anaesthetic, and I think of those starched white sheets spotted with blood.'

Regina sank into the chair and held her face in her hands.

'I mustn't cry. If I cry the make-up will run. Oh God, why does he keep doing this to me? Why is he so cruel? Look! My hand is still trembling. I am not well. There is a knot here – in my abdomen. I cannot go on. I am not well!'

'You can go on,' Eleanor said quietly.

Regina looked at Eleanor, her face taut with anxiety. Suddenly the muscles relaxed and she smiled.

'Yes. Of course I can. Thank you.'

Outside voices were arguing. Suddenly the door opened and Vincent came in, protesting. 'Who is this mad woman who is trying to keep me out of your room?'

'I don't like surprise visits,' Regina said.

'*Sono io*, Buonarotti. My friend, you are singing perfectly, which makes me very worried. Don't use it all today. Keep some for tomorrow night. Ah, you have met my friend Eleonora. A clever girl. *Intelligentissima*. And very pretty. Regina, *senti*. It's no good to anyone if the best performance is in the dress rehearsal. I want to hear it on the night! Whatever magic potion you are taking, don't stop. Take it again and again!'

'The "potion", as you call it, is hate.'

85

'Keep hating, *mia cara*, and sing like this on the opening night!'

These were the last few brushstrokes. In a few moments Eleanor would stop painting and the work would be complete. Vincent was in his seat, dictating to Sally Anne. Eleanor was not listening: her whole being was concentrated on the picture before her.

Suddenly Vincent began to shout, 'What do you mean – they've ordered second-class tickets?'

'That's what Mrs Buonarotti said – two second-class tickets to Geneva – one for herself and for your daughter Marina. Mr Kinski can't go with them. He's going to Cleveland but will be joining them later.'

'I'm not interested in Mr Kinski. I'm interested in my wife and daughter. Why does my wife book second-class tickets? Doesn't she think I can afford to send her first-class to Geneva? I earn a fortune and she knows it!'

'Maybe she likes the simple life, Mr Buonarotti. You know, I have just read this survey in *Time* about people's ambition, and you would be surprised, Mr Buonarotti – a great many people don't care about money.'

'A great many people don't have the choice, Sally Anne! They start poor and stay poor . . . God! I'm in a bad mood today! Stop painting, Eleanor, stop painting! I can't stand you looking at me like that.'

'I'm not painting you – I am just putting the finishing touches to the sheets of music . . .'

'I can't think with so many people around – why doesn't everyone leave me alone?'

'But you asked me to take dictation,' Sally Anne protested.

'Tell her to stop painting!'

Sally Anne looked at Eleanor helplessly.

'I can't stop,' Eleanor said. 'I must finish!'

Vincent stared at Eleanor, who held her palette firmly and with the long brush dabbed into the chaos of colours and then applied the short brushstrokes. And suddenly, to Sally Anne's relief, he laughed.

'*Tu te moques de moi*,' he said to Eleanor.

'Not at all. I'm just a simple craftswoman plying my trade.

86

I am nearly finished. Just a little more definition on the music . . .'

Vincent sulked as Eleanor continued to paint. There was a gentle knock at the door and Ethel Wingate walked in.

'Excuse me, I didn't mean to interrupt,' she said.

'Please,' Eleanor said, 'I've nearly finished.'

'This is ridiculous,' Vincent said, jumping from his chair. 'I haven't time for this nonsense,' and he waved his hand towards Eleanor and her canvas. Eleanor did not react. She continued to paint with the utmost concentration. Ethel, on the other hand, stiffened.

'That was an offensive remark, Vincent. I am disappointed.'

'I am tired, don't you understand? So tired. I could sleep for a hundred years.'

'Vincent is having a crisis,' Ethel said, sitting primly on the edge of a chair. 'He always has a crisis before the opening night.'

'Do you know what Dasha has done to me? Do you know her latest little ploy? I'll tell you. She is going to Geneva with Marina, in time to miss the opening – of course!'

'You know perfectly well that Dasha has to chair a conference in Geneva. She would not miss an opening night for the world, she is the most loyal and devoted wife, but this time she has no choice. Really, Vincent, shame on you for casting aspersions on the purest of characters!'

'*Va bene*. She has to go to Geneva. But she doesn't have to travel second-class. I earn a great deal of money!'

'I won't hear one word against Dasha. That wife of yours is an angel. There is not a mean bone in her body. Anyway, I can't see what you are objecting to. Most husbands would be only too pleased to be married to an economical woman.'

'She's not doing this to save money. She's making a point.'

'And what point could she possibly be making?'

'That she places no value on this material world of ours . . . that I am the one who is obsessed with money, with my work, with success . . . that I neglect my wife and my children.'

'You do, Vincent,' Ethel said drily.

'I live life on my terms. I don't accept psychological blackmail from anyone!'

'Vincent, I really don't know what is wrong with you. How Dasha puts up with you I shall never understand. And it hurts me – yes, Vincent, it hurts me to hear you being so uncharitable. I can only assume you are not yourself. You look tired. Perhaps you are overworked, although it would be hard to argue you are overpaid. I suggest you take a sedative!'

'There!' Eleanor said, 'the picture is finished!'

Ethel came round to the front of her painting and looked for what seemed to Eleanor an eternity. A slow smile spread across her face.

'Let me embrace you, child. I knew you wouldn't let me down. Excellent! The painting is excellent. Of course you have flattered Vincent. Only a touch of grey hair, and look at the body, trim, lean!'

'Let me see,' Vincent growled, but already his irritation was melting. He stood in front of the painting for a long moment, and in a new and mollified voice he said, 'It's a very good likeness.'

Eleanor smiled and waited. Vincent put his hand on her shoulder.

'It's a good painting. A very good painting. Everything about it is original. The composition. The colours. The mood. *Brava, Eleonora! Complimenti!'*

'With your permission,' Ethel said, 'I would like to put the painting on show tomorrow night for the opening.'

'But it isn't varnished yet,' Eleanor protested, 'and it has no frame.'

'It looks fine just as it is,' Ethel said firmly. 'And you needn't worry, we'll get a security guard to stand beside it.'

'Will you miss this picture, now that it is finished?' Vincent asked suddenly.

'No . . . no I won't . . . It's the act of creating that interests me . . . not the finished product. I mean . . . I like my pictures . . . yes . . . but already I want to get on with the next.'

'I am like that too!' Vincent said. 'We are the same, you and I. Already my mind has left *Otello* – my work is done, my mind moves on and now I am thinking of *Bohème*. I shall make the most beautiful film. And somewhere in between there is *Don Giovanni* at La Scala. Too much work, always too much work!'

Sally Anne put her head around the door and said, 'It's Paolo Contini's agent. There's a problem.'

'*Ma che problema?* We start rehearsals in January. Don't tell me he's pulling out! Where am I going to find a Don Giovanni between now and then? They should have booked Ruggieri. He's more reliable. Hello, hello? Yes, Buonarotti here . . . *dimmi* . . . well, that's very sad, but his father must have been an old man. Ninety-four? Well, at ninety-four you expect to die. His mother is upset? Of course she's upset. He wants to miss the second week of rehearsals? Well . . . he knows the part by heart. He should . . . he's sung it often enough. Yes . . . yes, he can miss the second week, as long as he turns up for the third, and the opening night, and for six performances thereafter, to which he's bound by his contract . . . If Paolo fails me I shall die! Yes, that's what I said, Mario, I cannot take any more disappointments. I'm having a crisis. The male menopause. No, thank you, I don't want any literature on the subject.'

'Every few months Vincent gives way to stress,' Ethel said to Eleanor. 'He won't take a holiday, he won't rest . . . he thinks he is superhuman, and of course he is not. There really is no help for those who will not help themselves. I am not sympathetic.'

Vincent was speaking louder than ever: 'I must have Contini by the twentieth, not a moment later, *capisci*? *Va bene*. There is plenty of time for him to bury his father and to comfort his mother. There is no problem. Oh, by the way . . . tell him I am very sorry. I shall call him tonight or tomorrow. It's very sad when our parents die. Very sad.'

Vincent put down the telephone and stretched out on the long leather sofa in his office.

'No more calls, Sally Anne. Not from anyone. Not even the Pope, unless he will lend me the Sistine Chapel for *Tosca*. Now, if you don't mind, *Eleonora, vado a dormire*,' and he lay back and fell asleep.

'Well, at least we have some quiet,' Ethel said. 'My dear Eleanor, come and have a drink with me . . . Yes now! We must talk.'

Oddly enough, Ethel Wingate had taste. The apartment was elegant and the art was well placed and discreet. A superb Khmer sculpture, a Bayon head with lowered lids, stood isolated in a corner; a Greek head was on a mantelpiece, a Ming buffalo in smooth green jade was set on another. Above the fireplace hung a beautiful Pisarro of a town by a river; it was not Pontoise, Eleanor noted. There was a Picasso drawing of a lady in a hat dated 1908; and a large David Hockney drawing of his mother. Eleanor was taking it all in, object by object, when her solitude was broken.

'You like my little collection? I chose everything myself. I shall tell you something, Eleanor. Until 1970 I had never set foot in a museum. It's true! And then I married my second husband, Hubert T. Maynard. Now he loved art. He taught me everything. Each phase of our lives enriches us, I really do believe that. Hubert Maynard brought art into my life, Edgar Wingate brought God into my life. You see?'

'I do see. You married interesting men.'

'I married positive men. Now sit down, my dear. Will you have champagne? Tell me, when are you getting married?'

'In the next few months, I suppose. It's not really up to me. Edward will decide.'

'That's right. Let the men decide. It makes them feel better. I am sure he is a delightful man.'

'Yes. Yes, he is.'

'I am glad you are going home, my dear. Vincent has taken a shine to you. And that is no good at all.'

Eleanor felt herself blushing. Ethel went on, 'There are times when I think I should no longer support Vincent. He is so negligent of his family. Those children hardly see their father – the boy Nicky began to steal cars, just to get some attention. And look at Marina – the child is anorexic because she wants to succeed in order to please her father. It's painful. And the worst part is Dasha. I am a great friend to Dasha, and the way he treats her – well, it's really not good. You may have heard he has an attachment with a lady in Rome. And who knows what else . . . there is always someone in tow.'

As she said this, Ethel looked straight at Eleanor, and then added, 'But you are much too sensible.'

Eleanor said nothing. Ethel handed out a glass of champagne and said, 'I congratulate you on your picture.'

'I thank you for your generosity, and for your faith in me. I'm so pleased I haven't disappointed you.'

'Far from it, my dear child, far from it! I have had faith in you from the start, and I am richly rewarded. Why, my dear, the first picture I bought from you at your exhibition – do you

90

remember? Why, it is the pride and glory of my church in San Antonio!'

'An afternoon in Covent Garden?' Eleanor said doubtfully.

'Our Saviour and Mary Magdalene,' Ethel replied firmly. 'When you painted the picture you were moved by the Spirit of God. So much so that when I asked Luis Brenton to add the halo . . .'

'You've *added* to my picture?'

'I bought that picture and paid handsomely for it, and what I do with it is my affair. Now don't look distressed, Eleanor. I asked you if you would add a few religious symbols, but you refused. So I turned to another hand. Now please, I value your friendship so very much. Don't be angry with me. Come to San Antonio and see for yourself. Come next week . . . I can fly you down in my aeroplane . . . My dear child, don't be angry. I have not spoiled your painting.'

'I'm not angry,' Eleanor said smiling. 'I never really felt happy with that painting – perhaps because I couldn't find a face . . . But I can't come to San Antonio next week. I would love to, but I can't. I must go home and get married and live in China. In that order.'

'Oh dear, what a pity, but you are not going to live in China for ever, I assume?'

'A few years . . .'

'On your return you must call me and stay with me, and bring your husband, of course. Now tell me all about him.'

Eleanor tried and failed to bring Edward to life, and after the briefest of descriptions, and filled with a sense of guilt, she began to talk about the magnificent art that filled the room and with genuine enthusiasm she asked Ethel about the paintings and the sculpture. She was surprised to discover that Ethel was sure of her own eye; she also voiced the one good reason, to Eleanor's mind, for collecting a work of art: 'You see, my dear, it gives me pleasure.'

Ethel invited Eleanor to a party she was giving at '21' after the opening night, and as she left, Eleanor said, 'I hope we always stay friends.'

'We shall, my child. It is ordained.'

For the first time in many weeks Eleanor had a day to herself. She walked from the Opera House across Central Park and then followed her instinct, turning this corner and that, passing brownstone houses and steaming manholes; stepping from bright autumn sunlight into the dark shadow of a skyscraper so tall that its summit seemed to touch the clouds; staring into fast food restaurants where, even at eleven o'clock in the morning, men and women and children were eating. All at once she found herself face to face with Alexei and Marina. Alexei smiled and showed his decaying teeth.

'I am a tourist,' he said. 'Marina is my guide.'

'He stays at home all day and smokes cigarettes and Mother says he will die of a heart attack. So I am showing him New York. We are going to the top of the Empire State Building, but we have to hurry. Tonight Mother and I are leaving for Geneva.'

'Shall we all have a cup of coffee?' Eleanor said. 'And perhaps a bun? I feel like a bun!'

'I'm not hungry,' Marina said.

They sat in a small plastic café and ordered coffee and Eleanor drank while Alexei smoked. Eleanor asked Marina about her dancing and the girl talked obsessively. The school was very strict; every morning for four hours they practised at the barre. In the afternoon they rehearsed and once a term they gave a performance.

'I am the prima ballerina of the school,' Marina said. 'I am rather tall but I am not fat.'

'No,' Eleanor said, 'no one could say that you are fat.'

'She never eats,' Alexei said. 'She would have been happy in the camps. There is no food – Marina would have been happy. She looks like someone in the camps – look at her arms!'

'Leave me alone, Alexei! Leave me alone!'

'Look at those arms,' Alexei went on, 'not arms – sticks! And Mother is so worried. You make Mother miserable. You must eat!'

'I hate you, Alexei . . . I hate you!' Marina burst out and ran out of the café.

Eleanor got up to follow her but Alexei put his hand on her arm.

'Let her go. She is all right. She is seventeen.' He drew deeply on his cigarette. 'Marina is ill. Vincent is not noticing. Not caring. I tell Vincent she must eat. Otherwise she will die.'

'What does Dasha think?'

'Dasha says to Marina, you must see a doctor. Marina – she is refusing.'

'Poor child,' Eleanor said. 'Starving herself for what?'

'For attention. From her father. She is in love with her father.'

'Everyone seems to be in love with Vincent,' Eleanor said.

Eleanor took Alexei to the Frick. It was the first time he had ever been inside an art gallery, and he walked from one painting to another in silence, until he came to 'The Polish Rider' by Rembrandt, when he stopped and stared.

Eagerly Eleanor said, 'It's so beautiful, don't you think . . . Look at the face. He's so young and brave. And the red hat! And look at his pose; the hand on the hip; so confident, so full of national pride . . .'

'Who is this man?' Alexei asked.

'He's a rider – the picture is called "The Polish Rider".'

'Name?'

'I don't think we know his name.'

'I am half Polish. I don't think he is Polish, this man.'

'Oh, Alexei, you are just being difficult!'

Alexei wandered round the room, looking at the Turners, the Velázquez, the Van Dycks, the Constable, but these paintings left him unmoved. It was only when he came to the Goya that he stopped, and for a long while examined the blacksmiths bearing down on a forge, pounding the anvil with weighty hammers. Alexei nodded in approval and said, 'This man understands . . . he understands the struggle of life . . . who was he? What is name?'

'Francisco de Goya. Born in Spain in 1746.'

'He was political – a fighter.'

'You are quite right, Alexei. He was.'

Alexei snorted in satisfaction at his own powers of perception, and on leaving the Frick he bought a catalogue.

The applause was tumultuous, and the star of the show, everyone agreed, was Regina Bruce. Eleanor overheard the cognoscenti talk of her 'new maturity', the richness of her tone, her fine handling of the difficult passages; and Eleanor, who was on her feet applauding in the auditorium packed with almost four thousand opera fans, sent her own silent message of congratulation: 'Well done, Regina and good luck with your art and your life!'

Ethel had taken over the restaurant '21' for dinner, and waiters scurried about, excited to have the room filled with famous opera singers. Eleanor did not enjoy herself: for most of the dinner she was silent, pretending to listen to the man on her left, who was talking about the state of opera in Bavaria to a Turkish woman opposite. She was on the point of leaving when Vincent announced that he was going home, and everyone was invited, and she was swept along by Karl Henkel and others who were still in a euphoric state after the triumph of the evening. At Vincent's apartment there was dancing and singing and bottle after bottle of wine. Eleanor was standing by the window staring out at the magnificent view of the city when Vincent came over to her.

'You're a fine artist,' he said to her. 'I should like you to do some work for me. An opera set. Do you like the idea?'

'I'm going to live in China.'

'Before you go' – Vincent hesitated and looked hard into her eyes – 'I would like to make love to you.'

'You're too busy and too tired.'

Vincent threw back his head and laughed.

'I like you, Eleanor Wynn! You are not – what do you call it? – hagiographic! You're right . . . I need a holiday. It's a pity we can't go away together. I suppose the fiancé would be angry?'

'He's angry already.'

Vincent smiled, and in his softest voice he said, 'I wish these people would go away and leave us alone.'

The last guests were leaving. Eleanor put on her coat to go. In a low voice Vincent said, *'Non mi lasci . . . non voglio stare solo questa notte.'*

The door closed on the last guest. Eleanor stood alone in the room, staring out of the window at the million lights of New York. She could feel him approaching. She did not move. He slipped his hands over her breasts and held them tenderly and kissed her neck.

'Mia bellissima Eleonora.'

With the tips of his fingers he massaged her nipples and felt them grow hard. His hands slipped down over her flat stomach and her pubis, which he pressed, and in so doing pressed her

94

whole body against his. He turned her round and took her face in his hands and kissed her hungrily.

In the bedroom they undressed quickly; all the while Vincent was smiling at her. They climbed into bed. He took her naked body into his arms and felt her nakedness against his and shuddered with pleasure and said breathlessly, 'I am married with a wife and two children, and I have a mistress in Rome. And now there is you!'

He turned his face to Eleanor and kissed her greedily, and his hand slid down to her pubic hair and his fingers began to explore, and her body tensed in expectation. Suddenly the fingers stopped moving; Vincent was asleep. Eleanor waited in the darkness for almost half an hour, listening to the ever-deepening rhythm of his breathing. She leant over the sleeping body and kissed Vincent on the forehead, and then got out of the bed and dressed. At first she worried that the slightest noise might wake him. Then she realized that his was a sleep of exhaustion, so deep that only an explosion would wake him, if then. In the drawing room the air was still thick with cigarette smoke, and the vibrations of voices lingered on; Eleanor looked around once more and closed the door behind her. Later that morning she booked herself on a flight to London.

The aircraft had taken off; the vertical pull threw Eleanor hard against the seat. Below, the skyscrapers of New York were getting smaller.

'That', she said to herself, 'was a narrow escape.'

11 'Edward, what's happened? Don't you love me any more?'

'I shall always love you.'

Eleanor was standing in Edward's bleak sitting room. The same books stood on the bookshelves; the ancestral portrait hung over the fire; the fire flickered with the same familiar crackle, and yet everything was different. The air was stiff with formality.

Eleanor had taken a taxi from the airport directly to Edward's house; her suitcase was in the hall. During the long hours of the flight she had, in her mind, closed the Vincent chapter of her life and prepared for the new life ahead, with Edward, as his wife.

Edward moved awkwardly and held out a glass of wine with an air of detachment that was new. He would not look in her direction but stared uneasily at his hands, his head bowed.

'What's wrong?' Eleanor insisted. 'You don't seem very pleased to see me.'

'I've had time to think . . .' Edward said slowly, 'and I'm not sure any more.'

Eleanor felt a coldness creep over the surface of her skin.

'I don't know how to put this,' he continued. 'You didn't write to me. You did not telephone. A woman in love would have written, she would have telephoned. For all I know you were having an affair.'

'No,' Eleanor said, 'I was not having an affair.' Her inner voice whispered, 'Nearly. Very nearly.'

'You're not committed to me, not in the way you should be,' he said, his eyes burning with resentment.

'I want to marry you and to have your children, and to live with you for the rest of my life. Isn't that enough?'

'This isn't easy for me, Eleanor. I may not get Peking. On the other hand the Head of my Department is very understanding, and he might just swing it. I won't know until I tell him.'

'Tell him what?'

'That we've decided to wait.'

'What are we waiting for?'

'I must feel sure.'

'Of me?'

'Yes. I'll be frank with you. I feel that I am convenient. You're at the end of your childbearing years. You want children, and I'm your best bet. That's how I feel you're looking at things.'

'Edward, we've been lovers for five years. We know each other fairly well.'

'Marriage is different. I must be sure.' Edward sat, his head bowed, the veins standing out in his neck, morose and miserable.

Eleanor felt the anger rise within her. She said, 'I see. So meanwhile I am on some sort of probation, reporting for the regular fuck, until you decide if I am worthy to be your wife?'

'You don't have to be crude.'

'Will you call me a taxi?'

'You can sleep in the spare bedroom if you like.'

'No, thank you.'

'Eleanor, you went off to America for six weeks and you didn't even ask me!'

'Why must I ask you? Am I your servant, Edward, tell me, am I?'

'We were getting engaged. I thought we would decide everything together. Instead, at the first opportunity you act unilaterally.'

'This is not an arms negotiation, Edward.'

'That was not funny.'

'What about *you*, Edward? Why didn't you consult me about the posting to Peking?'

'That's different.'

'Oh, is it? Really?'

'I have to accept a new posting. I'm in the Foreign Office. It's my career, my job.'

'And painting is *my* job.'

'I must come first.'

'Edward, do I come first in your life? Tell me honestly!'

'I love you, Eleanor. I shall always love you. But my work must come first, it's the same for any serious man. Men are different from women, whatever the feminists say. As a sex, we're in charge. We run this planet! It's a heavy responsibility. If we didn't put our work first, just think what would happen. Everything would collapse. Anyway, I think it's undignified for a man to be ruled by a woman. You can love a woman, certainly, but you can't let her dominate your life.' As an afterthought he added, 'Some men are better off as bachelors.'

Edward sat in his chair, his hands folded in his lap, tense and silent, until in a low and pained voice he said, 'I know what would happen. We'd get married, there would be children, and then after five years or so you would say, "I hate the life in the Foreign Office, I'm off." And you would leave me. I couldn't stand that, Eleanor. I couldn't stand it!'

Now was the moment to assuage his fears and to hold him in her arms and wrap him in her love. Now was the moment to say, 'Edward, I love you and I shall follow you to the ends of the earth. You are my lifeblood.'

Eleanor said nothing. She stood by the window and waited for the taxi. Edward, from across the room, spoke to her: 'I shall always love you. You know that, don't you?'

Eleanor turned in anger.

'What is this love of yours? Going nowhere, building nothing, creating nothing! It's a hoax, a sham. And it's dull! Brown, beige!'

Her eyes wandered over the room, picking up the sombre tones. She could not go on. Her feelings were in furious chaos, and words brought no solace. The taxi arrived and Eleanor travelled through the London night oblivious to rain and headlamps and glistening wet streets. She arrived at her studio and dragged her suitcase (which felt mightily heavy) up the wooden staircase.

There was no light in the studio. The door, she noticed, was slightly open. She staggered in, letting the suitcase fall, wanting to give vent to her anguish with one violent cry. Instead she opened the windows and gulped the night air. At the same time, involuntarily, the tears began to stream from her eyes, in one continuous, agonizing flow. She could hear her own crying.

Slowly Eleanor realized that she was not alone. She turned and through her blurred vision she saw the lighted ends of cigarettes shining like glow-worms in the darkness. A body moved on the floor, the shape determined by the pale light from a streetlamp outside. A cough broke the silence. Eleanor reached out to a desk light and turned it on. At least twenty people were asleep on her studio floor, punk rockers bedded down for the night, dressed, half-asleep. Many had put their hands to their eyes to shield themselves from the sudden and painful light. From a dark corner a figure emerged; it was Rosie.

She was hardly recognizable; she had shaved her head except for a coxcomb down the middle of her skull, several inches high and stiffened with some magic potion so that the hair stood on end. It was bright red, and either side the skull was smooth and bare.

'Eleanor . . . you said Thursday and it's Tuesday. I got your postcard . . . here, I'll show you . . .'

'Don't bother . . . I'll come back tomorrow. You said there would be you and your boyfriend . . .'

'He's got so many friends!'

'Yes. You promise to clean up the mess? I want to start work tomorrow.'

'You work too hard.'

'See you tomorrow.'

Eleanor went round to her sister Marcia. She asked for a bed. She must sleep. She could not explain.

Eleanor opened an eye and saw her nephew and niece staring at her, inches away. They clapped their hands and Rowley said, 'I told you she wasn't dead.'

'What time is it?' Eleanor asked.

'Teatime,' Beatrice said. 'And there's chocolate cake. Get up, Eleanor. Come and play with us. Please!'

'I'm a Roman soldier. Beatrice is my slave,' Rowley said. 'You can be Emperor Nero if you like. He sits in Nanny's chair.'

Eleanor turned away from the children.

'In a little while,' she said.

All at once Eleanor registered the full impact of what had happened. There was no future, nothing to look forward to. There was no Peking and no children, no little people to come and wake you up and smile at you with eyes of dazzling innocence. She would go back to her studio, take up her paint-brush and grow old alone.

Marcia stood in the entrance of the bedroom, holding her baby daughter.

'I'm so glad you're awake. I wanted to show you Clare. She's getting so big. It won't be long before she gets her first tooth.'

Eleanor thought, 'Don't torture me with your happy family and your gurgling baby.' She sat up and said, 'I have to go.'

Downstairs in the hall Eleanor sat on a wooden chair waiting for a taxi. She stared down at her hands which she had folded in her lap. Marcia knelt beside her and said, 'Talk to me, Eleanor, please. Tell me what's wrong.'

'It's over.'

'What is over?'

'Everything. My dreams, everything.'

'I'm not interested in dreams. I'm interested in facts. Your engagement to Edward – is that what you mean?'

'There's no engagement. There never will be.'

'Eleanor! Don't be a fool! You *must* marry Edward. This could be your last chance.'

'I *know* it could be my last chance. You don't have to remind me. Sometimes you can be so cruel, Marcia. As a child you were sweet, at least that's how I remember things. But later, after we had left school, in those years when we shared a flat, you had those rages and you said so many terrible things to me . . . You lashed out with such venom, and I remember thinking, "She's enjoying herself, inflicting pain!" I wanted to sue you for mental cruelty. I did! Can one do that in a family? Are there any legal precedents?'

'You always exaggerate,' Marcia said coolly. 'I'm not being cruel. I'm being clear-headed. You mustn't turn Edward down.'

'Edward is turning me down.'

Eleanor described the conversation of the night before; Marcia listened closely and then began to laugh.

'I see exactly what's happened. He's nervous. It's only natural. All you have to do is to woo the man! Flatter him! Tell him that you worship the ground he walks on.'

'I don't.'

'Look, Eleanor. You're a very successful painter. That's terrific. But you've made a mess of your private life up to now. Even in this emancipated age single women are . . . well, they're pathetic! A woman *needs* a husband. She's incomplete on her own. You can win Edward round. Use your charm, massage his ego. Pile on the flattery. You can do it!'

'No. I can't.'

'Eleanor, you're impossible. You'll never get married.'

'I know.'

As Eleanor was leaving Marcia said, 'Mummy has been ill.'

Eleanor looked up sharply.

'How ill?' she asked.

'There is something wrong with her eyes. She's been in hospital for tests. She won't say what's wrong.'

From New York Eleanor had telephoned her mother every week and not once had she mentioned a problem with her eyes.

'I'll go and see her at once,' she said.

As she stepped into the taxi Eleanor said, 'Thank you for letting me stay.'

'You're my sister. We may not be the best of friends, but I love you and I would do anything for you.'

Eleanor looked into her sister's eyes.

'I love you too, despite everything,' she whispered.

It was a day of Andrew Wyeth colours, hard, bleak, with spiky black trees set against a white winter sky. It was cold for November, and harsh, and winter seemed to stretch ahead indefinitely. And yet, the light was so clear that Eleanor looked in wonder at the dark brown earth and the black hedges and the black trees. It was four o'clock and the day was already closing in, and the thin sunlight was on the wane; soon the moon would creep cautiously into the sky, and the long night would set in.

Anne Wynn was in the garden burning dead leaves. She was wrapped in a sheepskin coat, and wore an old cloth hat; even so she looked beautiful.

'Darling, what a lovely surprise,' she said, embracing her daughter.

Eleanor inspected her mother's face for signs of illness but found none. All the same, the searching look did not go unnoticed.

'Oh dear,' Anne said, 'I can see from your gloomy face that Marcia has been dramatizing. I am perfectly all right. Now hand me those hedge clippers. I've got a few more lupins to cut down and then we'll go in and have a drink.'

'Mummy, what's wrong with you? You have to tell me!'

'Nothing's wrong with me. Nothing at all.'

'It's something to do with the eyes.'

'My eyes are perfectly all right.'

'I shall ring your doctor.'

'You certainly will not. I can't bear fuss, you know that. At my age nothing matters. I'm not one of those people who cling to life. I can't live for ever . . . something has to kill me. I'm not afraid. I just don't want any fuss.'

'Then something *is* wrong.'

'The only thing that's wrong is my herbaceous border full of dead plants.'

The trees were now black against the setting sun. There was a gust of cold wind and both women shuddered. Anne said, 'Come along, let's go in. And you can tell me about New York!'

They drank wine and laughed and Eleanor evoked the magical world of opera and was careful to sound detached when she mentioned Vincent Buonarotti. Her hero was, she said, Karl Henkel, her mother's old lover.

'You see, I know . . . I know everything,' Eleanor said, smiling.

'Is he still handsome? Is he still fun?' Anne asked eagerly. 'And did he really say that I had a good voice? Who knows what would have happened if he had not been married . . . perhaps I would have been Madame Henkel . . . perhaps I would have made a name for myself as a soprano . . . who knows?'

'He says he is coming to see you,' Eleanor said.

'No . . . no, he mustn't do that. I want him to remember me as I was . . . In those days I was pretty. Now . . . well, I'm an old lady. I don't *feel* old. That's part of the problem! It's a curious thing, but you'll find out for yourself . . . you grow old, lines and wrinkles appear, but you feel as you always have – young! Sometimes you wake up in the morning, you get out of bed with the spring of youth. You smile, you stretch and then all of a sudden you catch sight of yourself in the mirror and you want to cry out in horror, "Who's that old woman with that old face and body? Who's that hideous creature?'' '

'You're not hideous!'

'Thank you, darling, but there's no need to comfort me. Now, let's talk about something more interesting. Your wedding. Do you think I should buy a new hat or can I get away with the red one? You know, the one with the feather.'

'You won't be needing your hat. Edward has postponed our engagement.'

'How very odd. It is usually the women who get cold feet. Is that what's happened? He's got cold feet?'

'More or less.'

'I'm rather relieved.'

'I knew you would be. I'm beginning to feel that I'm unfit for marriage. I can't pay the price. But I want a child. Oh God, I want a child!'

'Then have one.'

Eleanor looked at her mother.

'Just like that?'

'I've told you before, if you want a child, have a child.'

They cooked a simple supper, talked and laughed and drank red wine and went to bed early. As she kissed Eleanor goodnight, Anne said, 'I want to see you settled, in one way or another. That's what I am living for.'

'Without you I'd be so lost . . . I couldn't cope.'

'Yes you could.'

It was in the early hours of the morning that Eleanor woke and for some reason the house felt strange. She got out of bed and walked on to the landing, where she saw a light coming from her mother's room. She heard a voice. It was her mother's; she was talking, but to whom? Eleanor went into the bedroom and found her mother sitting up in bed, her eyes open, staring at the wall in front of her. There was something strange about the eyes: they were open and unblinking; Anne was in a trance, talking to herself:

'We can't stay here . . . we haven't got enough water. We'll have to keep walking until we get to the lake. Oh, damn these leeches! I shall never get used to leeches . . .'

'Mummy,' Eleanor said gently, touching her mother's arm.

Anne stared at Eleanor and said, 'Is Marcia here?'

'Marcia's in London.'

'Tell her to come and see me. And bring the children. They can play in the garden. Where's Daddy?'

'Daddy is dead.'

'Oh dear, oh dear. How dreadful . . . Yes . . . yes . . . We buried him in a cemetery on the lower slopes of Kanchenjunga. He loved the Himalayas. And Karl . . . Where is Karl?'

'Karl is in New York.'

'He met my daughter Eleanor. And he remembered me. After all these years.'

She sat quite still with her unblinking eyes, and now tears spilled down her cheeks.

'Karl,' she said. 'Dear Karl.'

'Go to sleep, Mummy . . . Go to sleep.'

Anne Wynn drifted into sleep. For most of the night Eleanor lay awake, now and then getting up and staring out at the winter moon, and the frost glistening icy cold in its platinum light. 'He was the love of her life, and he still is, even though she's old. Still she loves him! Isn't there anyone out there for me to love? I don't ask to be loved in return. I ask only to love!' she thought.

The next morning Eleanor found her mother in the garden, tying back some rose bushes.

'Hello, darling,' Anne said. 'Did you sleep well?'

'Yes. And you?'

'I always sleep well in the country.'

Later that afternoon Eleanor drove to London, clearing her mind of the confusion, becoming a practical person once more, preparing herself to take up the paintbrush once again. As she walked up the stairs to her studio she remembered Rosie and her friends. What would she find? She opened her studio door. Sunlight was pouring through the skylight on to the studio floor. There was silence and emptiness and perfect order; Rosie had kept her promise. A telegram lay on the table. Eleanor picked it up. It read:

I AM WAITING FOR YOU IN PARIS.
ÎLE DE LA CITÉ. RUE CAMBON NO. 6

It was signed, VINCENT.

12 Eleanor could hear music. She stood in the half-lit corridor and listened to muffled notes beyond a mahogany door, and stared at the shaft of light that escaped beneath the door and fell on her shoes. The narrow, shaky lift, so typical of old Paris buildings, was shuddering down the shaft, leaving her alone and in doubt. There was still time to turn back to take the lift once more and descend the six floors, to escape into the streets of Paris and go home – to what?

Eleanor rang the bell. She waited. No one answered. She rang again. Vincent opened the door, waving his arm in the air as if he were conducting. The brilliant smile she had carried in her mind for days lit his face; without any hesitation he pulled her towards him and wrapped her in his arms, and held her tightly and tenderly as if she were a child.

'*Sei venuta . . . sei venuta . . .*' he murmured.

He led her on to the terrace and stood beside her in the cool air beneath a pock-marked moon and pointed out the grey slate roof of the Louvre, the white stone surface of the Sacré Cœur and the buttresses of Notre Dame.

Vincent put his hands on Eleanor's shoulders.

'You're trembling,' he said.

'I'm nervous.'

He took her face in his hands and kissed her softly.

'Give me one year of your life . . . and we shall create such beautiful memories . . . then I shall let you go . . . and you'll get married . . . and have babies and do all the things that everyone else does.'

'It doesn't look as if I shall marry. Edward has postponed our engagement.'

'How very considerate of him! I shall write and thank him . . . What a kind man! What a stupid man! What an idiot!' He dropped his voice. 'All the same, it's lucky for me! . . . *Tu sei bellissima, con una faccia così originale, bellissima fanciulla con questi occhi verdi! Capisci Italiano?'*

'Sì, capisco.'

'You speak Italian!'

'È la mia lingua preferita.'

'Why didn't you tell me?'

'You never asked me.'

Vincent touched her hair, softly.

'Clever girl, so full of surprises . . . I shall call you Schmetterling, my butterfly . . . my beautiful butterfly.'

He opened a bottle of red wine and they sat inside and drank. The room was a curious mixture of countries and cultures: red velvet Victorian chairs and primitive paintings from Bali; a Ming vase and a modern Italian table.

'What happened in New York? I woke up, I don't know when, in the middle of the night . . . I reached out expecting to find your beautiful body next to me, and what do I find? Nothing! No one!'

'You fell asleep, so I left.'

'I was exhausted. You have no idea.'

'I have a very good idea.'

Laughing, he took her hand and kissed it.

'Look on the bright side. It can only get better.'

Vincent took Eleanor into his bedroom. It was rough and frantic lovemaking. Vincent wanted her and he took her, but without delicacy or preparation. With great vigour and almost immediately, he thrust himself inside her until he reached his own powerful orgasm and cried out, 'I want a baby from you, do you hear? A baby!'

They drank champagne and looked out at the massive buttresses of Notre Dame flooded in yellow beams of light, and Eleanor said, 'I used to live in Paris. I studied at the Beaux Arts.'

'Alors tu parles français?'

'Evidemment.'

'My Schmetterling, so gifted and so accomplished. Tell me everything about yourself. Come, sit beside me and tell me everything.'

Eleanor could feel his affection, his love, and she was touched by it all. And yet she was not awed by Vincent; she never had been. She sketched her life in big brushstrokes, but filled in the faces of her family; she painted a generous, eccentric, brilliant father; a patient, loving mother; a spoilt, pretty and wilful sister; and herself, introvert, dedicated to her work, rootless, buffeted, hopeful. And Vincent laughed and enjoyed the anecdotes.

'Now it's your turn,' Eleanor said.

'It's my turn!' he cried. 'My turn to confess the sins of the Buonarotti family . . . We Buonarottis – how can I describe us? Libertine? Yes! But more important, artistic! We are not called Buonarotti for nothing. Michelangelo had no children – we are descended from his brother Gian Simone – and even today I have an aunt who lives in Caprese – that was Michelangelo's village. You know, it's very interesting, Michelangelo was given to a wetnurse who happened to be the wife of a stone-cutter. He always said it was her milk that made him a sculptor. Well, my grandfather was born in Caprese and he too was a sculptor . . . not too good . . . but not too bad either . . . his Madonna is in the church.'

'How lighthearted he is,' Eleanor thought, 'just like a boy . . . throwing his hands in the air in the Italian manner, laughing at his own jokes almost before they are told.'

'*Basta* . . . enough about me!' he said.

'No, no!' Eleanor said. 'It's not nearly enough. What about your father?'

'A conductor and a Communist . . . that was Papa. In the war he was imprisoned by Mussolini. Eventually he escaped and fled to the hills and joined the partisans. My mother joined him there – she was Scottish – Teresa Fadden from Inverness. An actress. But you know all that already! You know everything, my clever Schmetterling . . .'

'No, I don't. Go on, please!'

'Well, my mother and my elder brother, Luigi, they lived in the hills with the partisans. Luigi had a wonderful time. It was an exciting childhood for a small boy with all those guns and soldiers and freedom fighters. He used to tell me about it, and I began to feel that I had been there too. Sometimes it was dangerous . . . three men in our village were hanged for talking to the Fascists. I made a film about it all, my first film. It was about a small boy who spent the war in a mountain village near Arezzo. It was called *Pietro*.'

107

'I saw it twice,' Eleanor said.

'Good . . . no?'

'It was a wonderful film.'

'Ah . . . So you do like some of my work after all!'

He took both her hands in his and kissed them. He went on: 'Pietro won all the prizes. I was only twenty-six, a novice! Of course I was trained by Fellini – I learnt so much from him.'

Vincent paused and sank lower into the sofa.

'The first success is the sweetest. The awards I got for Pietro are my most precious. I was so proud!' He sat up and poured himself more wine. 'It's never quite the same again. You have more success. You become famous. You have fanmail, and secretaries, and your face appears in all the newspapers, and you can't conduct your love affairs in private, unless you hide away in your Paris apartment and there you can make love to a beautiful English painter . . . and snatch those brief hours that belong to lovers.'

He leant over and kissed Eleanor on the mouth, long and tenderly.

'Quanto sei bella e giovane . . . you look fifteen . . . no wrinkles, no lines. Dasha is so worried about getting old. She was fifty the other day . . . she minds so much!'

Eleanor thought to herself, 'I don't want to hear about Dasha!'

'My Schmetterling . . . my clever, clever Schmetterling. Let me play you some of Bohème . . . the first act where Mimi meets Rodolpho. It's great music and the libretto is poetry. Ascolti . . . amore.'

Vincent wrapped his dressing gown tightly around himself and led Eleanor into his study, a room fitted with books and records and compact discs, newspaper cuttings and photographs. They sat together on a sofa.

'You came into my life suddenly . . . just like Mimi . . . From now on I shall think of you . . . Listen to this aria – it is so beautiful – when she first arrives and tells Rodolpho about her life . . . listen!'

The voice of Vittoria de los Angeles rang out:

> 'Mi piaccon quelle cose
> Che han si dolce malia,
> Che parlano d'amor, di primavere,

108

Che parlano di sogni e di chimere,
Quelle cose che han nome poesia.'

Vincent said excitedly, 'Go on, translate, *tu che parli italiano!'*

'Let me hear it once more.'

Vincent played the piece again and Eleanor said, 'She is saying: it is the enchanted things that I like . . . things that speak of love and spring, of dreams and visions . . . all the things that people call poetic . . .'

'*Brava . . . bravissima!* It's beautiful, isn't it? Delicate and beautiful. She's not just a pretty face, our Mimi. Now, wait a moment and let's hear Rodolpho. There is one line of his that might have been written by Keats, or Yeats.'

They listened and Vincent sang out, '*Bello in allegra vampa svanir*: how beautiful to vanish in a flash of joy! It makes me think of "To cease upon the midnight with no pain" and also "Everything is changed, changed utterly . . ." Joy, love, passion, that is what *Bohème* is all about. That is what my life and your life is all about!'

They listened to the first act. Eleanor had heard it many times; it was so well known that it was almost a cliché and yet, she admitted to herself, it was the music of love. The conviction was there, in the notes, in the words, and like a tidal wave it swept over her and intensified her love for Vincent. She said, 'I don't want anything to spoil this.'

'People change, they get possessive.'

'But we are different.'

Vincent looked at her. 'Yes, we are different,' he said.

That evening they dined at a small bistro on the Île Saint-Louis and held hands across the table like young lovers, and the flame from the candle was reflected in their eyes.

'We have two whole days together,' Vincent said.

'Two whole days,' Eleanor said, hiding her disappointment. 'And what happens then?'

'Then Dasha comes to Paris and so does my assistant and my secretary, and we're off. It will take me one year to make *Bohème*. Next week we start on what's called the "pre-production". My headquarters will be in England at Twickenham.' He took her hand. 'I shall be close to you.' He went on, 'In the next month I get my technicians together. I only work with special people, all hand-picked – the lighting cameraman Dave Stuart and his team; I always have the same sound recordist, the same set designer – an Irish woman of genius – and then of course there's my cameraman, Giuseppe Negroponti, the best cameraman in the world. The singers – well, they've been booked for three years – Allen, Bruce and Domingo. In March we record the soundtrack in Munich because Carlos Kleiber likes to conduct his own orchestra, the Bavarian State Opera, and they live in Munich! No one conducts Puccini better than Kleiber. His music is so rich and romantic but never *kitschig* – you know that word? It's a good word. It means sugary – like a chocolate box painting. Also in March, while I'm in Munich, Giuseppe will come to Paris for me and film some hazy dawns and sunsets, some romantic slow pans across the Seine . . . maybe some exteriors of Rodolpho's house. First we have to find it! That's what we are going to do tomorrow . . . even if it takes all day . . . we are going to find Rodolpho's house, you and I.'

Eleanor said:

> 'Let us go then you and I,
> When the evening is spread out against the sky
> Like a patient etherized upon a table.'

And Vincent threw back his head and laughed.

The next day, in the sharp November air, they walked for hours along Paris pavements lined with chestnut trees. Brittle brown leaves floated tortuously to the ground. Eleanor dissected the autumn colours: red oxide mixed with cadmium orange, raw sienna and red ochre, cadmium and barium yellows, vermilion and cobalt violet. They hurried from one district to another: Montparnasse was too squalid, Montmartre too artificial, 'A toy town built for Japanese tourists,' Vincent pronounced. On the Pont Napoléon III they stood together, following the flow of water towards the Louvre and Notre Dame. Behind them rose the engineering miracle of the nineteenth century, the Eiffel Tower.

'That's where we have to be careful,' Vincent said. '*Bohème* takes place in 1870, the year of the Franco-Prussian war. In 1870 the Eiffel Tower wasn't built. We have to be careful, do you see? And look at all those television aerials – they are the curse of every film-maker. The camera must move stealthily among the monuments of Paris . . . We need to film when the light is hazy . . . either a sunset or a dawn . . . I like the idea of dawn, when nothing is too distinct. I have one idea I want to put to Giuseppe – he's my cameraman, I think I told you, the best there is. I keep thinking about an opening shot. We need a pigeon – just one pigeon – here on this bridge, on one of these statues of angels. You start with one tight shot of this pigeon and then you pull out and out and back and back until we have a view of the whole of the Seine and from here to the Louvre to Notre Dame and beyond! Obvious, dramatic and beautiful – just like *Bohème* itself!'

They walked all day. Through the Marais, and the Place des Vosges and the Paris of Louis XIII; they visited the Victor Hugo Museum, the Picasso Museum and Beaubourg. They crossed the river and began a long march through the Latin Quarter and here Eleanor took the lead. She turned down this street and then that; she pointed out restaurants and half-hidden museums; they saw the unicorn tapestries in the Cluny Museum, and the mosaics by Puvis de Chavannes in the Pan-théon; and then, without warning, they came upon Rodolpho's house. They both knew immediately this was the spot, a small circular *place* at the end of a twisting, uneven, cobblestoned street with a fountain in the centre encircled by a beautiful iron grille, and a house with tattered brown shutters which overlooked the street. At once Vincent began to fill the *place* with actors and props:

'And we'll have chimneysweeps and flowersellers and horse-drawn carriages in the distance; and urchins and women here by the well, drawing water. And Rodolpho can throw back the shutters and lean out of the window . . . Oh, this is perfect! I must contact Chirac immediately . . . Yes, I must! *Brava, mia Eleonora, bravissima* . . . here's the perfect setting for *Bohème*!'

It was dawn. Eleanor stood on the terrace in a towel dressing gown she had found in the bathroom. The moon was strug-gling to keep its titanium whiteness in a battle of light against a watery sun that was gaining strength and throwing a sheen of barium yellow across the thin blue sky. The view of Paris was the same as the night she had arrived; and yet everything had changed, changed utterly. Her eye wandered over the skyline from the Sacré Cœur so fresh and silvery white in the early light, to the Eiffel Tower with its criss-cross beams of steel to the Arc de Triomphe, so massive and triumphant. It was all so familiar and yet now it was all different.

'I have changed,' she said to herself, 'that is what has happened. It is I who will never be the same.' She breathed deeply and felt the morning air tingling in her lungs. 'I love this man totally. I want to be a part of his life for ever. I know he will never marry me; I know he will always have at least one other mistress. It doesn't matter. I shall take what time he gives me, as long as he loves me, in his way, whatever way he chooses.'

She found herself smiling; and the smile stayed on her lips. She reached out with her hand and took a handful of air. She told herself, 'I must hold this moment in my hand. I must cry out to the stars – "Thank you, thank you for giving me life so that I can live through a moment such as this!" '

Two black birds wheeled about in the air, their jagged wings cutting into the creeping sunlight. Eleanor shuddered and went inside; her father used to say that black birds brought bad luck. She looked into the bedroom. Vincent was sleeping. It was not an ordinary sleep; it was the sleep of the dead, absolute and total. He slept as he lived, with abandon. A telephone rang; he heard nothing.

In the drawing room, on every table, there were family photographs, landmarks in the familiar saga of family life. There was a photograph of Dasha when she was a dancer with the Bolshoi. 'It's an intelligent, sensitive face,' Eleanor thought, 'determined, brave but sad . . . always sad.' On another table was Marina in a white tutu, smiling; and on another table a handsome young man on a horse. Eleanor guessed this was Nicky, the son. 'How odd that Vincent never mentions his son,' she thought. 'I wonder why?' There were other photographs: a wedding picture, and a christening, and another christening; and a family holiday by the sea with Dasha and Vincent, their arms around each other, and the two children building sandcastles, laughing. Suddenly a coldness crept over Eleanor's skin; she felt like a burglar breaking into a family. 'I am not the first and I will not be the last,' she told herself. 'I am just another lover.'

For over an hour Eleanor browsed among the books, pulling out a life of Puccini, another of Mozart, of Michelangelo and

Donatello. She heard the high-pitched tone of the telephone. She went back into the bedroom, where Vincent was sitting up, propped against pillow, talking in Italian:

'What damage? The Colosseum has been damaged already, in case you haven't noticed! What is all this talk of damage? I want to stage an opera not a football match against England! We are not talking about an audience of hooligans – we are talking about the high society of Rome listening to *Aida*, *capisci*?'

Vincent saw Eleanor, smiled, blew her a kiss and beckoned her to come and sit beside him. One telephone call led to another. Eleanor sat down on her side of the bed and, without thinking, took a pad of notepaper and with a pencil that she found on the table began to draw butterflies. Vincent covered the receiver with his hand.

'This is Dasha's doctor . . . he wants her to have a hysterectomy . . . she doesn't want to have it – women hate the idea of a hysterectomy – they feel it takes away from their womanhood.'

Eleanor thought to herself, 'I don't want to hear about Dasha's hysterectomy.'

She sat on the edge of the bed, wondering if, when he had finished his telephone call, Vincent would make love to her again. ('How odd' she thought, 'to desire a man so much who gives me so little satisfaction.') She wondered if it would be more dignified to get dressed, but she waited. He stretched across the bed and took her hand as he talked on the telephone, and now and then he smiled at her. At last the telephoning was over; Vincent leaned forward across the bed and pulled Eleanor towards him.

'Come here, Schmetterling,' he said. 'Come and sit beside me . . .'

His arm slid around her shoulders and his hand fell on to her breast, which was naked under the dressing gown, and his finger tips touched her nipple.

'Dahsa knows,' he said.

'What does Dasha know?'

'She knows that I like you. She always knows. It is extraordinary. That night in our apartment in New York she watched me watching you and she knew. She is an extraordinary woman, almost psychic.'

And once again Eleanor thought, 'I don't want to hear about Dasha.'

Vincent took Eleanor's face in his hands.

'She doesn't know that I adore you!' He kissed her on the lips and suddenly turned away, threw off the bedclothes and stood naked in the room, stretching. 'No more of this indolence! We must get dressed . . . go out and find Rodolpho's house!' he said.

He turned back and looked at her with laughing eyes which said, 'I know that you want to make love, but you must wait. You must wait for me to pleasure you.'

All over Paris the church bells were ringing, calling the faithful to worship. They walked along the Seine. The branches of young willow trees trailed in the water, and now and then a coal barge slipped through the grey waters, sounding a mournful salute. Lovers were kissing beneath a bus shelter and a tramp was huddled beneath newspapers on a bench; and all the while Eleanor could hear the steady lapping of water against the banks of the river.

'Vincent, are you a Catholic?' she asked.

'Of course I'm a Catholic. In Italy everyone's a Catholic.'

'I don't know how you sleep at night.'

'I sleep very well at night.'

'You call yourself a Catholic and yet you are an adulterer and a fornicator! Do you ever go to confession?'

'Of course I go to confession.'

'My God! It must take all day!'

'Confession – like everything else – benefits from good editing. You don't want to say too much and you don't want to say too little. Just enough to convince the priest that you're human.'

'Have you always been unfaithful?'

'I don't think of myself as unfaithful.'

'You don't?'

'No! I love Dasha. She is the most noble woman I have ever met. I will never leave her.'

'I know that,' Eleanor said quietly.

'We're not together very often, but I make it up to her in other ways. Once a year, in July or August, I take her on holiday alone. You should see how happy she is! Just like a little girl!'

'And your mistress?'

'Who told you about my mistress?'

'You did.'

'I must have been drunk . . .'

'You were.'

'Well, I've known her all my life. It's true! We played together as children. And today Flavia – that is her name – she
works for me.'

'Don't tell me she's your secretary.'

'No . . . I started a music festival, Il Festival della Gioventù,
the Youth Festival of Rome – she's the organizer. She's married
to a banker . . . she hates him. Her daughter is a heroin
addict . . . It's all very difficult, but she loves me very much,
so what can I do? When I leave, she cries, not quietly, but
loudly, so that people in the street look up at the window and
wonder what is happening. Last time I left she took my coat
and would not let go. What can I do?'

'Does Dasha know?'

'Yes.'

'And?'

'And what? Dasha is an intelligent woman . . . She never
comes to Rome, so there is no embarrassment; and I never
take Flavia abroad, so the two never meet. Flavia is part of my
life. So is Dasha. I need Dasha. She is like a mother to me.
Every man needs a mother-lover.'

'Were you brought up by the Jesuits?'

'Yes.'

'I thought so! You exult in sin. If it's not sin then it's not
fun. Those Jesuits priests told you to stay away from the sins
of the flesh, didn't they? And here you are, flouting their
teachings in the most flagrant way, but always ready at the
last moment to confess and beat your breast and say, "*Mea
culpa*." I've come across this before . . . the Merry Sinner.'

'If I am a sinner, Schmetterling, then what are you? Answer
me that! Here with someone else's husband! Shame! *Vergogna!*'

'You are the husband. You took the oath of fidelity to
another person, not I! I took no vow. I am not breaking my
word.'

'And that makes you feel better?'

'Yes.'

'You are easily satisfied. Come, we are going home. Right

now! I must take you to bed . . . it's the only way to stop you talking . . .'

The lovemaking was fast and furious, without any delicacy or subtlety. For Eleanor there was no time to have an orgasm, and yet she was completely caught up in Vincent's enthusiasm; his smile was so brilliant and his affection so overwhelming, that she felt loved, even if the loving itself was incomplete. 'It doesn't matter,' she told herself, 'as long as Vincent desires me . . . Then he will want to see me and we shall be together. My own pleasure does not matter. Anyway, I love him.'

It was five o'clock and getting dark as Vincent and Eleanor walked arm in arm down the Boulevard Saint-Michel, and the clock in the courtyard of the Sorbonne rang out and students walked this way and that.

'How young they all look,' Eleanor said. 'But today, it is as if twenty years have fallen away . . . I am sixteen . . . this world is new!'

'That's what you look,' Vincent said. 'Sixteen.'

The sun was low on the horizon, a brooding vermilion, daubing the sky with fierce streaks of violet and purple. It was a magnificent sight. Eleanor and Vincent both leaned over the Pont de la Cité and stared down into the water. Eleanor imagined to herself that there would be many days like this, in Paris or in Rome or even New York, where they would spend hour after hour together, free from pressure. But she was wrong, just as she was wrong about so many things. Nevertheless at that moment she felt sure that the pattern for the future had been set. Vincent had given her one uninterrupted day sharing with her his thoughts. He would always be like this, she told herself.

It was Eleanor's idea to go into Notre Dame and listen to part of the evening Mass. A choir was singing the Mozart Requiem and the music filled the cathedral with a celebration of life and youth. At the end of the service the congregation moved slowly towards the great doors; Eleanor felt a hand on her arm, and she turned to see Alexei, who smiled at her until he noticed Vincent beside her and the smile vanished.

'Alexei,' Vincent said easily. 'I didn't know you liked churches – or music, for that matter.'

'I am interested in pagan rites.'

'You know Eleanor Wynn?'

'Yes.' Alexei hesitated and then said, 'I was with Dasha in Geneva at refugee conference. Work is finished early so we all come to Paris this morning. She went to country with a friend, back tonight. Asking me for dinner.'

'I'm delighted,' Vincent said with perfect ease. 'Eleanor, can you join us?'

'No . . . I'm afraid I can't. I have to have dinner with the people I'm staying with.'

'*Che tristessa*. Well, Alexei . . . see you later.'

As soon as Alexei was out of sight Vincent began to run. Eleanor followed, feeling ridiculous, running along the Seine, while Vincent called out, '*Forza! Fai presto!*'

Once inside his flat Vincent rushed into the bedroom and gathered up Eleanor's belongings and flung them at her.

'You must take everything. Don't leave anything, not your toothbrush, or your lipstick.'

'I don't wear lipstick.'

Vincent was not listening; he was agitated, almost angry, and his eyes darted about the room. Suddenly he said, 'Look at this bed! Oh God. Come on . . . help me! How can she change her plans like this? She was staying in Geneva until tomorrow. I think she's spying on me. I do! Of course Alexei knows exactly what's going on, but he adores Dasha so he warned us. Well done for saying you were busy tonight! *Brava!* My God – what is this? Something for your hair. Please take everything! Hurry, Eleanor, hurry!'

It was unseemly haste. Eleanor threw her belongings into her small suitcase and did her best to make the bed so that it looked as if one person had spent an innocent night between the sheets. The lift was rumbling upwards; was it Dasha? Vincent pushed Eleanor on to the backstairs landing where the garbage stood waiting for collection. The lift stopped at the floor below.

Breathlessly he said, 'It's all right . . . It wasn't Dasha! Come on . . . You can go . . . Quickly! *Ciao* . . . *amore* . . . *ciao*. Call me!'

'I don't know your number.'

Vincent pulled out a piece of paper and wrote at great speed as he spoke.

'In Rome you ask for Claudia . . . in Paris there's Michelle, in London there's Maureen . . . Now here's the lift. In you go . . . and hurry . . . if you meet Dasha in the lobby, just hide your face . . . That's right, pull your hat down . . . don't look up, whatever you do!'

He kissed her quickly and said, 'I love you.'

The words filled her mind for days.

13 Looking back, there were no difficulties; looking back their love was triumphant and passionate and inspiring. At the time it was agonizing; each perfect moment was overshadowed by either Dasha or Marina or *Bohème*. And yet perhaps these shadows were necessary; they were the darkness that made the brightness so bright.

Their love bloomed in winter, and whenever Eleanor remembered their time together, there was snow on the ground and Vincent's breath was steaming in the night air, and days were short and pale and the nights were endless and black, and beneath a diluted sun their love burned with beautiful intensity. It was snowing in Paris on that blustery day when Eleanor's black beret blew over the Pont de la Concorde into the grey slate water of the Seine and Vincent took her cold face in his hands and told her that he loved her. In Vienna the snow lay two feet deep as they huddled together in the back of a tram, and the snow muffled the sounds of the wheels on the track, and Vincent put his hand on her stomach and whispered, 'Schmetterling, our baby will be beautiful!' In London the snow was turning to brown sludge as Eleanor wrapped her scarf around her face and said to Vincent, 'Let's go to the National Gallery,' and he said, 'Let's go to bed.'

He was extravagant at all times; and he gave her wonderful presents: a drawing from Picasso's blue period; a watercolour by Turner; a beautiful bound set of Dante; a jade kitten to match her eyes.

In the 'Edward years' Eleanor was always apologizing for being herself, but Vincent delighted in her as she was, and the feeling was superb. He told her she could be a great painter and pointed her towards the stars in the sky, and for the rest of her life she would try to touch the distant universe; often she failed but now and then she succeeded and she always said her best work came from trying to paint the impossible, and this she had learnt from Vincent Buonarotti.

119

Her painting was changing in front of her eyes; it was more dramatic than ever (she seemed able to take extraordinary chances); there was more of it (she was never again so prolific); above all it was joyous.

She looked prettier – everyone said so – and Eleanor wondered if it were physical (a French friend of hers maintained that lovemaking was good for the skin). Marcia noticed and said, 'Who is he?' Eleanor smiled and kept her silence. Her mother also noticed a change but asked no questions. Instead she said, 'There's nothing like a new beau to bring out the beauty in a woman – you are looking well, my darling,' and she left it at that. Dominic rejoiced twice over: the demise of Edward was cause enough to celebrate, but the advent of Vincent, that was truly magnificent.

'This is a man for you – a creative force that will fill your life! Well done, Eleanor, well done! Of course, I was on to this long before you told me. Yes I was! Ethel Wingate gave the game away. She came over to London and told me all about your picture. She kept saying, "You should see Eleanor's picture. It's wonderful . . . so truthful and so affectionate. She has painted Vincent with love." I knew at once what was going on!'

Life itself changed; Eleanor was filled with goodwill to all women and men. Her inner tension had been replaced by patience and understanding; nothing irritated her, nothing saddened her. She found her sister beautiful and delightful, and she was glad that she had a rich husband; glad that she had a lover. Eleanor was glad for everyone.

In December Vincent set up his office in the Twickenham studios, and soon the soft Irish lilt of his secretary Maureen became a part of Eleanor's life. She spoke to her almost every day.

'I must talk to him, Maureen, it's so important.'
'He's in a meeting.'
'It won't take a second. It's very important.'
'I'll have to interrupt – '
'It's very urgent.'
A moment later he was there, anxiety in his voice as he asked, 'What is it, Schmetterling?'
'Do you love me? Tell me that you love me . . .'

He laughed softly. 'You've got a nerve, Eleanor Wynn. Yes, yes, I love you! Stay there, don't go anywhere. I'll come over.'

She waited, too happy to work, imagining the sound of his car outside, and his footstep on her staircase, and the ring of the doorbell, and his presence. And he came and stayed all evening and all night; and he possessed her with the same frenzied enthusiasm, burrowing his face between her legs, kissing her, touching her, loving her. She was caught up in this whirlwind of male desire.

The moment before Vincent reached his climax he cried out, 'I want a baby from you, do you hear?' and then his whole body shuddered and he fell back lifeless.

Later he said, 'Dasha knows.'

'How?'

'In Paris she found a drawing of a butterfly on the notepad. I pretended that I had done it but she said, "This is the work of a professional." You see, she knows.'

Eleanor thought, 'Why is he telling me all of this? It is none of my affair.'

'She looked so sad,' Vincent said.

14 This time she would not telephone. It was a matter of principle. She must make a stand on behalf of all women. She had left so many messages, what was the point of leaving another? Snow had fallen steadily all day, and the skylight was covered with layer upon layer of silent flakes, blocking out the winter light. Outside children were throwing snowballs in Hyde Park, while in the street cars turned the snow-whiteness black. Was Vincent in a car? Or was he walking? Was he in Paris or in Rome or in Munich? He had not telephoned. Eleanor's only contact was with his secretaries. By now she was familiar with the soft response of Claudia, the secretary in Rome, who greeted each caller with 'Produzione Buonarotti'; and she knew the clipped, efficient accent of Michelle in Paris, who said, 'Je vous écoute', and of course there was Maureen at the Twickenham studios with her Irish cadence.

These faceless women seemed to sympathize and Eleanor felt that she knew what they were thinking: 'So you are the latest . . . well, my poor girl, this is how it is. Days, even weeks go by, and he does not telephone. It doesn't matter how many messages you leave. He only rings when he wants to. Poor girl, you are new to all this, but you will learn.'

Eleanor lay back and rested her head on soft pillows. She was tired. She had slept badly. Her nerves were on edge. The painting on the easel had not been touched for three days: the new Lord Chancellor had only one eye, and that morning Eleanor had cancelled the sitting. Her hand felt unsteady and she did not trust her judgement. She might tamper with the picture and spoil the composition.

'This is terrible,' she said to herself. 'Just because I haven't heard his voice I am in such a state. How can I live like this? I need to talk to him every day! To hear his laugh. I drew such joy from the sound of his voice. It fills me with such happiness, and then I can work all day and all night, I can paint ten pictures!'

In the studio the silence was great, as the night closed in. Eleanor sat on her bed, her mind a blank. How would she spend the evening? What would she do?

The telephone rang. She picked up the receiver. The voice said, 'Schmetterling.'

Eleanor could not speak; tears came to her eyes; she was smiling and trembling.

'Schmetterling?'

'Yes . . . yes . . . I'm so pleased to hear you.'

'I'm staying at Claridge's. Can you come over?'

'I'm coming, I'm coming!'

And she played *Bohème* as she dressed, and the phrase turned in her mind, 'Tu sol commandi, amor' (love alone commands me), and she felt exultant and sang out loud. The moments passed in ecstatic anticipation: they would laugh and kiss and make love; she could feel his skin, his warmth, his hand. And then they would have a long and intimate dinner and go back to bed. She was startled by the sound of her intercom (a Christmas present from Dominic). She pressed a button and a voice said, 'It's Edward.'

'I can't see you.'

'You must.'

He looked wonderfully handsome in his fur hat flecked with white snow; his face was red with cold. He stood awkwardly in the entrance to the studio, holding a bunch of red roses which he held out to Eleanor. She thought of Manet's painting of the shy man hiding behind the flowers and took the roses.

'Edward, I . . . I have to go.'

'Did you get my letter?'

'Yes.'

'From Peking?'

'Yes.'

'I said that I missed you. I said that I wanted to marry you.'

'It's too late. Everything has changed.'

'You've met someone?'

'Yes, I've met someone. I'm in love, for the first time in my life. I should thank you, Edward. If we had married I should never have felt like this. That is unkind, I know, but it's true!'

'Do I know him?'

Eleanor said nothing.

'It's Vincent Buonarotti, isn't it?'

'Yes.'

'I knew it!' Edward cried out. 'I knew if you went to New York I would lose you . . . I felt it in my bones . . . I didn't want you to go . . . do you remember . . . I was angry.'

'I remember.'

'He will hurt you. You know that, don't you?'

'Everyone hurts me,' Eleanor said, 'except my mother.'

There was another long silence.

'You know his reputation?'

'Yes.'

'Then you know he just wants to fuck you.'

'Everyone wants to fuck someone, as far as I can see.'

Edward took a deep breath and said, 'I feel sorry for you.'

Eleanor swivelled round, her eyes shining.

'Well, don't. This is the happiest time of my life,' she said.

Edward stared at her in anguish and left the room. She still held the roses in her hand. She took off the paper and stood them in a white jar, and went to meet Vincent at Claridge's.

The eyes of the receptionist seemed to be saying, 'You have come to make love to a guest, I know, I can tell!' and Eleanor felt embarrassed as she waited at the desk while they rang Vincent's room. She began to tremble at the thought that in a few moments he would be holding her. She knocked lightly on his door; the door opened and Vincent enfolded her in his arms. He tore the button on her silk blouse in his hurry to possess her and once again she rejoiced in his desire.

His heavy breathing slowed as they lay naked beside each other, and he said, 'My poor Flavia is having a terrible time! Her daughter is a heroin addict – did I tell you? Last week the Italian police arrested her and took her to jail. Flavia was beside herself – she rang me in tears and I had to go to Rome and sort things out, and no sooner had I got back to Paris than Dasha rings me in tears because the doctor says that Marina must go to hospital because she won't eat. One cannot reason with Marina – it's better she goes to hospital, that's what I said, but how am I expected to concentrate with all these problems? And I have so much on my plate at the moment . . . too much. I should never have accepted *Don Giovanni*. I'm not in the mood for Mozart . . . my mind is locked into Puccini . . .

all I think of is *Bohème* . . . but what can I do, I leave for Milan tomorrow!'

'Can I come?'

'Oh, my Schmetterling, Italy I must reserve for Flavia. Otherwise I never see her. You do understand?'

'I suppose so.'

'And she's having such a hard time at the moment with her daughter . . .'

'You told me.'

'Schmetterling . . . I would like to take you to Munich when I record the soundtrack to *Bohème* . . . That would be nice, my Schmetterling! Munich is beautiful. But it may be difficult. Dasha likes Munich. She may want to come.'

'I don't care about Dasha,' Eleanor thought.

Vincent went on, 'So many problems . . . my nerves are on edge. Come here and let me feel you.' He pressed his naked body next to hers and stroked her smooth skin. 'Only you understand me . . . only you bring me something that is bright and joyful and uncomplicated. We have no problems, do we, my Schmetterling? Between us everything is so simple! *È vero?* Yes?'

'You must ring me. I can't stand it when you don't ring me.'

'Schmetterling . . . it isn't easy. I am so busy.'

Suddenly Vincent threw back the covers and jumped out of bed.

'Look at the time . . . I must get dressed!'

'Where are we going?' Eleanor asked gaily.

Vincent threw out his arms and with a gesture of despair said, 'My Schmetterling. I have to leave you. *Mi dispiace!* My good friend Carlos Kleiber is in town.'

'I would love to meet him.'

'Yes, but he's not alone. He's with his wife,'

'I am very good with wives.'

'She's a great friend of Dasha's. What can I do?'

They did not go down in the lift together; that would be 'imprudent', Vincent said. Instead Eleanor went ahead. As she crossed the lobby of the hotel she caught sight of herself in a large gilded mirror, and thought, 'All dressed up and nowhere to go!' She *must* go somewhere; she could not creep back to her studio, her body fresh from the lovemaking with Vincent, and sit alone.

Eleanor drove along the Embankment to her sister's house. Marcia opened the door; she seemed nervous.

'Ralph's in Scotland. I'm with . . . a friend,' she said.

'I didn't mean to interrupt. I'll go away.'

'No, no, come in. Come in. It's time you met Matthew.'

Eleanor did not expect to like Matthew, and yet she did. He was English-looking, tall and thin with an angular face and round brown eyes that were bright with intelligence. He had the pink and white skin of a child and wore round spectacles. Matthew was the editor of a literary magazine which surprised Eleanor; she had never imagined that her sister would fall in love with an intellectual.

Marcia announced, 'This is my sister Eleanor. She's the successful one.'

'I know,' Matthew said, smiling.

'Marcia isn't usually so complimentary,' Eleanor said, as Marcia laid another place at the table and gave her sister hot soup. In the middle of dinner Rowley appeared in his pyjamas.

'Go back to bed, darling,' Marcia said. 'At once!'

'Uncle Matthew . . . will you play Lego with me?'

'He certainly won't at this hour!' Marcia said.

'But will you play tomorrow?'

'I don't think I shall be here tomorrow.'

'When will you be here?'

'I really don't know . . . but soon. And then of course I will play Lego with you.'

Uncle Matthew! How many times did he come to the house? Did the children talk of him to their father? Marcia was playing a dangerous game.

Eleanor found it hard to concentrate. She forced herself to discuss the Lucien Freud exhibition, and 'The Age of Chivalry' at the Royal Academy, and all the while she wished that she had not come; she felt intrusive. They were sitting at the table drinking coffee when a key turned in the front door, and a man coughed in the hall. Marcia went pale and she stood up, her eyes wide and staring as her husband Ralph walked into the dining room.

'Surprise, surprise! I got on the last flight from Aberdeen. I missed my little ones and you, my darling. No point spending another bleak night in Scotland. It's so cold in Kirkenny and you should see the snow! Five-feet drifts, and hundreds of farms cut off. It's a miracle that we're not snowed in. Eleanor, what a delightful surprise. How pretty you look!'

Ralph's gaze fell on Matthew. Marcia, still deadly pale, said, 'Darling, this is Matthew Elton, a friend of Eleanor's.'

'How do you do? I'm so glad to see Marcia has her friends round in the evening. I feel awful leaving her alone so much, but at the moment I have to be in Scotland at least three days a week. Our estate manager died a few months ago, and there's no one who knows the estate except for me! And I must look after my forest. It's very exciting planting a forest, but I'm afraid it does mean that I'm a neglectful husband! I'm hungry – is there any dinner left?'

Eleanor did her best to appear relaxed and familiar with Matthew, but even so she found the situation excruciating, and soon after ten she made her excuses and left, taking Matthew with her. They stood for a moment outside in the street; it had stopped snowing and the sky was white and menacing.

Matthew said, 'Thank you. That was very kind of you.'

'What else could I do?'

'I want to marry your sister.'

'What does she say?'

'She says no. She can't leave Ralph . . . she can't break up the family. I suppose she's right . . . only it seems such a waste of our love.'

'I really can't say anything. I like my brother-in-law. He's a sweet man and he loves her.'

'Yes. We both love her.'

15 The filming of *Bohème* got underway in the spring. The blossoms were particularly rich that year and Eleanor walked in the parks beneath trees ringed with fallen petals, and she marvelled at their dying colour; and tried not to think about Vincent. 'When I am filming I can see no one . . . not even you!' he had warned. She braced herself for a long silence, but within a few weeks Vincent telephoned and invited her to the studio and asked her as a favour to bring Ethel Wingate, who was staying at Claridge's. Dominic got wind of the expedition and invited himself along.

They drove to Twickenham in Ethel's enormous black limousine, and as they passed through the security gates Dominic gave the guard a royal wave.

'This is how I like to travel,' he said.

Ethel Wingate patted Eleanor's knee with her jewelled hand.

'I'm very sorry to hear about your engagement,' she said.

'There is nothing to be sorry about,' Dominic said firmly.

'It must have been very distressing.'

'She was saved from a fate worse than death.'

'Dominic, I'm not asking you.'

'It seems a long time ago now,' Eleanor said.

'Is there someone new?'

'Yes.'

'Oh, how nice.'

'Not nice, but . . . interesting.'

Ethel studied Eleanor for a moment and then said, 'I have some good news for you . . . the Met calendar, do you remember? Well, the Board is delighted with your drawings and wishes to purchase twelve for $30,000.'

'What's this?' Dominic said, jerking forward. 'It's a deal. I accept at once.'

'I can put down a deposit on my studio,' Eleanor thought, 'and take out a mortgage.'

Inside the film studios Vincent threw out his arms and welcomed them all, and introduced them to his secretary, Maureen. Eleanor took her warmly by the hand and quietly she said, 'I feel I know you.'

'We've had so many conversations, haven't we? How nice to meet you at last.'

Maureen had classic Irish looks, green eyes and red hair and was pretty and plump. Eleanor wondered if Vincent had slept with her.

'Sit down, sit down,' Vincent said. 'I have seats for you over there,' and he led Eleanor by the arm, as if she were a stranger. His eyes were empty of love, and his smile was the professional smile of a man on the job. If only he would call her 'Schmetterling', if only he would say, 'I love you . . .' She argued with herself: 'This is ridiculous . . . he is working . . . he cannot pay attention to me . . . not now . . . be reasonable, Eleanor.'

Suddenly she felt immensely sad. Where was the blazing joy of those early days of love? Now she was anxious and fretful.

'This is Act II,' Vincent explained, 'and this is the café, where Musetta is flirting. The outside, the street, the band, the children, has been filmed on location in Paris. I found this wonderful street behind the Panthéon . . .'

'*You* found the street,' Eleanor thought. '*I* found that street, but I cannot say so. My love is secret and must remain so. Oh, Vincent, look at me, please . . . give me just one loving look!' But Vincent was busy with his cameraman.

The set was built with extraordinary precision; every detail, from the wooden benches inside the café to the wine glasses, were of the Napoleon III period. Eventually the singers appeared, and urgently a wardrobe mistress adjusted a bow here and a button there, and a make-up artist highlighted a cheek and smoothed an eyebrow, and Dominic pointed to Placido Domingo and whispered, 'That man is God.' And all the while Eleanor did not take her eyes off Vincent as he moved among the crew and singers, projecting his confidence and provoking laughter; and she longed for him to look in her direction, and with his eyes send her a message of love; but Vincent was talking to the floor manager.

'Eleanor!'

It was Regina Bruce, splendid in her costume.

'You're Mimi . . . of course . . . I'd forgotten,' Eleanor said.

'And you're in love with Vincent. Don't deny it! I've been watching your moonstruck face. My dear girl, there's something you should know, if you don't already. He's a heartbreaker. It's his metier. So be careful!'

'Are you an authority?' Eleanor asked guardedly.

'Of course I am. I was his protégée, which means only one thing. But that was a long time ago. Now we're friends.'

'Oh my God,' Eleanor thought. 'How depressing.'

'Clear the set!' the first assistant cried out. 'Going for a take – clear the set.' The cameraman settled himself in his mobile seat and adjusted his Panavision camera; and the gaffer lowered a spot here and opened one there; and Vincent put his eye to the camera and told Regina Bruce to stand back, and Placido Domingo to step forward, and Thomas Allen to sit more sideways, and there was dead silence, and gradually the studio filled with the glorious sound of the perfect soundtrack, and the shoot was underway. The singers sang to their own voices with perfect precision, but Vincent was not satisfied, and again and again he asked them to repeat the scene, until he cried out, 'That's the take – that's the one!'

'I can't stand this any longer,' Eleanor thought. 'I must go home.'

A hand settled on her shoulder and she trembled at the sound of his voice.

'Schmetterling.'

'It's a beautiful set.'

'I wish all these people would go away and leave us alone.'

'So do I.'

'I haven't seen you for so long . . . Have dinner with me tonight. Alone.'

'Just you and I?'

'Just you and I.'

She could not work; she lay on her bed anticipating the evening ahead, imagining his laugh and his loving. She took a leisurely bath and made herself beautiful, and felt so wonderfully happy, waiting for her love to arrive. She thought to herself, 'I must teach myself to be patient . . . not to mind . . . In the end he comes to me, and then I feel everything is worth it. I must not make demands . . . my love is unconditional . . .'

The doorbell rang downstairs and she pressed the button

130

which opened the door, and stood counting the seconds that it would take him to climb the stairs, and any moment now he would be there, his arms open, ready to embrace her.

'Eccola!' Vincent cried, but Eleanor was not looking at him; she was staring at the man who stood in the shadows.

'You know Giuseppe Negroponti – you met today on the set, Giuseppe is the finest cameraman in the world! Come here, Schmetterling, let me kiss you. Isn't she beautiful, Giuseppe, and you must see her painting . . . she's a fine artist, and she works very hard when I am not around to distract her!'

The men laughed. Eleanor thought, 'Perhaps the cameraman will leave us alone. Perhaps he has to go.' But Vincent said, 'I've booked a table in a Chinese restaurant. It's very good food. Giuseppe, ring your girlfriend and tell her to come to the Fragrant Garden in Frith Street.' Vincent lowered his voice. 'Poor man, his wife is a dragon . . . she never lets him out of her sight, and they have six children. No wonder he hates Milan. Here in London he can have his *divertimento*.'

'Like you.'

'Schmetterling, don't be difficult . . . Come . . . let me look at your paintings . . . what is that over there?'

Eleanor was working on a large painting of several figures listening to a man on a soapbox at Speakers' Corner. Vincent studied the painting carefully and said, 'Who is that man?'

'I don't know. He's a Palestinian but that's all I know.'

'Is he your lover?'

Eleanor stared at Vincent in disbelief.

'I've never met the man! I've only watched him on a soapbox at Speakers' Corner. Of course he's not my lover. You are my only lover,' she said.

Vincent shook his head. 'No . . . no, you should have someone else.'

'Why do you say things like that?' Eleanor asked.

'I cannot be the centre of your life. I will only hurt you.'

He was not smiling, and even his eyes were serious. Suddenly he laughed and turned back to the paintings on the floor.

'Show me everything! What's this? And this? Hold it up – I can't see properly. *Ma tu sei bravissima. Giuseppe, vieni qua . . .*

come and look, Giuseppe . . . She can paint, this girl. What else, what else can I look at? I want to see your art!'

Vincent picked up one canvas after another and paced about the studio excitedly, throwing his arms about, talking fast.

'In your paintings there is a sense of drama. You see the world from an interesting angle – buildings, people, objects – it's special to you. I think you could design opera sets. What do you think, Giuseppe? *Che pensi? Guardi, la ragazza ha qualcosa di molto originale . . . che pensi?'*

They made their way to the Chinese restaurant, where they were joined by Giuseppe's girlfriend, a woman in her forties, with dyed blonde hair and old-fashioned, heavy eye make-up and a blouse that opened to reveal a plump, appetizing bosom. Her name was Bella. She held Giuseppe's hand under the table but Giuseppe hardly looked at her. Instead he talked to Vincent in Italian about the day's work. Eventually Bella asked to change places, and after wriggling in her chair she settled next to Eleanor.

'Is yours married?' she asked in a whisper.

'Yes.'

'So's mine. They're all married these days. It's cheaper. He's got six kids and a wife in Milan. And God knows what else. Of course, I've got another. Rides a motorbike. Delivers messages. Lives in Shoreditch. He's twenty-two. And I'm forty-one. He's my toy boy. But I mean, there's no point pining over a married man, now is there?'

'You're right, Bella.'

'Don't look so sad, love.'

Bella reached across the table for the wine bottle and poured.

'Come on, drink up. What are they on about then? Hey, Vincent, what are you two on about?'

'We are talking about *Bohème*, the greatest love story in opera. But Giuseppe doesn't see it that way. He's a Communist. He doesn't believe in love!'

'You don't believe in love?' Bella giggled, putting her hand on Giuseppe's thigh. 'That's not very nice.'

'Schmetterling, you're very quiet,' Vincent said.

'I have nothing to say.'

Vincent lowered his voice. 'You are being rude to Giuseppe. I've never seen you like this. Eleanor, *per calita!'*

So, she talked, or rather she argued, first about politics

and then about art. She contradicted Vincent and Giuseppe in almost everything they said, solemnly and without humour. And eventually she withdrew from the conversation and drank her coffee in silence. And in that moment she saw the end of their love: like a meteor flaming across the sky, it would burn itself out.

'What was that all about?' Vincent said, as he walked with Eleanor after dinner through the silent London streets.

'I never see you alone any more. I'm just part of the admiring crowd. I'm sorry if I ruined the dinner. I was so disappointed.'

Eleanor hailed a taxi and said, 'It's my fault. I love you too much.'

'Get in,' Vincent said, laughing. 'Go on, get in!' and he followed her into the taxi.

That night, beneath the studio skylight studded with stars, he made love to her with a rare tenderness, and afterwards, as they lay together in the dark studio, he said, 'You'll feed the baby yourself, won't you?'

And Eleanor thought, 'Why does he keep talking about a baby?

'There is', Dominic said, 'something new about your painting. Now what is it? Let me see. It's an interesting mix of emotions. There's joy – oh yes, the joy is unmistakable. Look at the face of the man in your painting. He is excruciatingly joyful. But then, by contrast, look at the girl. She's sad. Like the Venetian masks – one smiling and one sad. There's a rich experience in your work, Eleanor.'

'There should be.'

'But it's the artist herself who gives cause for concern . . . Look at you! A skeleton. And your face is haggard. I am taking you out to lunch. No arguments, please! Put on your coat and we'll go and gorge ourselves on pasta!'

They went to a small and noisy Italian restaurant in the Fulham Road. Dominic was excited.

'I've just heard that you are on the short list to paint – wait for it – the Queen! I put your name down a year ago . . . and then I heard nothing, and so I thought those aged relics at the Royal Society of Portrait Painters had blocked you. But no! You're on the short list.'

'I'm not that sort of painter.'

'Exactly! That's why they like you. You're different. Oh, Eleanor, if you get this commission I shall retire in a blaze of glory. Just think, if you had married boring old Edward none of this would have been possible! Let's toast spinsterhood and freedom!'

He raised his glass and drank, but as he drank, his eyes fixed on the table opposite. Two men were sitting deep in conversation. One of the men let out a loud, high-pitched laugh (it had a cruel tone to it and sounded like the cry of a tropical bird), and then he bent forward and talked conspiratorially. Eventually he turned round and Eleanor recognized Dominic's friend, the art critic Hugo Kyle, who had been the first guest to arrive at the opening of her exhibition. She recalled a look that had passed between the two men: a look of love. Dominic sat staring at his plate; his mouth was set tight, his long fingers tapped on the tablecloth.

'He told me he couldn't have lunch with me today. He told me he was working. He's a liar.' Dominic raised his voice; heads turned. 'He's a liar!' he called out, and then suddenly he got to his feet and walked towards the table of his friend, the glass of red wine in his hand. He came right up to Hugo Kyle and then shouted, 'You are a liar!' and threw the glass in his face and left the restaurant.

Eleanor paid the bill and followed, to find Dominic standing on the street corner, his arms folded, leaning against a lamppost. The wind was fierce; people were closing their umbrellas, but Dominic did not seem to notice.

'Let's go somewhere else,' he said.

They walked together down the street.

'Perhaps there's an explanation,' Eleanor said.

'I don't want to talk about it.'

'That man . . . perhaps he's a business friend.'

'That man is Guido Crespi. He designs men's clothes. He was my lover, once upon a time, and I introduced him to Hugo. Oh, never mind, never mind! I shall wipe Hugo from my mind. Blot him out! I am not given to unnecessary suffering. The rest of the world can drown in neurotic distress. Not I! Anyway, if all else fails . . . I can turn to women! There are so many of them . . . wandering about . . . looking for love. It's pathetic!'

'I don't think you like women.'

'Of course I don't like women. I'm a man. Men don't like women, or haven't you realized this, even now?'

'I really can't accept that.'

'You will. In time. There is everything else between the sexes but no love. There is passion, envy, hate, jealousy. Above all there's boredom – years and years of boring boredom . . . but no love.'

'You would say that, wouldn't you?'

Dominic looked at Eleanor sharply.

'It's not a homosexual point of view. It's what I have observed,' he said.

A voice rang out in the raw afternoon, and a man could be seen in the lamplight walking towards them. He was calling out, 'Dominic! Dominic!'

Eleanor recognized Hugo.

'You had better go,' she said, and as she watched Dominic turn and walk towards Hugo she thought to herself, 'It's the same ghastly business for everyone.'

16 It was a miserable summer with bad light and no Vincent, who was doing the rounds of the music festivals, Salzburg, Tanglewood and Siena. Eleanor went to Scotland to stay with Marcia and waited for Vincent to ring, but he never did. Each time the telephone rang she held her breath and listened for Marcia to say, 'Eleanor, it's for you,' but it never was.

She walked across the purple moor behind Kirkenny and the wind blew hard and the rushing air cooled her mind. A fierce shaft of light burst through the clouds and raced over the moor, like a searchlight, over the heather and the rock, over the backs of Friesian cows and over the fullness of summer trees, on to the river Dee which seemed to catch fire as the blinding light touched its metallic surface. Eleanor thought of the great Australian artist Arthur Streeton and his translucent landscape, 'The Purple Noon's Transparent Light', and she smiled at her painterly mind.

Surrounded by her family, Eleanor felt utterly alone. She could not hide her melancholy mood, and her mother kept looking at her anxiously. One afternoon Anne said, 'Let's walk in the garden.'

Together they strolled in front of Kirkenny, a large, grey stone house, and watched the children playing croquet on the lawn. They were heading for the steps leading down to the rock garden, when Anne lost her footing and stumbled. Eleanor caught her by the arm and held her back from the steep slope.

'How stupid of me,' Anne said. 'I wasn't thinking.'

'Mummy, you didn't see those steps, did you? Tell me, go on! Tell me the truth!'

'It only happens now and then.'

'What happens now and then?'

'A grey cloud comes down. And I cannot see.'

Anne put her hand on Eleanor's arm, and looked at her.

'I have seen a doctor. There is nothing to be done. Now don't go on. You know I hate discussions about health.'

They walked in silence. Ahead stretched the valleys and hills of Aberdeenshire. Bright yellow fields of corn were scattered across the landscape like squares of patchwork quilt; and in the air was a smell of harvest and the distant sound of tractors.

Eleanor held her mother tightly by the arm, and said, 'I love you so much. Don't die . . . please . . . don't die.'

'I'm waiting to see you settled, one way or another.'

In early September Vincent walked into the studio, suntanned and smiling.

'Schmetterling.'

'You didn't ring. I waited, day after day and you didn't ring.'

'I wanted to see if you would miss me.'

'I did. Every moment.'

'That's what I like to hear!' he said, and he kissed her and made love to her in frantic haste in the middle of the day.

As he was leaving, Eleanor said, 'It's my birthday next week. Dominic is giving a dinner. Will you come? Please? It would mean so much to me if you were there.'

'Of course I shall be there! Dominic rang me in Sydney, didn't he tell you? He said, "Will you come, Vincent? I should like to impress my friends!" I shall be there, Schmetterling, to celebrate our love . . . I want everyone to see how much we love each other. I want everyone to know!'

On the evening of her thirty-seventh birthday Eleanor lay on her bed and imagined the evening ahead. She pictured Vincent laughing, bewitching the guests and whispering to her now and then, and pressing her hand; and later they would make love and she would forget the loneliness of the summer in the turbulence of his warmth. The telephone rang.

'Schmetterling.'

'My love.'

'Listen . . .'

A terrible tension rose in her throat: he was going to cancel.

'You are coming tonight?' she asked.

'Of course I am coming.'

'I can't wait to see you.'

'Schmetterling. I want to bring Dasha.'

Dominic had filled his drawing room with flowers arranged in the Japanese style to match the hanging scrolls. He greeted his guests with champagne and caviar on toast.

'How very nice to see you again,' Dasha said to Eleanor, holding out her hand. 'It's very nice of you to invite me. It's your birthday? Here – this is a small present,' and she handed Eleanor a bottle of expensive French scent.

'Is she always so charming to the women in Vincent's life?' Eleanor wondered. 'Perhaps it's the only way to keep sane. Perhaps in her shoes I would do the same. In her shoes! How I wish I were in her shoes. Tonight she will go home with Vincent and they will go to bed, and perhaps they will make love – Vincent makes love to her when she's nervous, to calm her down – and then tomorrow she will see him for breakfast and talk to him. Oh, the lucky woman!'

Vincent was in his most ebullient form and kept the dinner table enthralled with opera stories. Now and then his gaze fell on Eleanor, but there was no intimacy in his eyes. After dinner Eleanor sat on the sofa beside Dasha; she wanted Vincent to see what a great effort she was making with his wife. She wanted to please Vincent and to prove that she could handle any situation, however difficult. She wanted Vincent to feel that she was a woman worth keeping. At the same time she despised herself. Out of the corner of her eye she saw Vincent, laughing, and she asked herself, 'Does he realize what an effort this is? Does he realize how I hate the falseness of my position, and how much I like his wife . . . and how that makes it all worse? Why is he doing this? What is he trying to prove? That we are all his slaves? Is that it?'

Eleanor could not bear to hear the sound of her own voice so she took refuge in Russia and kept asking Dasha questions.

'And is Russia changing – do you think so? Tell me!'

'How changing? Go to a bookshop in Moscow – there are no books. Go to a newsagent – no foreign newspapers. Information is banned – only official information is allowed. You want to go from Moscow to Kiev – you need a passport. When I go to see my aunt, I need a passport. On the other hand, I can go back to Russia. Before Gorbachev I could not go back, so perhaps that is a change. But it will be slow. Very, very slow.'

'Madame Buonarotti, it's my turn to talk to you,' Dominic said, sitting at her feet. 'Is Russia as beautiful as people say . . . do you miss your homeland?'

'I miss the hugeness of the land,' Dasha said, 'and the horizon that is absolutely bare, leading nowhere, simply going on for ever; I miss the miles and miles of steppe, especially in winter when everything is covered in snow and there are only two colours, black trees and white snow. You see, I grew up in the country, and you never forget, and your soul longs to go back . . . Not to live! No! I would never live in the Soviet Union, but I would like to see the forest once again.'

At this moment Dasha gave Eleanor a look of anguish which had nothing to do with what she was saying. It was a look which told Eleanor that she knew everything, and that she too was suffering. 'But you are his wife,' Eleanor thought. 'You have children . . . What do I have? Nothing! And here we are, you and I, in the power of this man . . . too weak to pull away . . . I cannot speak for you . . . you are his wife . . . but I must be mad . . . mad!'

The dinner was over and the last guest had left.

'Was that . . . very difficult?' Dominic asked.

'Yes.'

'Madame Buonarotti, does she know?'

'Yes.'

'If you ask me, it was a pointless exercise. He didn't talk to either of you.'

'He enjoyed himself.'

'Yes, I think he did. He was superb . . . I haven't laughed so much in a long time.'

The next day Eleanor waited to hear from Vincent. The day wore on and she grew apprehensive. 'He must ring . . . I made such an effort for him . . . I tried so hard with Dasha . . . surely he noticed?'

Eventually she telephoned Maureen in the Twickenham office, who told her, 'He's not here, Eleanor. He's gone to Rome.'

17 *'Addio, addio senza rancor.'* Eleanor played the haunting music from *Bohème* again and again. The decision was made: she would not see Vincent any more. She repeated to herself, 'It's over. Over!'

She could not sleep; she could not paint. Hour by hour the days crept past. Even the most perfunctory task demanded colossal effort; she instructed her hands to mix the paints and reluctantly they obeyed, and all the while desolation swept her soul. Vincent was no longer part of her life. An infinite bleakness stretched ahead; she was a barren and lonely woman. In her mind she went over and over their moments together and tortured herself as she remembered every touch and every look, and at times she could hear his laughter ringing in her ears. All that was in the past, and in the future there was nothing. She repeated to herself again and again, 'It's over'.

Dominic could not understand what was happening; for months she had worked at the most frenzied pace, and all of a sudden the painting stopped. Why? What was wrong?

'I want a rest,' she told him. But there was no rest; only torment.

One afternoon Eleanor called on Dominic in his gallery. It was a few weeks before Christmas and the shop windows were full of tinsel, and the Christmas lights spanned Oxford Street. In Dominic's office Eleanor noticed Vincent Buonarotti's name and telephone number scribbled on a piece of paper and she began to cry.

'What *is* going on?' Dominic demanded.

'I shall never call that number again.'

'You wouldn't get an answer if you did. They're closing the office next week. The film is in the can, as they say; and tomorrow night there's going to be a wonderful party at Annabel's to celebrate. Our beloved Ethel Wingate is footing the bill and Vincent is acting as host. They're taking over the whole place, and you and I are going!'

'No, Dominic, I am not. You don't understand, it's over.'

'Really?'

On the evening of the party Dominic had called to see if she would not change her mind, but Eleanor was obdurate. A few hours later she was less so. She kept imagining the party, and Vincent laughing with his friends. She could be near him once more, she could see him one last time. The thought became all-powerful. She dressed quickly and drove herself to Berkeley Square.

'It would make a good painting,' Eleanor thought as she walked into the nightclub, with its glimmering square pillars, and velvet sofas, and glamorous people crowding at the tables. It had an atmosphere of intrigue, of secret assignations. It was not easy to paint people at night in the lamplight of dark rooms; not easy to paint shadows in darkness. Eleanor thought of the Moulin Rouge and the cancan women and the tophatted gentlemen of Toulouse-Lautrec; and Degas's haunting picture of a half-lit bedroom, and a man and a woman conspiring.

The cast of *Bohème* were there, although Eleanor could not see Regina Bruce, and so were the crew and the technicians and Maureen.

Ethel was unmistakable in jewellery that dazzled, and when she saw Eleanor, she called out, 'My dear, we thought you weren't coming. How perfectly lovely. Vincent, look who's here!'

Vincent, who was talking to Karl Henkel, jumped to his feet and embraced her.

'Schmetterling! I was told you weren't coming. *Ma sono così contento!* You remember Karl?' Beneath his breath he whispered, 'Will you dance with me, later?'

It was a family affair, with Dasha and Marina and the handsome son, Nicky, whom Eleanor met for the first time. Vincent paid lavish attention to his wife and children, putting his arm around first one and then the other, sitting beside them, and filling their glasses. 'They are not often together,' Eleanor thought. Vincent did not even glance in her direction; instead he was enchanted with his daughter, Marina (the hospital had cured her, she was healthy and smiling), kissing her in front

141

of everyone, putting his arm around her shoulders. Suddenly Eleanor longed for this same affection: a kiss, a hug, an arm around her shoulders; instead it was her role to stand in the sidelines and watch as Vincent gave his love to others. Despair hit suddenly with a force so violent that Eleanor felt sick and stumbled past the dinner tables towards the exit. In her head she was shouting, 'I am nothing to him . . . nothing . . . He has a wife and children . . . I am a *divertimento* . . . that's all.'

But Eleanor did not go home. She reached the far end of the nightclub and turned and saw Vincent joking with his son, and she stood quite still and realized, for the first time, that she did not have the strength to leave him. She could not live without his love; he was essential to her. This realization plunged her into the deepest gloom, and slowly and miserably she walked back to the dinner table. Alexei came and sat beside her. He was chainsmoking and held a glass of vodka in his hand. The bow tie around his neck was undone and his shirt open. A Bruce Springsteen record was playing loudly.

'What is this place for?' Alexei almost shouted.

'It's a nightclub.'

'What is function?'

'You can have dinner here. Or just come in for a drink, and talk.'

'Talking is impossible. Music is too loud.'

'You can dance. Most people to come here to flirt.'

'Flirt? What is flirt?'

'Oh God, Alexei, in Russia people must flirt!'

'Sexual?'

'Exactly.'

At another table a man had his arm round a girl and was kissing her neck.

'They have no home?' Alexei asked.

'Of course they have a home – but it's more romantic here – at least that's what some people think.'

Alexei threw back his head and once again showed his black teeth.

'A club for kissing . . . crowded, expensive, noisy . . . and not allowed inside without a tie . . . I cannot wear a tie . . . I feel I am choking! You know, the world has gone mad! Completely mad!'

Vincent danced with his wife and daughter and several other

women, but not with Eleanor. Suddenly she felt in desperate need of sleep and she slipped out of the nightclub into the cold December air. She began to cry and was too tired to check the tears. A man was standing beside her; she turned and saw Alexei.

'I'm sorry, Alexei,' she said, inhaling in short sharp breaths. 'I do this sometimes . . . I'm like a child . . . I can't stop. It's so silly.'

'You cry for Vincent,' Alexei said.

'I suppose so.'

'Why not cry for Dasha?'

'He will never leave Dasha . . .'

'He tortures her.'

'Vincent is cruel, I know.' She wiped her face roughly with the back of her hand; mascara was streaked across her cheek.

Alexei said, 'In West everyone cries for himself. Everyone suffers for himself. No tears for men and women in Soviet labour camps who sleep at night with no blankets – who die from cold or from hunger or from both. No tears for these people. In West no pity for anyone but self.'

'Have you ever been in love . . . when you were young?'

'I was never young.'

The next morning Vincent telephoned.

'Dasha has gone to Paris. I shall come to your studio tonight. We can talk,' he said.

They did not talk; they made love, slowly and tenderly, and without the usual frantic urgency, and Vincent let his hand drift over her limbs, as if he were a sculptor, feeling his own creation.

'I tried to leave you,' Eleanor said.

'I know.'

They lay in silence.

'No one should leave their lover in winter, isn't that what Mimi says? We must wait till spring. When we have the sun for company.'

'*Dolce svegliate,*' Vincent said, smiling.

'*Dolce svegliate.*'

'In a few weeks I am going to Barbados for a holiday in Ethel Wingate's private jet. Will you come?'

'Yes . . . yes . . .'

143

'I want a baby from you, d'you hear?'
'Yes.'

Eleanor took the pack of green contraceptive pills and threw
them into her wastepaper basket. She stood staring down at
the neat rows of tiny green capsules, shedding her old life like
a dead skin. She was a new woman, ready to bear Vincent's
child and to bind her life to his for ever.

The little boy (she was sure it would be a boy) became a real
person in Eleanor's imagination. She could see him standing
up shakily on his small, fat legs; and she could hear him
speaking his words of one syllable, and she could watch him
running, faster and faster into her outstretched arms.

She would move to Italy and live in the countryside (far
from Rome and Flavia), and Vincent would come and see her,
and their little boy; her affection for the child would be intense
and he would spend more and more time with them . . . and
less and less time with Dasha and Flavia and eventually –
'Stop,' she told herself, 'I am being ridiculous.'

'You seem happy,' Dominic said to Eleanor one morning.
'I am.'
'Is Vincent behaving better?'
'No.'
'Are you spending Christmas with him?'
'No.'
'But you are happy?'
'Ecstatic.'
'I shall never understand women.'

18 The Challenger jet was on the tarmac at Luton airport. Eleanor and Vincent stood at the foot of the stairs leading into the aircraft, waiting for the steward. Eleanor said to Vincent, 'Is Ethel meeting us here?'

'Ethel isn't coming! Ethel is a great admirer of Dasha's.'

Eleanor took Vincent by the arm. 'Darling, how wonderful. We're alone.'

At the top of the stairs, framed in the doorway of the aeroplane, a woman appeared.

'Hello, Vincent, we're here! Inside. Hello, love!'

It was Bella, and behind her stood Giuseppe Negroponti.

'Giuseppe needs a holiday almost as much as I do,' Vincent said.

'Of course he does. How very nice . . .' Eleanor's voice trailed off and inside she was laughing at her own optimism as she told herself, 'A holiday with Vincent alone! What a funny idea! He hates to be alone. The adoring flock must follow wherever he goes . . . But that's fine . . . everything is fine . . . We're going to have a child, and the boy (it will be a boy) will have his huge dark eyes and he will laugh from morning till night and my happiness will be complete.'

The colours of Barbados were primary colours, undiluted and unequivocal and perfectly suited to Eleanor's positive mood. 'I've made a decision . . . I'm committed . . . It's as if these undiluted blues and reds are saying to me, "Yes, that's right! Be clear, be strong, don't hesitate!" '

Vincent had rented a large house on the beach, and a black maid was waiting to greet them. She swayed slightly as she stood, her feet apart, balancing her huge body on her tiny feet. An enormous smile spanned her face and she waddled down the corridor and showed Vincent the rooms. The master bedroom opened on to a lawn of elephant grass, and the sea and the viridian green met manganese blue head on, as in a Gauguin painting, Eleanor thought.

Vincent closed the door.

'I want you now,' he said.

'I've stopped taking the pill . . . so we can have a baby.'

'You are sure?'

'Yes.'

'No second thoughts?'

'No.'

Later, he lay on his back awake, his long, delicate fingers resting listlessly on Eleanor's flat stomach. He said, 'The only way a woman ever gets a man is to have his child . . . children are an ambush.'

'I don't want to ambush you . . . I love you . . . I want to have your child.'

Bella wanted to walk by the sea. The sand was warm and silken under Eleanor's bare feet. The coastline curved into a bay, and large white villas stood back from the ocean, half hidden by huge palm trees swaying smoothly in the evening breeze. The air was filled with a rustling sound. Vincent walked ahead with Giuseppe. A pregnant woman came slowly towards them, her large stomach round and flagrant in her bathing suit. She stared at the two men, and then she waved and shouted out, 'Vincent! . . .' Eleanor watched with dismay as he embraced the intruder, who joined the men on their walk. Bella went into the sea for a swim and Eleanor sat down alone on the sand and let the warm, salty sea slip over her toes. She would be pregnant soon; her stomach would swell with the child; perhaps even now conception had taken place; perhaps even now the miracle of life had begun . . . She smiled to herself. It was all wonderful, wonderful, and perhaps within nine months a new tiny creature would be sleeping in her arms, and after so many years the agony would be over. No longer would she stand in dumb defeat before the laughter of small children. In her grown-up hand she would hold the small hand of her own child.

The pregnant woman was called Kate. She was Irish and her husband was an American oilman; this was their fourth child. She never took her eyes off Vincent. When he got up to make a drink she followed him with her strange, almost mad Irish eyes.

'Vincent was a friend of my father's,' Kate said. 'Dad was a poet. He's dead.'

'He was a fine man, your father,' Vincent said. 'We had some good times together.'

'I've known Vincent all my life, haven't I, Vincent? You've known me since I was a little girl. Now I'm a mother of three' (she touched her stomach) 'and three-quarters and I'm twenty-eight.'

'You're doing the thing that women do best,' Vincent said. 'Having babies . . .'

'You will let me come and see you, won't you?' she said to Vincent, with an eerie wildness in her eyes.

'Of course you can come and see us. What are you doing tonight? Join us for dinner.'

'Thank you, thank you.'

'What about Bob, will he come too?'

'He's in Houston. I'm alone.'

As they were dressing for dinner Vincent said, 'The girl's on cocaine. She'll get busted if she goes on like this. She's crazy, but I'm sorry for her, and Bob. Well, I do business with Bob. He wants a share of my film company. I've been thinking of selling him five per cent. Oh, Schmetterling, there's no such thing as a holiday!'

'Not for you,' Eleanor said sadly.

They dined in a small fish restaurant beneath an alcove of palms, which filled the air with the sharp rustle of their knife-edge leaves. Giuseppe and Vincent discussed *Bohème* once again, and Bella winked at Eleanor and whispered, 'Men – always talking shop!' Kate said very little, and now and then laughed hysterically. They stayed late, and it was after two when Vincent fell on to the large bed.

'I am tired through and through and I want to sleep for ten years. No one can understand how tired I am! Don't wake me, Schmetterling, don't wake me ever . . . ever . . .' he said.

He slept until one o'clock the next day. Bella and Giuseppe had gone into Bridgetown; Bella wanted to shop. Eleanor was swimming in the pool; Vincent came to the water's edge in his dressing gown and kissed her wet lips.

'Come back to bed,' he said.

She was climbing out of the water when the haunting pregnant shape of Kate moved across the lawn.

'Would you like to come to my house for lunch?' Kate asked.

'He will refuse, of course,' Eleanor thought. 'He will put it kindly . . . Can't she tell that we are in love?'

'That's a nice idea,' Vincent said.

'Did we have to?' Eleanor said quietly as they were dressing. 'She's all alone, poor girl.'

She was not all alone. Her house was filled with guests, mostly Irish with racing connections. It seemed absurd on an island of black inhabitants in the Caribbean to be talking about Trinity College Dublin, but it was that sort of lunch. Eleanor felt miserable. If only Vincent had not forced her to come, at least she could have stayed by the swimming pool alone. Pregnant Kate, cocaine-snorting Kate, witch-eyed Kate put herself next to Vincent and did not take her eyes off him. She kept resting her hand on his arm and whispering confidences in his ear. Vincent enjoyed the attention; he laughed, ate well, and said what a wonderful lunch.

It was late in the afternoon. The sun rolled blood red in the white sky. They walked back to the house on the beach. Bella took Giuseppe's arm and led the way, and in her heart Eleanor thanked Bella for her tact. Deep red flashes of light were stroking the swaying surface of the ocean.

'We have to talk,' Vincent said.

'What about?'

'This crazy idea of yours.'

'What crazy idea?'

'This idea that we should have a baby. There must be no baby, Eleanor.'

'But it's what you wanted.'

'It's what *you* wanted.'

Eleanor stood quite still. She was finding it hard to breathe; a pain was stabbing at her heart and for a moment she said to herself, 'I'm going to die . . . I feel that I'm going to die . . .' and immediately another voice from within countered, 'You're not going to die. You will survive.' She could not move. Vincent took her arm to lead her along the beach; she pulled away, rooted to the spot where she stood.

'Now come on, Eleanor' (no more 'Schmetterling', she thought). 'This is not *Bohème*, you know – we are not characters in an opera. This is real life.'

He would not look at her; instead his eyes followed the gulls that swooped and wheeled above the frothing waves of a breeze-blown sea.

Struggling to control the tremor in her voice, Eleanor said, 'But you kept talking about a baby. The first time we made love, the very first time, you said, "I want a baby from you!" Don't you remember? And you said it again . . . and again. "I want a baby from you, d'you hear?" – that's what you said.'

'Of course you want a child,' Vincent said, his voice softening. 'You're thirty-eight.'

'Thirty-seven. I'm still thirty-seven.'

'You're thirty-seven and you want a child. It's normal! But it can't be mine, Eleanor.'

Slowly Eleanor sank down on her knees, into the warm, soft sand, and took her head in her hands. She moaned, 'You said that you wanted me to feed the child myself . . . you did . . . you said you wanted a baby from me . . . you did, I swear it!'

Vincent crouched beside her and stroked her hair; hot tears were streaming from her face, dampening her loose hair.

'Of course I was tempted . . . very tempted. I wanted to see myself reproduced in you . . . but it was a fantasy. I'm a director of opera, Schmetterling, drama is my life!'

Eleanor was swaying from side to side, holding her head and weeping.

'I must think of Dasha . . . it would kill her,' Vincent continued.

'And what about me? What will happen to me?'

'Why don't you get married? Then you can have your children and we can still see each other. It would be so much easier if you were married. Is money the problem? I can give you some money. What about the ex-fiancé? What's he called – Richard?'

'Edward.'

'Edward . . . Look, go and marry Edward. As I say, I can give you some money. Have your children – you should have children, every woman should have children – and then when you're settled we can see each other again. I'm no good to you, Eleanor. You mustn't stay with me – I'll only make you unhappy. I'm trying to help you, Schmetterling! Now, dry your eyes and come with me. I've booked a court at five.'

'I don't want to play tennis.'

Vincent's voice changed, it became hard.

'Don't sulk, Eleanor. I have earned this holiday – my God, how I've earned it – and I'm not going to let you spoil it. The others are waiting for us on the tennis court. Come on!'

'You're a bully, Vincent. Leave me alone.'

Vincent turned away and walked down the beach. Eleanor was too stunned to move. Buildings were crashing down, walls collapsing in huge, dusty heaps, columns splintering into a thousand pieces. Time passed. Eventually, dragging each foot, she walked back to the house.

The smiling black maid handed her an envelope which contained a sketch map and directions to the tennis court. Keys to the jeep were also in the envelope. Eleanor went into the bedroom, pulled out her suitcase and packed her clothes. Suitcase in hand, she passed the black maid in the hall.

'Please would you tell Mr Buonarotti I had to leave for London. I shall park the jeep in the car park at the airport and leave the keys in the glove pocket.'

The woman began to laugh and her huge round shoulders heaved.

'An' they be thinkin' you are goin' to play tennis – and you flyin' away! What a good joke!'

'Goodbye. Thank you.'

'Come back an' stay longer. Come back for the Carnival . . .'

There was no flight to London until the following day, so Eleanor flew to New York. She kept asking herself, 'What happens now?'

The picture of her life with Vincent and their child lay shattered in her mind. A thousand canvases had been destroyed: scene after scene of herself playing with the child, reading stories to the child, chasing the child across a park, holding the child against herself – those and countless other pictures had been obliterated by a black brush.

'It is as I foresaw,' she told herself. 'Our love has burnt itself out. It blazed like a meteor, and now the sky is empty.'

As she said those words to herself, a physical pain burst inside her soul, so sharp that she caught her breath, and again the tears started to stream down her cheeks and she struggled for a moment to control the flow and failed, and she sat in her seat, her head leaning against the window of the aeroplane, shuddering in misery.

In the baggage hall at Kennedy she was waiting for her

suitcase, her head bowed to hide her swollen eyes, when a hand tapped her shoulder and a woman's voice said, 'Eleanor? Are you all right?' It was Regina Bruce.

'No . . . but I will be . . . I must go home!'

'To London?'

'Yes. I must go home to London.'

Cautiously Regina said, 'Can I help?'

'No one can help. My heart is broken.'

'I warned you.'

'Yes.'

'Give me your luggage. Go on! You need a rest. I'm the world's living expert on broken hearts. Come along. I'm taking you home.'

In the arrivals hall a newspaper photographer took pictures of Regina, and a bunch of flowers wrapped in cellophane appeared from nowhere. The chauffeur helped with the luggage while the Portuguese maid took the coats, and within minutes Eleanor found herself sitting in the back of a black Mercedes heading for Manhattan.

Eleanor spent a month with Regina Bruce, by which time her life had lurched on to a new and irreversible course.

19 The sense of loss was overwhelming. It was not anger nor hurt that dominated, but loss. For the rest of her life she would be without Vincent. They might meet again; they might share a joke, a memory, and there might be a flicker of former intimacy; but it was over. The meteor had run its course.

Vincent had been unkind; she repeated this to herself over and over, but no palliative surges of indignant anger came to her rescue. She tried and failed to be stout-hearted. Again and again she repeated to herself, 'You're better off without him,' and again and again, as she said these words, desolation swept over her soul. Every moment of every day she missed Vincent, and the thought of missing him for the rest of her life was almost unbearable. With all her might she hoped that she was pregnant. She was not. Her misery was intense.

'My heart is breaking. It's as if I have broken my leg, or my head, only this time it's my heart. Shall I go and have an X-ray? What will the doctor say? "Miss Wynn, this is most unusual. Here we have a heart that has a crack right down the centre. It is amazing that you are not dead." But I am! Don't be misled by my breathing. Inside I am dead.'

Eleanor was alone in the apartment; Regina had gone to Washington. Every morning Augusta, the Portuguese maid, laid out breakfast which Eleanor did not eat, while a secretary sat in a small office taking telephone calls. Any moment she would turn and say, 'It's for you,' and Vincent would be on the line, laughing, and he would take her to Avignon or to Aachen, and sit upon Charlemagne's throne.

'It's for you,' the secretary said.

'What?'

'For you – the telephone.'

Already she could hear Vincent's deep laugh; she pressed the receiver to her ear. She heard Dominic's voice:

'And what exactly do you think you're doing? Buggering off

like this, telling no one where you are! The Mintos are waiting, Miss Wynn, or have you forgotten? Family portrait complete with dogs in front of their hideous Victorian pile, yes? It was *your* idea . . . I've said you're ill, which you are, brain dead by the sound of it. It's all very well being in love, but *come home*, Eleanor – that's an order!'

'I can't. But I will, eventually . . .'

'Eventually . . . are you completely mad?'

'Goodbye, Dominic.' Eleanor put down the receiver.

It was the edge of spring. Eleanor walked in Central Park and saw the new green of young leaves. The world was awakening. A man with a scarf hung loosely round his neck crossed the road. It was Vincent! Eleanor ran towards the man shouting 'Vincent!' and people turned and stared. She ran faster and shouted louder, until the man turned round; it was not Vincent but a complete stranger, who looked irritated at being disturbed.

On a Sunday afternoon Eleanor saw Vincent's film of *Bohème* in a cinema on Third Avenue, and memories flooded back, and the beautiful words reminded her of the different episodes of their love. She saw the film through for a second time, and now and then she cried in her seat, and the woman next to her said, 'Opera always makes me cry.'

It was the dead of night. Eleanor was sitting on the edge of the sofa, still dressed. Tears were falling and had been falling for hours upon her hands that now felt sticky. So many conflicting emotions: love, rage, disappointment, fear, pulled and wrenched and turned within her, and left her exhausted. In a mirror she stared at her face; the eyes were so swollen from crying they had become tiny, dark currants wrapped in bloated eyelids. She had never looked so ugly, a fact that added to her distress and made her cry all the more. At some point she stumbled into the bathroom to wash her face and her hands, and to feel the cool water on her skin, and to instruct her own self to take command once again of her emotions, to hold the love and the rage in check, and not to fear the future, because in the end it would not last for ever; in the end, like everyone else in this world, she would die. The thought was comforting. She breathed in, and the breath came in broken, short gasps, as it does when a person has been crying for a long time. Slowly, her legs feeling so heavy and tired, she walked back into the dark sitting room and fell asleep on the sofa.

Moonlight, healing rays falling on her face, touching her skin with love. A figure standing against the window. Vision blurred and then sharpening. It was Regina.

'I see . . .' she said quietly, 'I see . . .'

Slowly, her body aching, and the heaviness of her eyelids throbbing (a reminder of endless hours of darkness and crying), Eleanor sat up.

'You poor sweet,' Regina said. 'I shouldn't have left you alone.'

'I'm fine.'

'You look it! My God, I should have known that you were not as strong as you looked – no one ever is. But you're alive . . . no slashed wrists? No, and no overdose – but you're as white as a sheet. And so thin! If you didn't look so God awful I'd be jealous . . . when did you last eat?'

Augusta, standing vigilantly by the open door in her dressing gown, said, 'I make toast every day. She no eat. I say, "Why you no have fried egg?" She say she no hungry. For supper time I say, "Why you no have soup and roast chicken?" and still she say, "No hungry!" '

'Go to bed, Augusta,' Regina said gently. 'It's very late.'

'You no want hot soup?'

'Well, that does sound rather delicious. Thank you, Augusta, hot soup for both of us.'

Regina looked intently at Eleanor and said, 'You've cried and cried and cried. And now your eyes are swollen and your head is beating. Oh, don't I know! Don't I know! Well, from now on things are looking up, kid. I am going to put you back on your feet, if it's the last thing I do. Dry your eyes, Eleanor – the period of mourning is over!'

Augusta brought the soup, beautifully set out on a tray with toast, and watched sternly as Eleanor hesitated and then took a slice.

'Is it so hard to be happy?' Eleanor said.

'You're asking me if it's hard to be happy – am I hearing right? It isn't just hard, it's impossible. You know why? Because happiness doesn't exist! It was invented by delirious poets in the nineteenth century who were dying of consumption. They fantasized and told the world that joy was elastic – it could stretch across decades! And then, poor bastards, they died! Joy is momentary – you know that – I know that – and in between we have to contend with a lot of humdrum living. Eleanor, believe me, happiness is a myth. Once you hoist this aboard, you'll feel much, much better – and you won't feel that you're missing out.'

'Life, liberty and the pursuit of happiness,' Eleanor said.

'Come on! Jefferson was talking about sex! He had a black mistress who bore him several children – that's what *he* meant by "pursuit of happiness", not some ludicrous generality. You've misinterpreted the Founding Father, I'm telling you!

'If happiness is not the goal, then what is?'

'Creativity! Experience! And indeed, when you are creating, and experiencing, you may well feel happy, but it will be a by-product, a transient mood, not a state of mind. Eat up. You are what you eat! I have gone down this path myself, Eleanor. I know about these things.'

'I miss him so much.'

'That will pass.'

'The other thing won't pass.'

'What other thing?'

'It will come back again. I can feel it. That longing to have a child that nearly drove me mad a year ago. I thought I was going mad, I did! I wanted a child so much that I couldn't think about anything else. Everywhere I went I only noticed the children; it became an obsession. And you were going to have a child with Vincent?'

'The first time we made love he said, "I want a baby from you".'

'He said that to me the first time I slept with him. But I didn't take him seriously! Men often say things like that. It's sort of sexy to talk about babies. It makes the woman seem more erotic, especially to men with giant egos. It's the "you're the lucky lady" routine – you're going to receive *my seed* – wow! And a little baby *me* will be born. Did he lay that number on you? I bet he did, if I know Vincent! Don't look so embarrassed. You're not the only one who has fallen for it. Vincent's a pro. He knows his lines by heart.'

'Please,' Eleanor said. 'Don't go on.'

155

'Eleanor,' Regina said, 'listen to me. If you want a child. Have a child. What's to stop you?'

'I love Vincent. I want his child!'

'Then go back to him and have his child. You're a bright girl, you can do it.'

'I can't go back . . . he was too cruel. And I was too abject. I can't go back.'

'All right then, let's take this step by step. Vincent is no longer a candidate for fatherhood. He's struck off the list. So you have a child with someone else. It's the child that matters, not the man. I know what I am talking about, Eleanor – do I *ever*! The father of my child talked me into an abortion. I can't believe I gave in, but I did, and I still have nightmares about the blood on the sheets. I'm only telling you this because I want you to learn from my mistake. Have that child, Eleanor!'

'How . . . how do I have a child with a man I do not love?'

'By sleeping with him. It's very simple. Don't tell me you have only slept with men you have been in love with? Eleanor, sometimes you talk as if you are out to lunch. What is this? Millions and millions of women all over the world – particularly Muslims and Hindus – marry men they hardly *know*, let alone *love* – but they still have children by them. And you and I have countless friends who have married men they like, but don't love.'

'Yes, but they *marry* the men.'

'So you're different. You don't. What's the problem? You earn enough to support the child on your own. That's what really matters. You can go it alone.'

'A child needs a father.'

'A child needs a mother. It's the women in this world who bring up the children – it always has been and it always will be. Generations of men have been wiped out by war, but their children have survived, and grown up and written great books and composed great sonatas. I'm telling you, Eleanor, a father is a side attraction. He can be loving and erudite but he's still a side attraction. My father was a delightful man, but as a child my world revolved around my mother. She was and always has been fundamental to my life. Is it the same for you? Tell me!'

'Yes.'

'There! We agree! In personal relationships the axis of the

world is mother–child, and not man–woman. But I don't want to digress. I haven't made my point yet, which is that a child does not need a father. Not really. I have a friend with really nice teenage kids and the father died years ago. Their mother has nurtured them in love and generosity, and as I say, they're great kids – they haven't missed out. On the other hand, I have another friend with a really screwed up daughter, and she sees her father all the time, and she's miserable!'

'Of course there are bad fathers,' Eleanor said, 'but there are also wonderful fathers, like mine. My father brought so much into life – he taught me so many things, he opened so many doors. Men are more interesting than women, on the whole, I think.'

'Yes, on the whole.'

'Well then, it must be good for our children to draw from their influence, and their paternal love!'

'Our children need *male* influence, and *male* love – forget about the paternal. And you will find your male, and so will I. But we must have our children now, before it's too late! The male seed is what we're after, delivered in person or in a tube. I've settled for the tube.'

'*What?*'

'Yes. I have been to a sperm bank and I've been inseminated with test tube P.897, belonging to a man who is white and a professor of biology, name provided on request.'

'Are you serious?'

'I most certainly am. That's how I've spent my long week-end. Visiting the sperm bank in Washington.'

'I don't believe it! You may be pregnant! Now – this very minute! Let's drink a toast to that thrilling possibility. Open some champagne, Regina, this is so exciting!'

'It's good to see you smile.'

They drank and talked until streaks of curious mauve were lighting the sky, and you could hear the garbage trucks rumbling through the streets.

'I'm telling you, Eleanor, we women suffer too much. I for one am tired of it all. I'm sick to death of feeling miserable. I've got to L.U. – Lighten Up. Put sorrow behind me. But to do that you have to understand the cause of female suffering. In my opinion it's always the same: we submit to men who wish to control us – we allow them to dominate our lives, and we watch them destroy us. Look at me! I was so mesmerized by Loder that I let him kill my child. I allowed it! But not any more! As far as women are concerned, there's a Brave New World out there! You don't believe me? There is, Eleanor, I'm telling you! Give me some more champagne and I'll explain.

'A revolution has taken place, don't you see? In America, in Western Europe – women are *free*. For the first time in human history they can earn their own living. Have you any idea how important this is . . . how it has changed their lives? Look back in time – you don't have to look far – take our great-grandmothers. They couldn't go out and get a job. There were no women barristers, or policemen, or teachers – all the professions were closed to women. So what could they do? Well, they could go into "service", and slave away for forty years for some creep of an employer; they could be a prostitute or work in the mines alongside their children, or they could be a nun or a nurse, or a governess, but very little else, except a wife. That was *the* job – to be a wife. And those who didn't make it were hangers-on like the spinster sister, the maiden aunt, both at the charitable mercy of the rest of the family. But let's get back to the wife. She was owned by her husband. Literally. In law she had no rights, Eleanor – just think of it! No rights over her property, or even her children. She was owned lock, stock and barrel by her husband. And there was no escape, because as long as women did not have the right to work they had no independence. They *had* to live off a man, as wife or mistress. But today everything has changed! Women can work, they can earn their own living, they're independent human beings who can decide what they do with their lives. They even have the power to decide when to have children. Contraception has given women control over our own reproductive system. You realize what this all means? For the first time in human history women are independent of men. All the age-old reasons for getting married should be reconsidered, and carefully reconsidered. A woman used to marry to have a man provide for her, and for their children. That reason is no longer valid. A woman used to marry so she could have a sexual life. That reason is no longer valid. A woman used to marry to have social status, to get away from home, even to travel. None of those reasons are valid. So where does this leave homo sapiens? Uneasy, Eleanor, I'm telling you, especially in your country! Last year, in England and Wales alone, twenty-three per cent of all births were illegitimate! That's nearly a quarter! It's true, I swear it . . . I read it in a magazine.'

'Yes, I know it's true . . . but what about the family – father, mother and children? I grew up in a wonderful family. We were very happy. Our family seemed to have a natural balance.'

'Great! But father, mother and children is not the only cast of characters in a family. It can be bigger, as in India or Italy, with Granny and Grandpa, and it can be smaller. Much smaller. Mother and child doesn't sound too bad, does it? In fact it has a beautiful ring: mother and child. That's going to be my family. Today we can choose, Eleanor, don't you understand? I'm not against the old idea, but it's not the only idea, that's all. Don't think I am being flippant, because I am not. Oh no! This decision may well be the end of my career. My doctor thinks I'm mad, not because of my age – I'm forty-three – but because I'm risking my voice. Well, I had a good run, nearly ten years at the top, and perhaps it's not a bad thing to stop at the height of one's powers. At least I'll never disappoint my public – not for me those angry boos and catcalls when I can no longer hold the high notes or master the coloratura. Anyway, I'm clear in my own mind that I'd rather have a baby than a career. Callas never made that decision. She had an abortion and I don't think she ever got over it. She longed for a child and you could see the anguish in her face. Of course, some people say it made her a greater singer, but that is a price I'm not prepared to pay. My God, it's light outside. Eleanor, it's bed and beauty sleep for us both, and I must rest my larynx or I shall never sing Lucia!'

Eleanor stayed with Regina for a month, living disembodied in luxury. The diva's apartment paid homage to modern creativity: everything was contemporary from the ashtrays to the bidets; everything was new, made yesterday or on order. Sometimes it was hard for Eleanor to identify objects: a small china horse was in fact a teapot; a minimalist sculpture was a reading light; a wooden tree trunk was a television. Paintings were by Wesselman and Frank Stella, Pierre Clemente and Helen Frankenthaler, and once again Eleanor tried to respond to their world, and once again she failed.

The only classical piece in the room was the piano, a Stein-way built in 1930. Every morning at eleven the *répétiteur*, Henri Fauré from the Julliard, came to rehearse his diva. He greeted Regina with reverence and ceremoniously sat himself in front of the keyboard and together they tackled *Lucia*. At one o'clock Larry Stein, Regina's agent, came for lunch and Augusta brought a grilled sole or an omelette aux fines herbes or an avocado salad, and Larry would report on the latest offers from the intendants of the opera houses for the spring and autumn seasons three years away. It seemed to Eleanor a dazzling choice: *Tosca* at Covent Garden in May, *Bohème* in Salzburg in June, *Traviata* in Rio in October, unless she would rather do *Rigoletto* in Frankfurt. Larry was good-looking and grave and discussed large sums of money with a deadpan face.

Lunch was over; Larry was gone; Regina threw out her arms and laughed.

'Poor Larry! I should have told him. It's going to come as such a shock. You see, Eleanor, I've just found that I'm pregnant!'

The two women danced a jig around the room, and Augusta, coming in with coffee on a tray, looked on in astonishment.

That night Eleanor vowed, 'It's my turn next.'

Eleanor fastened on the image of a newborn child. It filled her mind with love. She knew that it was essential, once and for all, to disentangle the birth of a baby from the need to have a husband. She wiped the man from the canvas and there remained only herself and her baby. One day she might meet someone and marry, and he could adopt her child and act as stepfather, but she could not count on that. She could only count on herself.

'You've made me whole,' she told Regina, 'and now I'm going home.'

'I shall miss you.'

'I can never thank you.'

'You are my friend – for life.'

'Yes.'

'One thing I want to ask you . . .'

'Anything.'

'Will you be godmother to my child? Oh my God, Augusta,

bring a handkerchief. We've got a weeping woman in our midst. I take it you accept?'

From the aeroplane Eleanor stared out at the sea of white clouds tinged with purple and pink from an invisible sun and the world seemed vast and full of hope.

'So,' she asked herself, 'whom shall I choose as the father of my child? I shall not choose, I shall leave it all to fate and wait for the next man to step into my life. I'm taking no contraception. Let nature take its course! He must be nice to look at, and intelligent, and cheerful. I should like the father of my child to be a smiling man. Also, he must not be married. That is one condition I set myself. He must be a single, free person, so that, perhaps, who knows – oh, here I go again, looking for the impossible – but still, why not? I shall have my child, and one day I might marry the father; or perhaps I shall marry a man who is not the father but who is kind and loving, and life might work out after all, in reverse order, first the child and then the husband! Yes . . . yes . . . I do want a husband. Regina, I'm sorry. Perhaps it's the centuries of conditioning, but I cannot throw off this hope that one day I might share my life with a man and a child – or a child and a man – both are necessary to me as a woman. For the time being I shall think only of my baby. Let it happen soon!'

For the first time, on the aeroplane, on a sheet of blank paper spread out on the plastic tray before her, Eleanor calculated the cost of bringing up a child on her own. There were so many things she did not know: the cost of a nursery school, of a baby-sitter, of a part-time nanny (she did not envisage a live-in nanny). How much was school? Should it be private? Could she afford it? Was state education really so inadequate? There was so much that she had to find out. She had no idea how much it cost to have a baby – and should it be on the National Health Service or should she go privately? There were many questions to ask and many answers to unearth, and for the six hours or so above the Atlantic her mind was filled with pragmatic details about life with a child (she even found herself thinking about where she would put the cot, and the playpen and the clothes).

'First things first,' Eleanor told herself as she stared down at the huge spread of London. 'I must find a man.'

161

20 It was spring at its most triumphant. All over London, streets were brightened by trees in full bloom; puffy clouds of white apple blossom lit up dark corners and cherry pink exploded in gardens and parks. The sky was the clearest blue, and everywhere Eleanor saw her favourite colour: the biting, newborn green of spring. The air was wonderfully pure, and as Eleanor walked in St James's Park she said to herself, 'Something will happen today, I can feel it!'

From St James's Park she had walked along the Charing Cross Road and browsed in the second-hand bookshops until she reached her destination, the British Museum. She stood on the steps and wondered what she should look at: Chinese painting, the Elgin Marbles, the illuminated medieval manuscripts, Etruscan vases, or the Rosetta Stone? No! She would go down to the Assyrian basement and lose herself in the world of King Ashurburnipal and his lion hunt. It was Edward who had first taken her to see this masterpiece. The bas-relief extends over a hundred feet, but the sculptor is unknown (another unsung hero of art). Whoever he was, it is clear that his sympathies were with the lions. These noble creatures were bred to be slaughtered by Assyrian soldiers with bows and arrows. The proud King with his jutting square beard rides in his chariot to watch the hunt; he shows no emotion, unlike the lions, who rise up in human agony as arrows pierce their bodies; some thrash in death throes; others turn on their persecutors for one last suicidal assault. Eleanor stood in front of the bas-relief, over two thousand years old, and imagined the roaring of the lions and the cheers of Ashurburnipal's army, and she started as a hand was laid on her shoulder.

'You saw this first with me,' Edward said.

'I was thinking about you just a moment ago.'

They decided to have a cup of coffee in the café opposite the Museum.

'How are you?' Eleanor asked.

'I go back to Peking next week.'

'You didn't need a wife after all.'

Edward sat back and smiled, and Eleanor thought how beautiful he looked when he smiled.

'I was waiting for you to say that . . . I knew you would say that.'

'Well, it's true, isn't it?'

'I would rather have married you than go to Peking.'

'You could have done both.'

'You look lovely.'

'Do I?'

'Are you happy? I want you to be happy – you know that, don't you?'

'You mean am I still with Vincent? Well, the answer is no. It was wonderful, for a while, but then I fell from grace, or he did. Something happened and it all fell apart. For a while I was absolutely miserable – '

'Poor you.'

'Please, Edward, spare me your sympathy.'

'I hate to think of you being hurt. I want to see you happy.'

'Edward, don't talk to me in platitudes, I can't stand it!'

'You are upset, I can tell.'

'I'm upset because you're not honest. You're never honest.'

Edward smiled indulgently and sipped his coffee, and he did not take his eyes off Eleanor. He reached out and took her hand and held it.

She said, 'Tell me about Peking. What sort of life do you lead?'

The question did not seem to register with Edward, he said, 'You look lovely. Whenever I see you I want to make love to you. Do you suppose it will always be like this? Perhaps we could come to an arrangement, lovers for the next fifty years, what do you think?'

'Why not?' Eleanor said; she was not smiling.

For a week Edward lived with Eleanor, and for the first time Eleanor bolted her studio door. There were to be no interruptions; no friendly visits from Dominic. The first time they made love, Eleanor prayed, 'Dear God, please let me conceive a child.'

'Ours is a loving friendship,' Edward said as he lay naked on Eleanor's bed, staring at the skylight above. He seemed a different man; there was no tension and no criticism even; he even seemed amused by Eleanor ('because he is going away' she thought), and found time to look at her painting.

'You're very talented,' he said.

She drove with him to the airport and waved him off to China.

'I'll send you postcards,' he called out.

'Yes, do.'

21 Eleanor was pregnant. She had taken a urine sample to a chemist in Victoria Street and the result was positive. A smile settled on her face and stayed there for days. There was no hurry to spread the news; for three months she told no one. Eventually the time came to make the journey to Oxfordshire to see her mother.

It was an evening of Brueghel colours, of yellow-ochre cornfields and red-ochre tractors. The round bales of hay cast long shadows over the raw sienna ground. But it was the light that caused Eleanor to stop her car and breathe the air filled with the sounds and smells of harvest; the sweetness of corn and the saltiness of straw, and the steady drone of bees. A light of extraordinary clarity lit the world that evening, a light so translucent that all colours were rendered absolutely pure. There was no mist, no indecision. Everything seemed to be of the essence: the viridian green of the beech trees and the green black of the hedges; the black and white starkness of the Friesian cows; the purple blue of the stream and the silver grey of the willows that drooped so sadly; the grey and green jagged teeth of a Cotswold stone wall; the blazing pink roses in a front garden; the flapping red pub sign above a thatched cottage. That evening nature seemed to proclaim a heightened existence.

'Or is it me?' Eleanor wondered. 'Is it because I am expecting a baby and suddenly everything looks so different? Or has the world always been this beautiful and I have not noticed?'

Anne Wynn stumbled in her garden, caught a branch of an apple tree and steadied herself, adjusted her wide-brimmed straw hat, took deep breaths of the harvest air and went on dead-heading her roses, until she caught sight of Eleanor and cried out with joy. At that moment a painting formed itself in Eleanor's mind: her mother, in the garden, looking up from the rich yellow rose bush, the face grown old but still beautiful, still joyful.

Eleanor told her mother that she was expecting a baby, and there were hugs and tears and Anne said, 'I am so pleased for you, my darling. What joy you will discover! What great joy! I am so pleased for you, my darling . . .'

Later she said, 'And who, may I ask, is the father?'

'I'm not saying.'

'Does he know?'

'No.'

'Will you tell him?'

'I don't know.'

After a moment of silence Anne said, 'It doesn't matter. Nothing matters except you and the baby. I am so happy for you, darling! We must prepare ourselves to welcome this little one into this world. I only hope – '

'What do you hope?' Eleanor asked, urgently.

'I hope when he is born . . . I still have my sight. The edges are blurred; even your pretty face is hazy now . . . Don't cry, my darling, don't cry. I've been so lucky in my life.'

Eleanor dreaded her meeting with Marcia, although she did not know why. Over the last year the two sisters had hardly seen each other; this had been mainly Eleanor's decision. She wanted to keep her love for Vincent private, and so she avoided Marcia. But on the few occasions they had met, Eleanor noticed a new anxiety in Marcia's manner; she was on edge, and was easily annoyed. The composure was no longer there.

Eleanor called on her sister in Cheyne Walk. The leaves were curling on the branches of birch trees, and for the first time she heard the rustle of autumn.

Marcia opened the door, and stood for a moment staring at Eleanor, before she said, 'Come in, come in, this is a surprise. We've just got back from Scotland. The house is in a terrible mess. People think Scotland is so beautiful, but I think it's so boring. Miles of barren land. I don't know . . . it just doesn't appeal to me. Let's go into Ralph's study. Do you want tea or a drink? It's almost six . . . well, five-thirty. That's near enough. I'm going to have a drink.'

'I'll have tea.'

Eleanor waited for Marcia to notice the gentle swell of her stomach, but it was covered by the loose dress, and anyway,

Marcia seemed preoccupied. Eleanor drank tea while Marcia sipped her wine.

Suddenly Marcia said, 'It's no good! I can't go on much longer. I shall do something rash. I know I will. We've been in bloody Scotland all summer . . . Ralph's had all his dreadful shooting friends to stay. I haven't seen Matthew for eight weeks. He's gone to South America. If he'd asked me I would have gone with him, but he didn't . . . he likes to travel alone. Oh God! I miss him so much! My whole being longs to be with him every hour of the day! He's coming back next week. Thank God! Thank God!'

'Ralph still doesn't know?'

'Of course not!' Marcia snapped. 'He trusts me. We're married till death do us part. Didn't you know?'

'Then everything is the same?'

'Nothing is the same! I cannot bear to be in the same room as Ralph. I cannot bear to look at him; or to hear his laugh, or his bad jokes. Even his manners – his perfect manners – I find infuriating. I don't know how I will stand it. Without Matthew I'm not alive. I just sit thinking about him. You wouldn't understand.'

'Why do you say that?'

'You're not the sort to fall in love. Anyway, you've got your painting. You don't *need* a man. I do. I'm not clever or good at anything. This man, he's my life! I suppose you think I'm silly and frivolous, but I'm not. I never meant to fall in love. I only wanted an affair, an amusing diversion . . . but it's taken over my life. It's become an obsession. I don't pay attention to the children any more . . . it's terrible. You know, Eleanor, you're very lucky to be a painter, to have a gift. Your whole life has a purpose, you know what you're doing. But for me, it's harder. I'm just an ordinary person who drifts along . . .'

'You're not very "ordinary", Marcia. Ordinary people aren't beautiful, and they're not rich, and you are both.'

'I knew you wouldn't understand. I don't know why I bother to talk to you . . . you are always against me, whatever I do, whatever I say! I know you don't like me! You've never liked me! Go away! Leave me alone! You've no idea what it's like to be in love. You're just an old maid and that's what you'll always be! Look at you! Nearly forty. No children. No husband. Nothing but your paintbox!'

'I came to tell you I'm expecting a baby.'

Marcia stared at her sister in astonishment.

'My God, so you are. I should have noticed before. Oh, Eleanor, that's wonderful! I'm so sorry for what I said . . . my dreadful temper. I haven't changed, have I? Do you remember my terrible rages as a child? I tried to kill you with a croquet mallet. Do you remember?'

'I remember.'

'I . . . I feel awful . . . I didn't mean what I said just then. You do know that, don't you? I just wanted to hurt you. Nothing I said was true. Please forgive me. I'm so happy for you. It's lovely news.'

Marcia came forward and put her arms around her sister and hugged her, but Eleanor stood stiff and still. She felt worn out from a lifetime of quarrelling.

Dominic was the last to know. He had spent his summer with Hugo wandering along the North African coast, sending the odd postcard from Marrakesh and Tangier. It was mid-September when he walked into Eleanor's studio to be told that she was five months pregnant. Dominic felt faint and had to sit down.

'Are you sure?' he asked.

'Of course I'm sure! Oh, Dominic, be happy for me! If you knew how I've longed for this baby.'

'Give me a minute. Let me catch my breath. Perhaps you could furnish me with a few essential details. The father is . . . ?'

'I'm not saying.'

'I beg your pardon?'

'I'm not naming the father.'

'Is he . . . happy with this arrangement?'

'Don't pry.'

'All right . . . all right! Don't get on your high horse. I was only asking. Well, well, so you've taken the plunge. Look at you! Smiling from ear to ear. I have got to give you one enormous bear hug. Well done, my star painter! Well done! It's what you've always wanted, I know. Get out the champagne and let me toast the embryo!'

They held their glasses high and Eleanor said, 'Dominic, here's to you, my dearest friend!'

'To me!' Dominic said, jumping to his feet. 'To my short and happy life!'

'Don't talk like that.'

'And why not? The odds are against me, I know that. I hate to say this, but my mother was right. She always told me that if I indulged in unnatural vice I would incur the wrath of God. That's what the righteous in this world call AIDS, did you know that? The wrath of God!'

Eleanor went deathly pale and put down her glass.

'Have you . . . have you got AIDS? Tell me. Tell me now!' she said.

'Relax, relax. I was tested last week and I got the all-clear. I must say, my doctor has a sense of humour. He left me a message on my answering machine. "Well done," he said.'

'Then why are you so worried?'

'Hugo is HIV positive.'

'My God!'

'Indeed. And I shall be by his side to watch him die.'

'Oh, Dominic, I'm so sorry. So very sorry.'

'Hugo doesn't really want to live. For the last ten years he's been bored to death. He keeps saying the world is too crowded and too noisy. He's wonderfully iconoclastic, which is why I like him so much, but it's also why, sooner or later, he'll die of AIDS. You see, Hugo would never restrict himself to the better class of lover. He likes the rough trade and that's very dangerous, but Hugo doesn't care. He is a hedonist. Pleasure is all.'

'How is he taking it?'

'Showing off. Laughing. Feigning stoicism. Only when he is alone with me does he sit with his head on my knee and cry.'

'Oh, Dominic, I'm so sorry.'

'So am I.'

'And you, what about you?'

'From now on it's a waiting game. I'm not a carrier for the time being, but the virus can lie dormant for several years, undetected, and suddenly it could show up in my blood, just like that! Even if I were to give up *all* my unholy practices, I could still be doomed for the sins of my past. The AIDS virus is a cunning little devil. I may escape, and on the other hand

169

I may not. Death may be round the corner, who knows? Death, are you there? Are you?'

Dominic ran towards the studio door and threw it open, and stared into a dark corridor and laughed. He sauntered back into the studio, whistling.

Eleanor took both his hands in hers and said, 'Dominic, I forbid you to die! I forbid it! Already my mother is touched with death. I can see it in her face. She says it's creeping blindness, but I think it's more . . . Her eyes are clouding over and so is her spirit, her soul. I can feel it! She's shrivelling up, like a plant, and each time I see her I feel such an agony, knowing that one day I shall lose her. But you, you are young, you've got to live!'

Dominic clicked his heels and saluted.

'As you wish, mademoiselle! I proclaim myself immortal! Let's finish the bottle, let's drink to life without end!'

The gynaecologist, Stephen Budd, was a handsome man in his early forties and sat behind a large desk on the sixth floor of No. 70 Devonshire Street. Impassively he took down the details. Thirty-eight. Unmarried. Does not smoke. Drinks moderately. Eleanor was in excellent health, he declared. For the next visit it would be nice if she came with the father.

'The father is abroad.'

'But he knows you're expecting a child?'

'No.'

'Are you going to tell him?'

'I don't think so.'

'Miss Wynn . . .'

'Eleanor.'

'Eleanor. Let me be clear. This pregnancy is accidental? You didn't plan the baby together?'

'That's correct. We didn't plan the baby together. I planned it on my own.'

Stephen Budd put down his pen and sat back in his chair.

'I see. You are fulfilling yourself as a woman,' he said.

'Yes.'

'It's not easy bringing up a child alone.'

'I won't be alone. I have wonderful friends . . . Oh, Mr Budd . . .'

'Stephen.'

'Stephen – don't be so severe with me! I'm so happy to have this baby. I feel such love for this child already! I've longed to have a baby year after year . . . I don't think any man can understand how deeply a woman longs for a baby. And now I'm pregnant and it's wonderful. What is wrong about wanting to love a child? Tell me!'

'I'm not here to judge you. I'm here to look after you. You know it's all the rage these days – single motherhood. Three days a week I'm on duty at the Westminster Hospital. I have a great many patients on the National Health, and seventy per cent of all women who come to see me in the early stages of pregnancy are not married. Half of those women get married by the time they have their babies. Half don't. The fathers bugger off. It's as simple as that. As your gynaecologist I urge you to let the father of your child know that you're having his child. You will need his emotional support. That's my advice, but from the look on your face I doubt if you will take it.'

'I must do what I think is right.'

'A child needs a father.'

'Then I shall find a father!'

Stephen Budd smiled and closed his notebook and said, 'Good luck. Come back in a month. And don't eat too much. There's no need to get fat just because you're pregnant.'

A few weeks later Eleanor received a letter from a Sister Edwards at the Westminster Hospital asking her to come in person and to register for a bed. Eleanor went immediately. In a small office filled with photographs of newborn babies and smiling mothers Eleanor filled out the application form leaving the name of the father blank. Alongside her own name she wrote 'Miss'. The nurse scanned the sheet carefully.

'I'm sorry,' Eleanor said, 'but I'm not married.'

'Oh, that's all right, love. Happens all the time. Especially among the West Indian girls.'

For Eleanor there was a wondrous, almost biblical feeling about the state of pregnancy. A seed in her womb had been fertilized, and from now on a miraculous process would be taking place: from one egg, invisible to the naked eye, a human being was taking shape, hour by hour, second by second. She was guarding the tiny creature with her body, nurturing it with her blood.

In the past, whenever Eleanor had imagined herself alone and pregnant, she had thought of all that could go wrong: the child would be deformed; he or she would be a heroin addict; the child would hate her. Now that she was pregnant she had no doubts. She would love her child, and the child would love its mother. This event was meant to be; it was *right*. The moment was solemn, almost holy. She said, 'I give thanks for the miracle of life; for the foetus in my womb and the child that is to be, I am profoundly grateful, I bow my head.'

For the first time in her life she was without anxiety. For so many years she had longed to give birth with a longing that had driven her to the brink of madness; now, at last, that longing was to be fulfilled and for the first time in her adult life Eleanor felt at peace.

She watched herself grow and the waiting in itself was wonderful. With intense joy she felt the strange stirrings inside her own being, those first movements of a new life. She sketched a self-portrait as she stood at her easel, her hand on her back, easing the ache, her large belly protruding; her eyes glowed with excitement.

Edward sent a postcard from Ulan Bator. He was travelling in Mongolia by train, sleeping in tents. He wrote, 'Love, as always'.

22 'What do you mean, there's no work?' Eleanor said as she sat on the edge of her bed staring at Dominic, who languished on the chaise-longue fanning himself with a newspaper.

'Everyone has a bad patch, Eleanor . . . things will get better . . .'

'But this has never happened before . . . you've always lined up more commissions than I can cope with!'

'Look, I'm just as astonished as you are . . . but what can I say? Five clients have rung to postpone their sittings. It's bizarre.'

'Charles Swallow?'

'He's gone to Australia to design a new tennis club.'

'The Minto family?'

'Now *there* you've only yourself to blame . . . you buggered off to America and that was that . . . you missed the deadline. And several others, by the way. It wasn't your cleverest move.'

'But this is terrible.'

'You've been earning very good money over the last few years . . . you must have plenty in the bank, for God's sake.'

'Where's it gone?'

'I don't know.'

'This is ridiculous. No . . . I do know. Of course I know. I paid my mother back . . . she lent me some money when I was really broke. And I paid off my car, and then, this was the big step, I paid off the mortgage. That was forty thousand in one go. And the rest I suppose I've just spent. I've got a little bit in the bank. But a baby is expensive, Dominic, you must find me work!'

'Calm down, calm down. Don't get excited. Let's take things step by step. What are the immediate costs?'

'The birth and a four-day stay in the hospital will cost £1,500 if I do it privately . . . which I would like to . . . Now I thought the drawing of Judge Barket would cover that.'

'I'm afraid not. He's dead. Choked on a chicken bone.'

'Oh my God!'

'Relax, relax! The Media Museum hasn't paid for the portrait of Sir Robin Day. That's £8,000 coming in.'

'I'd forgotten that . . . that's wonderful news. Eight thousand pounds . . . it's a lot of money . . . it will cover the hospital . . . Then there's the cot, and the clothes and help – I've got to have help. A part-time nanny. Or a daily. And then there's school. I was awake all last night worrying about school. The figures are horrific. They bear no relation to what most people earn. I'm talking about private school, of course, but state education is no good – at least that's what everyone says. In Italy it's excellent, and in France and Germany everyone goes to state schools, but not in England. I've worked it all out, Dominic. Look! Private school will cost about £80,000, and then there's university. It's about a £100,000 to educate a child privately from five to twenty-one. That's what I've got to earn, Dominic. Don't tell me there's no work, don't give me this sort of worry, not now, please . . .'

'Calm down, calm down. Everything will be all right.'

'But you said there was no work.'

'I will get you work. All right? All right?'

'Yes. Thank you.'

'I don't want you worrying about money. I can help you out . . . you know that. I can always lend you some money. Don't worry.'

'It's very kind of you, Dominic, but that's not the point. This child is my responsibility, and mine alone. I've never for one moment imagined that I would not be working. I've had such a good run.'

'And you'll have another good run. Leave it to me.'

'I can paint right up to the birth.'

'I think you should paint during the birth. We could call it "between contractions".'

'Don't be idiotic.'

At last Eleanor was smiling. Dominic put his arms around her shoulders and said, 'That's better.'

Suddenly Eleanor said, 'The Queen! What's the news on that front? That's the sort of commission I need, something that will hit the headlines.'

'There's a cloud on the horizon, alas.'

'You said I was on the short list.'

'Alas, no longer. They've given the wretched commission to Sir Archibald Stuart. What a choice! That man has not had a new idea since the First World War, when he startled the art world with his daring compositions – he would half-paint a man – '

'How do you half-paint a man?'

'You paint half the man, fool! The other half is not on the canvas. It's Somewhere Else. So your subject looks as if he's been cut in two by a pair of scissors. Oh, it was all the rage in 1910. Now Sir Archibald paints all the man, only badly. Our only hope is that he dies before he can complete the painting. He's very frail, so the odds are reasonable.'

'I'm out of luck, Dominic.'

'Not altogether. Dasha Buonarotti rang this morning to make an appointment. She wants to talk about a portrait – hers, or her daughter's, or perhaps another picture of Vincent?'

'I won't do it.'

'You need the money.'

'I won't do it.'

'That's your decision. I told her to come here at three o'clock.'

'But it is three o'clock.'

'That's why I'm here. You don't think I came to discuss your birth budget?'

There was no time to prepare. The doorbell rang, and moments later Dasha and Marina had walked into the studio.

Marina rushed forward to kiss Eleanor, and told her breathlessly, 'Have you heard my news? I have joined the Royal Ballet! They say I am going to be a star.'

'Do you eat?'

'I eat mountains of food. All the time!'

'She eats a little. Better than before,' Dasha said, 'much better. Hello, Eleanor.'

'Hello, Dasha.'

'For years I have wanted to have a portrait of Marina, and Vincent said I should come to you. You are the best, in his opinion.'

'I am very flattered, but I'm sure you could find an American artist. It's a little extravagant to cross the Atlantic for each sitting, don't you think?'

'We live in London.'

'I didn't know.'

'Vincent is directing *Fidelio* at Covent Garden.'

'I didn't know.'

'Alexei is here too – he's written a book.'

'Eleanor,' Marina said suddenly, scrutinizing Eleanor's stomach, 'are you expecting a baby?'

'Yes,' Eleanor said, smiling.

'But that's lovely. Isn't that lovely, Mummy?'

'Yes, it's lovely.'

'I have to fly. We have a class at four. Mummy will make the arrangements, won't you, Mummy? Can I be painted in a tutu with a white lily in my hand?'

'You can be painted any way you like,' Dominic said. 'Eleanor is infinitely versatile. I can take you to the West End if that is where you are going. I must fly too. Come, child, gather yourself.'

Eleanor and Dasha stood facing each other in the studio. Dasha had not changed. Her hair was scraped back; the eyes were black and infinitely melancholy; the face was beautiful.

'I ought to reassure you . . .' Eleanor began.

'There is no need.'

'This is not Vincent's child.'

'I didn't ask.'

Eleanor sat down on the edge of her bed and stared hard into Dasha's eyes. She saw mile upon mile of resignation.

'And why not? It is your right! You are his wife!' she said.

'I don't stand on ceremony.'

'Where do you stand? Tell me? Where?'

Dasha turned her head away, and Eleanor continued, 'You never smile. You never look happy. How can you live like this? If it's not me it's another girl. There is always someone, isn't there? And the mistress in Rome – what's her name – Carla?'

'Flavia.'

'Why am I doing this?' Eleanor said to herself. 'Why am I being so unkind? Vincent has hurt me and now I want to hurt his wife. I want my revenge.'

'I am sorry,' she said.

'You didn't tell me anything I didn't know already.'

'I don't know how you stand it.'

Dasha looked down at her hands, which pulled at the rope handle of a shopping bag; she was twisting the rope in her long, artistic fingers with their bloodless knuckles.

'I don't expect to be happy. I'm Russian. I believe that it's not a weakness to love, but a strength. I believe that love is stronger than hate or anger. I love Vincent. It doesn't matter how he behaves to me. I love him.'

'You hang your head, like an animal that has been cowed. That's what Vincent has done to you. He almost did it to me. Very nearly. You should fight back! Don't you see? Our inner being is sacred, we cannot allow it to be destroyed! If someone is trying to crush you, you must resist! If that person is your husband, or your lover, then leave. Leave! It's better to live alone.'

'You have your own philosophy. I have mine. I'm happy for you that you are having a child.'

'So am I. I am very happy.'

'Will you paint Marina?'

'Yes . . . yes, of course. Head and shoulders? Full length? What do you want?'

'You choose.'

'Full length. I shall need twelve sittings of an hour and a half. The cost is £15,000. There's a deposit. Dominic will sort it out.'

Eleanor held out her hand; Dasha took it. Solemn and unsmiling she left the studio.

The day was spoiled; Eleanor could not work. Memories of Vincent intruded into her thoughts, and she grew resentful. He could have telephoned himself and asked her to paint Marina; he did not have to send Dasha. And then suddenly she sat down and cried and beat the soft bed with her fist and cried, 'Damn you, Vincent, damn you! You still have the power to hurt me, even though I have not seen you for months! Damn you!'

She was startled by the sound of a man's cough. It was an unhealthy, smoker's cough. In the doorway stood a short, thick-set figure in an ill-fitting suit.

'Alexei!' Eleanor said, wiping her eyes.

'Is Dasha not here?'

'She was here but she's left. Come in, come in, Alexei. I am very glad to see you.'

'You're always crying.'

'I'm sorry. You think it is bourgeois to cry. If you had loved someone you would understand.'

'If I had loved someone I would be dead.'

'What do you mean, Alexei?'

'Vodka, please, and then I talk.'

Eleanor gave Alexei her best Russian vodka. Then she stretched out on the chaise-longue while he sat on a large red cushion on the floor and drank and inhaled deeply on his cigarette.

'You expecting baby?' he asked.

'Yes.'

'And husband?'

'No.'

He laughed and his shoulders heaved and he blew out a stream of white smoke.

Eleanor said, 'It's not Vincent's baby, Alexei. I've told Dasha that.'

Alexei shrugged his shoulders as if to say that he was not interested.

'What do you think of the human race? Do you think people are terrible?' she asked.

'I don't think people are terrible . . . I *know* people are terrible! And then you meet one man, or one woman, who is so remarkable . . . so different from the others, and you say, "There is good in man after all!" '

'When I look at the twentieth century, I am filled with shame,' Eleanor said. 'It's the century of mass murder, people have behaved like animals . . .'

Alexei banged the table.

'You insult the animals! Animals do not murder their own. They kill to eat. Only human beings kill for pleasure, or for political ideas, or for power . . . or whatever you want to call it. Only human beings do that. Do not compare us to animals! Animals are better . . . much better . . .'

His thick Russian accent gave even greater weight to his words. Eleanor touched his hand and felt the coarseness of his skin.

'Alexei, you are a good friend to me. Thank you,' she said.

'I don't know. I have no practice. For years I have no friend. No one. It was not possible.'

'Didn't you have family? Parents?'

'KGB use human relationships, especially family, for black-mail. You cannot fight because if you do, KGB threaten to harm your father, mother, sister, brother. They are very open: they said, "If you don't obey us then your father will lose job. Your mother must work to clean lavatories. They must leave Moscow, live in small town. Worse flat, less food. Brothers and sisters cannot go to good school. Cannot go to university." It goes on. I was arrested by KGB at eighteen. I am only child. But straight away I told them, "I hate my father and my mother." KGB brought my parents to detention centre. I would not look at them. I turned away. I told KGB for me they were dead people. In the end KGB felt so sorry for my mother and father and they said, "Isn't it terrible this younger generation with no respect for their parents!" '

'My God!' Eleanor said. 'Did your parents understand?'

'Not my father. He screamed at me in front of KGB. He cursed me. But my mother, she knew. And now I am trying to get her exit visa. She is old woman. No use to Soviet Union any more.'

'Alexei, how did all this start? What happened?'

'I was at school. In school we were taught lies. I began to argue. They said to shut up. I asked questions. They punished me for asking questions. In the end I was furious. I wrote poems and I read my poems aloud in Red Square. And I was arrested. But inside I was always furious. In detention centre, in labour camp, in mental hospital, I was furious.'

'And you never allowed yourself the luxury of making a friend?'

Alexei shook his head.

'Impossible. I could not fight with emotional ties. It would be used against me to make me weak. To bend my resolve. I made decision to be alone. Absolutely alone.'

'Do you believe in God?'

Alexei threw back his head and roared with laughter, and his crooked black teeth were prominent.

'What sort of God is allowing such injustice in our world? A God of evil, perhaps! I said to those priests in the labour camps, this God of yours, is he enjoying himself, watching the suffering of innocent people? Is he smiling? They were angry with me. They call me blasphemer. For a moment I nearly change my mind. You see, the priests were tortured so badly, and they did not lose their faith, and I was profoundly impressed. Is there a God? Is there? I don't know!'

'It must have been terrible to be so alone. And for so many years.'

'In between prisons – after I have finished one sentence and before next – I walked through Russian forests and drank vodka until I was unconscious. And then I would go back to Moscow and begin again with poems and go to Red Square and read my poems and wait. And they would come and beat me up and take me away. I would not respond to "re-education" so I was declared criminally insane and went into mental hospital.'

'My God, Alexei.'

'I survived. They did not think I would . . . nearly I was killed by forced feeding . . . but I survived. And I tell you this: in my whole life I have never betrayed another human being!'

For a while Eleanor sat in silence then she said, 'You're in England, now, Alexei. It's safe to make friends.'

It was a good evening. They laughed and Alexei drank vodka and Eleanor cooked spaghetti, and slowly the studio filled with smoke from Alexei's cigarettes until Eleanor threw open the windows and breathed the damp air of an October night.

Suddenly Alexei announced, 'I have written book. I have written about my years in prison. I have it here in briefcase. Dasha has made translation into English, and now she has found publisher. Gorton and Green. You know Gorton and Green? I would like you to read my book.'

'I'm very honoured, Alexei.'

'Important the people understand situation is still very bad in Soviet Union. Everyone is talking about Gorbachev, but what has he done? So far very little, and still they are force-feeding people in mental hospitals, and still political prisoners are freezing to death in Siberia. I want world to understand! Please read my book.'

He smiled and smoke seeped through his black teeth, and his round eyes were bright with courage. 'Those eyes,' Eleanor thought, 'are the windows into his soul.'

'One day,' she said, 'when you have time, I would like to paint you.'

'Then you must come to Afghanistan! That is where I am going!'

'You're not going to join the Mujahedin, Alexei?'

'I am too fat!' he said, laughing. 'No, no, I shall transmit radio messages in Russian from border with Pakistan. I shall talk to troops and tell them the truth . . . You see, Soviets have been telling soldiers they are an army of liberation . . . Of course this is not true. We must tell them, "You have been lied to! You are here to kill innocent people, you are being used to occupy foreign land! The local people hate you, look into their eyes." If soldiers realize they have been lied to it will undermine army . . . and eventually Soviet system. First we tackle soldiers in Afghanistan. It is possible some Soviet troops will be so disgusted they will desert. That is my aim – to get the soldiers to desert . . .'

'That will be a long, slow process, surely . . .'

'We must defeat Soviets in Afghanistan . . . that is beginning of collapse of Communist power! You will see, everything will follow – the countries of Eastern Europe will begin to strike, to protest, so will the Baltic states, there will be unrest all through the Soviet Union, but it all depends on Afghanistan.'

It was two o'clock before Alexei left. The next day Eleanor started his manuscript and she read continuously for seven hours. She found herself horrified, then amused (Alexei was very funny at times), then angry and then filled with admiration. The tone was understated but the effect was devastating. She had nightmares about the torture that Alexei had endured along with fellow inmates in the mental hospitals. He described a young man whose poetry was so beautiful and so powerful that the KGB destroyed his mind. Was he Dasha's brother, Eleanor wondered, or just another victim?

Eleanor wrote Alexei a long letter about his book and sent it to an address he gave her in Paris, and a few weeks later she telephoned, but she was told, '*Il n'est pas là. Il est parti pour l'Afghanistan.*'

23 'Bloody hell. You an' all!'
       'Rosie!'
       'Got myself knocked up, didn't I? Just like you!'
Rosie moved slowly into the room, her hand resting on her
huge stomach. She was even more pregnant than Eleanor. The
two women laughed and sat down and drank tea and Rosie
told her story; the boyfriend (no, not the punk, someone else)
had run a mile once he knew. But it was all right. She has
been given a flat by the council; unmarried mothers went to
the top of the housing list; and she got supplementary benefit
and housing benefit and it was all right. As for her Mum,
she was knitting bootees. (Somehow Eleanor had never asked
about Rosie's Mum and Dad; she thought they were dead, or
far away.) Mum was coming for the birth. She couldn't stop
her; Mum loved births and babies.

'It's good to see you. I've been worried about you. What a
fine pair of heavily pregnant women we are! When is your
baby due?' Eleanor said.

'Yesterday.'

Rosie had changed. Her hair was no longer bright red and
spiky; it was a dull brown colour, cropped short; and there
was less of the make-up, and the clothes were ordinary.

'I've turned over a new leaf,' Rosie said. 'My salad days are
over. I'm so tidy, my Mum can't believe it. My Dad's opened
a savings account for the baby, now he says I'm acting responsible. I wash my hands eight times a day. I don't have to. I
mean, they're not dirty eight times a day, but I've got this
obsession about keeping clean. And my nails. You remember
they were black. Look!' She held out neat hands and clean
fingernails.

'That's terrific.'

'My kid is going to grow up right. No drink. No drugs.
You're looking well. Who's the dad?'

'I'm not saying.'

'That's a laugh, innit? I mean, you and me, knocked up and no dad in sight!'

'We'll have wonderful children, Rosie, and they will have fine lives. We must see to that!'

'I want to ask you something. A favour.'

'Anything.'

'When I've had this kid – would you teach it French?'

'French?'

'Yeah. I like the sound of French. It's posh. I'd like my kid to speak French.'

'Of course I'll teach your child French. I'll teach both our children. They can learn together. In fact, Rosie, I have a better idea. Why don't you come here every day, bring your baby, and look after mine so I can do some painting. I need help and you need a job, isn't that right?'

'You serious?'

'Yes.'

'I've been to classes. I know about not getting water in the ears, and all of that. And winding and wiping and all the rest of it. And I've been reading books.'

'You'll do a great job, Rosie.'

'I'll do it proper. No mucking about.'

'They'll gurgle at each other, your baby and mine!'

Rosie smiled and held her huge stomach with her hand and said, 'He doesn't half kick.'

She gave birth to a little girl, Dolly, on 11 May, and Eleanor visited her in the Westminster Hospital in a ward full of screaming newborn babies and tired mothers. She brought flowers and a new baby blanket. Rosie's mother was sitting by the bedside, a fat, kindly woman. Both women stared at Eleanor's stomach.

'Can't be long now,' said Rosie's mother.

'Four weeks,' Eleanor said.

'Your kid and my kid – they're nearly twins,' Rosie said.

Eleanor spent a quiet Christmas in London with her mother. It was a bleak January day as Anne sat in the wicker chair by the studio window reading a book with a magnifying glass; but Eleanor noticed that she was not turning the pages. She was breathing more rapidly than usual and there was a ghostly whiteness in her face. She could no longer walk alone; even her white stick was not protection enough. Even so, she wanted to be by Eleanor's side.

'I may be old and nearly blind,' she would say, 'but I still have my wits about me, and we can always get Marcia to come over if there is an emergency. And in hospital I can make sure you have the papers and clean nighties.'

One afternoon Dominic came into the studio and found Eleanor clapping her hands. She held out a newspaper.

'Look, look! Regina Bruce has had her baby! Here's her picture in the *Herald Tribune* – that's my godson Harry!'

'What's wrong with you women? All you think about is procreation.'

Immediately Eleanor rang New York to congratulate Regina, and she could hear the joyfulness in her voice.

'He's right here beside me, Eleanor, the sweetest baby in the whole world, aren't you, my love! Do you like the name Harry? I do hope so. Oh, Eleanor, there's nothing like a baby. You must have one!'

'I am.'

'What?'

'I'm having a baby next month.'

'Just run that by me again. Next month you're having a baby. Is that what you said?'

'Yes. It's all your fault. You persuaded me. That's why I am asking you to be godmother. Will you?'

'I am going to cry – and crying is the worst thing for my voice. Tonight I have a recital – Schubert *Lieder*. I'm so excited I can't stand it. You are having a baby. Oh my God, Eleanor. This is the *best* news. You *bet* I'll be godmother. I feel totally responsible. Oh, just you wait! Babies are the best things on earth. They're better than men. They're better than work. They're better than your painting or my singing. What treats you have in store, my friend! Now listen. I have to tell you a few things. Stay away from *all* drugs. When they say epidural, you say "No". Any woman can handle childbirth. It's a natural process. I'll bet you are going to those pre-natal classes? Well, don't. All they do is put the fear of God into you with their videos of women writhing in agony and covered in blood. Don't look! But if you can arrange it, have the baby under-water. That's what I did, and I tell you it's painless. I didn't feel a thing. Oh, and something else. Don't be alone. Take your mother. That is what mothers are for. OK? Now you take care, see? You look after my godchild. And write. Long letters. That's what I like. I love you, Eleanor.'

'I love you too, Regina.'

Eleanor pressed her hand on her belly and thought of the coming joy. It could be at any moment; there was nothing to do but wait.

It was the time of the Chinese massacre in Tiananmen Square, and with horror Eleanor watched television and saw the soldiers gunning down students in Peking, and she thought of Edward; and then suddenly he was on the screen, part of a procession of British Embassy staff leaving the country. A few days later the telephone rang.

'I'm home.'

'Edward!'

At the mention of his name Anne looked up.

'You were on the television – driving to the airport in a jeep draped with a Union Jack. We saw the most terrible film of soldiers shooting unarmed students . . .'

'They killed thousands,' Edward said. 'And they took the bodies in the night and burnt them, and the parents were not even told. And now they are executing the so-called "ring-leaders". One bullet in the back of the head. Some of them are teenagers. Of course, there's no such thing as a defence lawyer. It's barbaric. I hate China.'

'Mr Chen was right,' Eleanor said.

'Yes, he was. I would like to see you.'

'Edward, I'm about to have a baby.'

There was a long silence. Then he said, 'I must come and see you.'

'I don't think – '

'I'm coming round now.'

Anne decided that Edward would be allowed half an hour and no longer. She greeted him at the studio door; he was clearly taken aback to find her in the room.

'Hello, Edward. I'm going into the next room, but I shall be back in half an hour. On no account are you to upset her, do you understand?' she said.

'Of course I won't upset her.'

Eleanor led her mother into the next room and came back

and lay down on her bed. Edward stared at her and her huge stomach and pulled at his fingers nervously and tightened his lips. Eleanor knew the signs; he was very angry.

'Well, are you going to tell me?' he demanded.

'Tell you what?'

'If the child is mine! God, you can be so irritating.'

'I'm not naming the father.'

Edward stared at Eleanor.

'It could be. The dates fit. Of course I don't know who else you were sleeping with. Vincent Buonarotti, no doubt. And perhaps others?'

'I've told you, Edward,' Eleanor said softly. 'I'm not naming the father.'

There was a long, tense silence. Then Edward said, 'I'm sure it is mine.'

Eleanor said nothing.

'I wondered why you were so nice to me . . . so agreeable . . . so unlike your usual self. I didn't realize that I was the chosen stud!'

Edward looked at Eleanor, waiting for some response. She said nothing. Eventually he said, 'I suppose you were taking no contraception?'

'That is correct.'

'That was unfair! Very unfair!'

'I let nature take its course. But let me assure you, Edward, this was no immaculate conception. A man was involved.'

'When I made love to you, of course I assumed that you were taking the pill. You didn't tell me you were not.'

'You didn't ask.'

'It's not up to me to ask you! You should have stated your intentions honestly!'

'Why? I wanted a child and I'm going to have a child. I accept the responsibility entirely. I am asking nothing of anyone. I am not asking the father to recognize the child; the child will have my name. I do not ask for money. I ask for nothing. No one is involved except me.'

'That is not true!' Edward exclaimed heatedly. 'As you said yourself, this is not an immaculate conception. A man is involved. That man is the father. He is involved whether he likes it or not. That is what is so unfair. You are forcing parenthood upon a man. It's a violation of one's rights.'

186

'You didn't have to fuck me. Or are you going to say that you were raped?'

'You don't have to be so crude.'

Again there was a long silence. Finally Edward asked, 'What do you want, Eleanor? Marriage, is that it? You want me to marry you?'

'Edward, I've told you, I want nothing.'

'You are unprincipled and stubborn,' Edward said.

'Aren't you glad we're not married?'

Edward hesitated, and looked at Eleanor with anger and hurt. Then he said, 'No, I'm not! And that's the pity of it all.'

On his way out Edward passed Anne Wynn, who was moving gingerly down the narrow passage, tapping her stick against the wall. He nodded but did not speak. Eleanor helped her mother into the studio.

'Was he – ' Anne began.

'He said it was unfair.'

'Unfair? How interesting. That *is* an unusual point of view.'

24 It was a Caesarean birth. Eleanor regained conscious-
ness on the trolley as she was being wheeled from the
operating theatre. Beside her, wrapped in a blanket,
lay her newborn son. He looked unbelievably solemn. Eleanor
was too weak to reach out and hold him; instead she stared
in wonder. A joy flooded her whole being: here was a person
to love and protect and cherish for the rest of her life.

It was wonderful for Eleanor to see the expression of infinite
tenderness on her mother's face as she leant over the hospital
crib and marvelled at the sleeping infant, whispering, 'Babe,
sweet babe, I wish you a long and happy life, dear child . . .
sweet child.'

Eleanor tried and failed to breast-feed her child. Within a
few days her boy was sucking greedily at a bottle, and Anne
swept aside any notion of guilt.

'You have no milk – there's nothing to be ashamed of. The
bottled stuff is just the same. Enjoy these moments – they are
precious,' she told her.

Precious indeed they were, and never to be forgotten. Eleanor would hold the tiny creature in her arms and stare trans-
fixed, watching every movement of his eyes or mouth. The
perfection of his newborn body was marvellous: the feet, the
hands, the tiny, tiny nails. His fingers moved like the tendrils
of an underwater plant, fluttering, trembling fingers feeling
air, and vibrating life. His smell was pure and fresh, and as
she held him nervously in the bath, and as he screamed his
strange, rat-like cry, she could feel the silken texture of his
virgin skin. She called him Orlando.

Rosie came every day with her daughter, Dolly, and every
day she wheeled Orlando and Dolly round St James's Park in
a double pram. She was clean and neat, and she cleared out
the storeroom, tossing Eleanor's old canvases into a corner,
fumigating the air, until she had her own nursery where the

babies could sleep, and where she could curl up on an old sofa and doze.

Dominic came every day to inspect the infant. One afternoon he arrived with a toy lamb made out of the softest fur, and he stroked the baby's cheek with the brown foot.

'What do they mean, a baby doesn't smile until it's six weeks old – before that it's wind! What nonsense! That was a smile. He likes me, the discerning fellow. Now give me another smile, my little friend . . . Look, he did it again! We understand each other, don't we, Orlando?' he said.

'Dominic, will be a godfather?'

For a moment Dominic was so astonished that he did not move, and when he did turn to face Eleanor his eyes were filled with tears.

'Me? Really?'

'If not you, who? No one's closer to me than you . . . except for my mother.'

'I'm *very* touched, Eleanor . . . and I accept with the greatest, greatest of pleasure! Did you hear that, Orlando? I'm to be your godfather. That's the nicest thing that's happened to me in a long, long time. I shall be circumspect in my behaviour. I shall set you a good example.' Dominic drew himself up, straightening his back. 'Even if he shows signs of being homosexual – which I doubt, but for the sake of argument let's imagine that he does – I shall discourage him. It's no longer safe. And it has never been a road to happiness. I shall encourage his heterosexual tendencies. On that front you needn't worry.'

'I don't.'

Dominic took Eleanor's hands in his and kissed her forehead.

'You do me great honour.'

'No . . . it is you who do me the honour by accepting. I expect a lot from you, Dominic. If I die you have to bring him up. You realize that?'

'I am the one most likely to die, my dear. Don't look so alarmed! There are no sinister developments. But, like every other homosexual, I walk in the valley of death.'

Eleanor fought to keep her sister at bay. Marcia came into the studio, surveyed the chaotic scene and said it would not do –

babies needed routine, and order, and absolute cleanliness. Rosie was indignant: the day was carefully programmed, and all bottles and teats were scrupulously sterilized. Nevertheless Marcia told her sister that she should employ a properly trained nanny, like everyone else.

'I don't want to live like that,' Eleanor said.

'You always have to be different, don't you?' Marcia said bitterly.

'What's wrong? You look miserable.'

'Oh, nothing,' Marcia said, and then, after hesitating for a few moments, she laughed nervously and almost in a whisper said, 'Everything, everything's wrong!'

'Can I help?'

'No, no you can't . . .' Marcia looked at the tiny child lying on blankets, gurgling at the skylight. 'Enjoy your little one . . . enjoy every moment. There's so little happiness in this world!'

Eleanor caught her sister's arm.

'You couldn't lend me some baby clothes?' she asked.

'Baby clothes?' Marcia said vaguely. 'I gave them all away to my daily.'

The scrawny limbs fleshed out; the wrinkled face of an old man (now she understood the fifteenth-century Christchild portraits of the early Renaissance) grew into a plump-cheeked, full-blown baby. His every mood, his every grimace fascinated Eleanor. The pleasure she derived from his laugh was immense. The laugh came from deep within the throat, a gurgle so gleeful and so spontaneous that Eleanor laughed and clapped her hands.

She found herself smiling all the time. The reason was before her, crawling across the floor, reaching out for the telephone cord, muttering strange sounds, concentrating intently, looking up now and then to make sure that she was there, then returning to the task at hand. Eleanor put the cot at the far end of the studio away from the paints and the smell of turpentine and white spirit. Each morning she was woken by a cry, and her day began with a sight of such sweetness that she would smile and jump out of bed. Orlando was standing up in his cot, peering through the bars as he held on tightly with his tiny hands. The day had begun; it was time to explore.

They had breakfast in bed. The small form snuggled against

her, propped against the pillows as she gave him his bottle with one hand and read the newspapers with the other. These were golden moments; and there were so many others. When he was teething he would wake in the night with a cry of pain, and Eleanor would rub ointment into his gums and then hold him to her, and sit in a rocking chair, which she had never used before, and rock him back to sleep. This was a sublime moment for Eleanor, the feel of the child against her own body, the small head resting against her chest, the hands dangling, the child totally relaxed and trusting, resting against his mother in confidence, whimpering slightly as he fell asleep to the sound of her voice speaking softly in his ear, and all of this in the dead of night. No further happiness seemed possible: she would live her life again just to experience this one moment. To an invisible being, a God, she gave thanks.

Eleanor was still out of fashion and the 'bad patch', as Dominic called it, continued. Even Dasha telephoned to 'postpone' the painting of Marina.

'Did she give a reason?' Eleanor asked, as she cradled Orlando in her arms.

Dominic shook his head.

'She just said, "I'm so sorry but we cannot go ahead for the moment." She'll come back.'

'I don't think so. Is there anything else on the horizon?'

'Nothing – for the moment. But the Robin Day money is in – and I'm working on Mrs Kluge, if she'll just stop flitting from house to house. Something will turn up.'

'I don't understand what's happening . . . You've always told me that I was so successful, so much in demand, and I believed you! And now look. The summer is here and there's no work. Nothing! You said things would get better, Dominic, you promised!'

'They will get better, they will. Now look, I can lend you some money. How much do you need?'

'I'm fine. I don't need your money. I'm fine. Just get me some work, Dominic!'

Alone in her studio, with Orlando asleep in his cot, Eleanor shivered with fear. How would she pay for his schooling, and for his skiing? (She had always imagined they would go skiing together.) If people did not like her portraits any more, then she would go back to teaching. Or perhaps she could become a commercial artist.

'I must earn money, I must look after Orlando,' she kept saying to herself.

As if her anxiety communicated itself to the child, he began to cry. That night Eleanor hardly slept; the child cried hour after hour. Eleanor walked up and down her studio floor cradling him in her arms. The anxieties about the future swirled in her head and she was gripped by fear.

'Don't cry, please don't cry,' she said to the baby, placing him back in his cot. She spoke louder: 'Orlando, please don't cry.' Suddenly she was shouting, 'Don't cry, please don't cry!'

For a moment the child stopped crying, terrified by the sudden harshness in his mother's voice, and then he began to scream. Eleanor picked up her baby and pressed him to her and whispered, 'Forgive me, I'm so sorry . . . I'm so sorry . . . There is nothing to be frightened of . . . We are together, I shall love you and protect you . . . and we shall manage. I love you, babe, sweet babe, precious babe . . . Sleep, sleep, my love, everything will be all right.'

That night Eleanor realized that her only enemy was fear. She was not afraid of life itself; but fear could eat into her soul and destroy her peace of mind and even her love for Orlando.

'If I worry about the future I shall ruin everything . . . everything . . . I have no right to spoil things . . . no right at all. My babe, my precious babe, I am so happy to have you in this world . . . nothing must destroy this happiness . . . I shall not give way to fear . . . I must not!'

There was no work, and therefore no reason to stay in London. Eleanor decided to spend the summer in the country at her mother's cottage in the Oxfordshire village of Dyne, while Rosie moved into the London studio with her baby.

That summer Eleanor began a new phase in her life as a painter and, looking back, it was as if the sudden absence of work was ordained. It released Eleanor from pressure; instead of forcing the pace, producing one picture after another, she stepped back, and waited, and life came to her in all its glory as she spent day after day in the unchanging rhythm of village life, in clear light, beneath a warm sun, watching the elongated shadows of evening slither over rooftops and rose gardens.

Eleanor was tired of faces, of mouths and noses in all their variations; she was tired of mixing white lead and yellow ochre and red oxide for unshaded skin, and then wrestling with white lead and raw umber to make up the ambiguous colour of shade. She was tired of long arms and narrow wrists and necks; the human form was altogether familiar. For months she felt frustration growing; then, all at once, she was set free. Here, in the tranquillity of Dyne, was a new backdrop, a new setting. She embarked on a cycle of paintings, watercolours and drawings which she called 'Summer at Dyne'.

Trees were the greatest challenge. Would she go for a wet look, *à la* Corot? Or the shimmering, almost dazzling high summer contrast of a Manet? Or the dense tones of a Claude? She went to London for the day and roamed the National Gallery and the Tate, and came back to Dyne, to the cedar tree on the village green and saw only Edward Lear. But she did not panic; her own style was evolving; she could feel it.

'And I have time,' she said to herself, laughing, 'I have all the time in the world!'

The land in all its richness spoke to her; browns and blues crept out of woods, and oranges and purples jumped out from haystacks, and sunlight danced on the surface of a stream and seemed to say, 'Paint me if you can!'

It was that same summer, among the grey stone houses and uneven walls, and the twisting footpaths at the backs of houses, that Eleanor discovered a new world of women and babies. Strangers (always women) would stop her in the street and look into the pram and ask about the baby – was it a boy or a girl, and how many months old? She would walk down the main street of the village, past a herdsman leading a slow-moving line of cows to milking, with her child strapped to her front in a canvas babyholder, and women would smile and cross the road and talk to the child. And they would talk about their own children and their grandchildren and their friends' children; and they would patiently wait for a wince or a smile or a splutter, and then they would throw back their heads and laugh and walk on contentedly. Neighbours delivered knitted coats and boots and offered to take Orlando to see the horses in the field. Eleanor realized that babies had magical powers to bring happiness; their innocence and affection spilled over into the lives of others, casting their aura of joy. Eleanor entered this fundamental world of mothers and infants, and she found it a revelation.

'Why didn't you tell me?' she asked her mother.

'Why didn't I tell you what?'

'Why didn't you tell me that it was so wonderful to have a baby? I should have married years ago and had five children, but I didn't know!'

'That's right, blame me! Mothers are always to blame. Nothing would have got you to marry at twenty. You looked down on marriage, and babies were a bore!'

'I never said that!'

'Yes you did, more or less. When people are young they don't want ties – it's natural.'

'We've got everything wrong . . .'

'And who is "we"?'

'We – the modern women of this world. We're obsessed with our work and our careers. And with our men. Children aren't fashionable. And yet the glory of a child outshines both man and job! What are fame and fortune next to my baby's smile?'

Anne said, 'Women need both. A job and a baby. If you had the baby and nothing else to do you would go mad, like your sister. Any minute now that child is going to do something rash. She's at breaking point, poor love. She shouts and screams the minute I try to talk to her. And of course it's all my fault. I pushed her into marriage – I ruined her life! Do you remember how I begged her to wait? I even offered to send her to an American university to get away, to grow up. But all of this is forgotten in her unhappiness. I'm very sorry for her.'

Eleanor was selfish in her joy. She blocked out Marcia and her troubles; all summer she indulged her love, for her mother and for her son. At night she would stand over the cot and watch her baby sleeping; the cheeks were so round, and the nose so small and snub, and the breathing was regular and sound, and the small arms were stretched above the large head, abandoned, and all the body was at rest; and the sight of it moved her so deeply and she said in a whisper, 'My darling child, I shall be at your sleeping and at your waking, and my love for you is infinite.'

It was early September and the blackberries were ripe. Dominic was pressing Eleanor to return to London, but she lingered on, unwilling to break out of her magic circle.

Marcia came quietly into the garden. Anne was raking leaves into a pile; Eleanor was lying on the grass with Orlando.

'Darling!' Anne said. 'What a lovely surprise!'

'It's a beautiful day,' Marcia said, as she offered her cheek to Eleanor to be kissed. From her pink and swollen eyelids Eleanor could tell that she had been crying.

They had tea on the lawn on a rug spread out beneath an apple tree while Orlando crawled excitedly after the cat, which jumped elegantly up the bark of the tree on to a branch, and licked its paws in serene superiority as the infant looked up in wonder at this magical creature.

Marcia said, 'I've come to tell you that I'm leaving Ralph. I'm moving to Wales. Matthew has a house there. I'll take the children, of course. They can go to school in Cardiff. I've arranged everything. The schools in Cardiff are very good, you know. Anyway, at their age school doesn't matter. I want to get out of London and start a new life with Matthew.'

'You're going to marry Matthew?' Eleanor asked.

'I don't know,' Marcia said, irritated. 'I've got to get away from Ralph. It's a trial separation, if you like. We'll see how things go . . .'

Marcia spoke in a voice brimming with tiredness.

'I feel like a bird in a cage, flapping my wings against the bars. I can't stand it! It's driving me mad. Perhaps I won't marry Matthew . . . I don't know . . . But I can't stay with Ralph . . .'

She stared at Eleanor and said, 'Why do you look at me like that? Who are you to judge me? Look, Mummy, look how she hates me . . .'

'Marcia, Marcia . . .' Anne said softly. 'Eleanor loves you . . . we all love you . . . no one is judging you . . . It's good to have a trial separation. You will have time to clear your thoughts. And then you can think it over quietly. You may feel differently. What you need is peace and quiet, my darling.'

Suddenly Marcia burst into tears and threw herself into her mother's arms and cried as a child would cry, in huge, convulsive sobs.

'That's right, my darling, you have a good cry . . . my little girl . . .'

'This is how we live,' Eleanor thought, 'our feelings are sovereign. Duty and convention have no power next to the rule of emotion. I do what I feel; Marcia does what she feels. Are we right? Is it right? Was the world a better place when feelings were contained within a tighter framework? Marcia's children will not live with their father; my son will not live with his father. Does this matter? Are we building a world more true, more stable, based on feelings? Are the feelings stable? Will we change our minds and cause chaos later? I don't know the answer to any of these questions . . . We do what we want to do. We are driven. Let us hope we do not cause too much harm along the way.'

The rest of the evening passed in a sombre mood. They had an early supper and immediately afterwards Eleanor went to bed in the spare room, leaving Marcia alone with her mother. They talked until the early hours. The next morning Marcia left early.

Anne said to Eleanor, 'You must go back to work, Eleanor . . . the holiday is over!'

And so, the idyllic summer ended. Even so Eleanor could not bring herself to hurry. She took her time and packed slowly. As the day drew near for Eleanor to leave, Anne played more than usual with Orlando; she would feed him and bath him and sing songs to him, and smile and laugh with him. On their last evening together she held the smiling baby high in the air and watched him laugh and she laughed back and said, 'You adorable little man . . . I would not have missed you for the world! I am so glad . . . so very glad to have lived long enough to see you . . .'

25 Anne Wynn slipped into blindness. The spectacles were ever stronger, the ugly, thick lenses magnifying objects several times, and magnifying her own dark pupils, which seemed to float like dismembered dark spheres in front of her face. She would take off her spectacles, wipe them with a silk handkerchief and blink. How much could she see? Less and less. She moved cautiously, one hand stretched out before her, fingers fluttering, acting as an antenna while in the other hand she clutched her white stick. She did not walk any more, she shuffled, inching her way forward in case there was a step; even so, she banged into doors and chairs, and there were dark bruises on her legs.

Eleanor watched her mother and suffered. She wanted to protect her from blindness and old age, but there was nothing she could do except to see that she was cared for. Even this was not easy; Anne would not be 'looked after', and there was no question of anyone living in; but eventually, and after burning her arm in the steam from a kettle, she agreed to abandon the kitchen, and a farmer's wife from the village came in to do the cooking. Anne never complained. Occasionally she would say, 'The world is closing in.'

Eleanor came back to London with eleven canvases and thirteen watercolours and waited anxiously as Dominic, swaying back and forth on his cane, looked at her work.

'Well?' she asked.

'Who would have thought?' he said.

'Yes . . . yes?'

'Who would have thought you had such a melancholy sense of colour . . . Look at those trees, the sky . . . that river of brown and mauve . . . Like Vuillard . . . just like Vuillard, only modern.'

'Do you like my new style? Do you? Tell me!'

'I like it very much,' Dominic said, throwing his cane high

into the air, 'and your timing is perfect. I'm holding a rather special exhibition in November of *plein air* painting. You can have a room. The front room.'

Eleanor threw her arms around Dominic and they laughed and opened a bottle of wine, and Eleanor said, 'Do you think they will sell? Really? Then I can go away . . . to Italy . . . that's where I want to live . . . and paint more. Dominic, do you see what I'm getting at? Do you? Up till now I've been a painter of portraits . . . mostly . . . with the odd exception . . . Now I want to be – a painter. That's all. Just a painter.'

'That's what you are! Eleanor Wynn the painter.'

'If these paintings sell . . . I can start a new life.'

'You are always starting a new life, it's so exhausting. And where, may I ask, does that leave me?'

'What do you mean?'

'Have you forgotten? Before the summer you begged me to find you work. That's exactly what I've done. Four commissions – that's what I've lined up. You're not going to let me down?'

'Of course I'm not going to let you down . . . I need the work. I'm so broke. The bank manager said to me the other day, "Miss Wynn, what are your prospects?" and I said, "Ever hopeful, Mr Lewis." Now I can be a little more concrete.'

'Bank managers are pests. Now let me have another look at these paintings. They really are very unusual . . .'

'Mama.'

'Yes, my darling?'

'Mama.'

'Yes, my love?'

'Mama.'

'My love, my little love.'

'Mama.'

'Rosie, come here, quick . . . he's talking.'

But Rosie was not herself. Eleanor watched her as she cared so lovingly for the babies, and bathed them and held them and covered them with kisses, and all the while there was an anxious look on her face. All summer long she had lived in Eleanor's studio, taking her daughter Dolly to the park, reading art books from Eleanor's library, enjoying motherhood, but now the first leaves of autumn were falling she was troubled.

'What's wrong?' Eleanor said.

'He wants to get married.'

'Who?'

'Rick. You remember Rick.'

Vaguely Eleanor remembered a punk with earrings.

'Is he Dolly's father?'

'Dunno. Maybe.'

'Do you want to marry him?'

'You must be joking! He's got no job. No money. He just wants a place to live. I told him to bugger off. But he keeps following me.'

'He'll go away . . . in the end.'

'He's got that mad look in his eye.'

Edward first met Orlando that autumn. He came into the studio, his face sunburnt from a trek in Nepal, and stared at the child.

'He has blue eyes, like me. And look at the chin . . . That's definitely my chin . . .' he said.

'Do you think so?'

'Of course it is!'

Edward kept his distance. He made no move to touch the child. He spoke wearily: 'All right, Eleanor. You win. I'll marry you whenever you like, but it should be soon. I am being posted to Hong Kong in November. It's cold. You'll need warm clothes.'

'I have no intention of going to Hong Kong in November.'

His face grimly set, oblivious to the baby, who was smiling at him and bursting out with unknown syllables, 'Bah . . . bah . . .' Edward said, 'I knew you'd say that. I knew you didn't want to live with me. You just wanted my child . . .'

'Not your child,' Eleanor interrupted. 'My child.'

'Look, I'm not here to argue with you. As I said when I arrived, you win. I'll marry you. You live in England, I'll live in Hong Kong, if that's what you want.'

'It's not what I want.'

'There's no point in being vindictive.'

'Edward, I don't want to marry you under any circumstances. I'm perfectly happy as I am. In fact, I can tell you in all honesty, I have never been happier in all my life. Oh, Edward, don't look so angry – try to understand. We had our

199

chance, you and I; our moment is past. We never made each other happy. I was not right for you and you were not right for me. Each of us resented the other. What about your favourite saying of Mencius – "Happiness is the quality of your thoughts"? When we were together my thoughts were bitter and begrudging, and so were yours.'

'I loved you.'

'We loved each other in our fashion, but we were not happy. We never laughed – do you realize? We never laughed! We were solemn and serious whereas love needs laughter, just as a flower needs rain. Anyway, all that's in the past now. I've embarked on another road. I don't know where it will end, but I would like you to be my friend.'

Eleanor took Edward's hand, but it was cold and limp. She let go. He stared at her, his face devoid of expression, and said, 'My son deserves to carry my name.'

'What is wrong with my name? I am his mother. I gave birth to this child and brought him into the world. It's only custom and prejudice that have led us to name children after their fathers. Certainly there's no logic in it.'

'And when he asks, "Who is my father?" '

'I shall tell him.'

'You will allow him to meet his father?'

'Of course. Whenever he wants to. And I hope they have a long and loving relationship.'

Edward stared down at the baby, who lay on the floor chewing a plastic brick, and then he walked slowly towards the door, where he turned and, in a voice filled with defeat and resignation, said, 'I hope you find what you are looking for.'

'I have found it.'

In the stillness of the studio Eleanor stroked her son's head and told him, 'Don't worry, my darling boy, you and your father will be friends. I shall see to it.'

'Summer at Dyne' – that was the title under which the paintings would be exhibited in Dominic's gallery. Carefully and lovingly Eleanor applied the varnish. In a few days they would be collected for framing and in a few weeks they would be on view, and then her life might take another direction. If the paintings sold well she would spend some time in Italy. Italy! The word filled her mind with beauty.

'And you can eat *gelato*, Italian ice cream, my sweet,' she said to Orlando as she pushed him along the pavement towards her studio. They had been walking in St James's Park; Rosie and Dolly were behind. The front door was open. Eleanor frowned; she knew that she had closed it. She carried Orlando up the flight of stairs to find the door into the studio also open. Suddenly she was frightened. She stood quite still and listened. There was no sound. With her foot she kicked open the door, able to look into the studio without going in; she held Orlando in her arms tightly. At first she saw nothing strange, everything seemed the usual chaos; and then she saw the Dyne paintings. Each one had been slashed with a knife and the canvas curled back in strange shapes.

Eleanor walked slowly into the studio, her eye moving from one picture to another. Out of the eleven canvases from her summer in Dyne not one had survived. She sank on to the edge of the bed. Orlando was pulling at her hair; she did not notice. She remembered the watercolours and jumped to her feet. The folder had not been touched; each sheet of paper carefully protected with tissue was intact.

'Thank God,' she whispered. 'Thank God.'

'Bloody hell!' Rosie stood in the doorway, holding Dolly. 'It's Rick. He's done this. I knew he'd do something. He had that mad look in his eye . . .'

Rosie went into her own room and found all her clothes and all Dolly's clothes cut to pieces. The women sat in silence. Eventually Rosie said, 'I don't know what to say . . . I don't give a stuff about the clothes. You can always buy new clothes . . . but this is your art. He's murdered your art . . .'

'No, he hasn't murdered my art,' Eleanor said. 'He's destroyed some of my work. But I'll paint it all again. Another time. Oh, Rosie, it's not your fault, but we've got to be careful. He may come back. I'm going to buy new locks. From now on we must be careful. I'm frightened for the children.'

'I'll kill him.'

Later that day Eleanor sat in the stillness of her studio staring at the violent gashes in her gentle summer scenes, mourning their destruction. She did not notice a man in the doorway, and it was only as he walked towards her that she recognized the step.

'Vincent!'

He was laughing and his arms were open. Eleanor ran towards him and for a moment he held her.

'What is it? What's happened?' Vincent said, stroking her troubled face with his hand. And then he noticed the damaged paintings. Eleanor explained what had happened. Vincent crouched beside one of the torn canvases and held the jagged pieces together.

'But this is something new . . . how interesting . . . nature dominates . . . not people. I always thought of you as a painter of people . . . Now let me see. This is very good. A child, yes, a child running, across a lawn . . .'

'It's me,' Eleanor said. 'I used to run across the lawn chasing my shadow. I thought if I ran fast enough I would fly . . . I honestly believed that!'

Vincent withdrew his hand, and the ripped canvas curled back to its mutilated shape.

'England is a violent place,' he said as he stood up. 'You must begin again, while the idea is still in your mind. And the pictures will be even better. Don't be discouraged. Begin again!'

'They were going on show next week.'

'Never mind about the show. Start again! What matters is your development as an artist. *Capisci?*'

'I have other work to do . . . portraits . . . that's how I earn my living, Vincent. I just don't have the heart to begin again . . .'

'This does not sound like you. There is always time. Where did you paint these pictures? At your mother's house? Then go at weekends . . . and begin again! Come here, come here, let me look at you, my Schmetterling. *La bella Mama* . . . motherhood suits you . . . yes . . . how pretty you look . . . Now, where is the little one?'

Moments later Vincent held Orlando in his arms and smothered him with kisses, exclaiming, 'I love babies . . . their smell is so delicious . . . Aren't you handsome, my sweet prince! Why aren't you mine? I wasn't good enough for your mother. She chose another man!'

'Vincent, how *can* you say that?'

'Well, of course we should have had a child.'

'Now don't start that. I longed to have a child. You know that.'

'You should not have asked me. You should have gone ahead.'

'Perhaps. But I was honest.'

'And you were very dramatic. I can remember every detail. You sank on your knees in the sand, white as a sheet, in a state of shock. It was a tremendous performance. You know I used that in *Don Giovanni* in Salzburg when Donna Elvira – '

'Don't,' Eleanor said quietly, 'please don't.'

'Truly, it's a scene I shall never forget. Oh, that desperate face of yours! Divine! In those days you did not have the courage to act alone . . . that courage came later . . . with someone else . . . But the joke is, Dasha is convinced that this delightful infant is my child. I tell her with my hand on my heart that I am not the father and she does not believe me . . . Nothing I say will make her change her mind . . . What can I do? *Che posso fare?*'

'How is Dasha?'

'The same.'

'She came to see me. She asked me to paint Marina and then she backed out. She didn't say why.'

'I told you, she thinks your little *tesoro* is my child!'

'But then you shouldn't have sent her to see me. That was very cruel.'

'I have no time for jealousies! Anyway, she was happy to see you. It didn't bother her at all. Dasha is not like other women – she is superior. And so am I! Have you heard about my new project? Let me tell you, my Schmetterling – '

As he said the word 'Schmetterling', Eleanor caught her breath, and memories flooded back.

'Bertolucci was the first European to make a feature film in China – *va bene*, he did it well – but I am the first to film in Russia. I am making *Boris Godunov* in Leningrad. I shall astonish the world! I shall do it all in modern dress and I can use the Red Army as extras. Imagine, imagine the impact! And dearest Ethel is paying for my gigantic fantasy, as usual. She's in London now. She asked me to tell you that she would love to see you. Ring her up! She's at Claridge's.'

'I'm very pleased to see you,' Eleanor said. 'You're always at the heart of things . . . involved, excited.'

'*Sono eccitato, è vero* . . . We are alone . . . just the two of

203

us . . . Let's make love. You look so pretty, like a flower in full bloom. Come, let me kiss you.'

Eleanor pushed Vincent away.

'You said yourself, when a thing is over it's over!'

'But it's always amusing to lapse from one's resolutions . . . to make the odd exception.'

Eleanor moved over to the window and saw, waiting below, a large black Mercedes.

'Vincent! You have a car waiting below!'

'Of course. It's impossible to get a taxi these days.'

'You were going to make love with a car waiting?'

'You know it doesn't take long, not with me! How many times did you tell me I was like an express train, too quick, *ma che posso fare*? I have so many faults! I just like to feel the naked flesh of a woman. It's so delicious!'

'Vincent,' Eleanor said.

'Yes, my Schmetterling.'

'There's a woman in the back of the car.'

'Yes. A very pretty, very young, very good soprano. Hungarian.'

'You are a rascal. Now get out of my studio and let me work,' Eleanor said, smiling.

'Why don't you come to New York . . . I'll give you a job. You can design my new production of *Tosca*.'

'I don't want to go to New York. I want to go to Italy.'

'I have a house near Lucca. It's yours! Use it whenever you wish! Ethel was there last week. Call her, Schmetterling, she's very fond of you. Look at you, so pretty and so maternal! We should have a baby. Any time you want another let me know!'

'I should like to have another child.'

Vincent began to take off his coat. His eyes were laughing as he said, 'I am at your service!'

'Vincent, your soprano is waiting.'

'I'll be back after Christmas.'

'I shall always be glad to see you.'

He took her face in his hands and kissed her lips lightly, and said, 'I kiss you and I love you.'

Suddenly Vincent went over the damaged paintings and picked up the canvas of the child chasing its shadow, and he fumbled in his pocket, and scribbled, and handed Eleanor a cheque for £5,000.

'I wish to buy this painting. I shall have it restored. Today they can mend anything. You have no objection?'

'Vincent, I can't take this.'

'It's not for you, it's for your work. You are in a new phase of your painter's life . . . You must continue. Not too many portraits . . . Go forward, always go forward. Promise me!'

'I promise you. And I thank you.'

'*Addio, senza rancor.*'

'*Senza rancor.*'

Orlando was standing, shakily, against the bed, pulling at the blanket. Vincent looked at the small, unstable creature and smiled, and said to Eleanor, '*Bravissima,*' and then he left.

Eleanor stood by her studio window and watched Vincent as he climbed into his car. She thought she saw him lean over and kiss the woman in the back seat. Her heart was pounding. She could not take her eyes off the large black limousine, and she watched it glide slowly down the street and turn a corner and disappear. She breathed deeply and thought to herself, 'I shall always love him.'

Eleanor did ring Ethel Wingate, and the following afternoon she found herself sitting on one of the ornate sofas of Claridge's tearoom, while a Hungarian orchestra serenaded the assembly of elderly women sipping Lapsang Souchong, while Ethel talked on her portable telephone to the press officer of the Metropolitan Opera House. Meanwhile Eleanor, with nothing better to do, doodled on a notepad.

Eventually the call came to an end and Ethel said, 'I do apologize, my dear, but that call was important. Now, let me look at you. I hear you have a baby. I congratulate you!'

'I thought you might disapprove, since I'm not married.'

'On the contrary, I applaud your courage. You see, I am President of the American Women's Anti-Abortion League. I am delighted you went ahead and had the baby. And if you should ever need any financial assistance, you come to me, is that understood?'

'That's very generous of you, but I'm fine.'

'Are you as happy as you look, my dear?'

'Yes.'

'I'm so glad. The Lord be praised. Now, let's talk a little business. I want you to paint a mural at the Met, an allegory of opera, twenty feet long, in the foyer on the first floor. I should like the legends to stand side by side, Tosca and Siegfried and Carmen. You can bring your baby and settle in at the Pierre. If you don't have a nanny I'll get one. You are shaking your head. Does this mean that you do not accept?'

'Thank you for the offer . . . thank you very much, but I must not be diverted from my path . . . not for a moment. My work has changed – I should like you to see it. I paint the fields and the trees and the sky, and I have this strong feeling that the trees have souls and I want to paint their souls. It's a Chinese idea. Perhaps I took it from a man I once knew, I don't know. I keep feeling that everything has a soul, the river and the sky. They are not objects to me, but spirits. Forces. I get so involved when I am working . . . it's hard to describe . . . but I know that I must not stop. Not now!'

'This sounds very interesting. I would like to see your work.'

'I have nothing to show you . . . but I will, the next time you come to London. But come and meet my little boy. Come to my studio!'

'Another time, my dear. I have to catch Concord this evening. But I'm so pleased that we got together, even if it was rather short. Please think about my proposal. I can wait until you are ready. Now what's this drawing?'

'It's nothing . . . just a doodle I was doing while you were on the telephone.'

'But my dear, this is Vincent, portrayed as a devil.'

'It's not really Vincent – '

'It most definitely is!'

'It's just a doodle – I wasn't even thinking.'

Eleanor took back her drawing and tore it up, but Ethel continued her train of thought: 'He *is* a devil. You are right! The way he treats that poor Dasha . . . this drawing of yours could be a sign from God, Eleanor!'

'It's only a doodle,' Eleanor said desperately.

'I don't think so. Now if you will excuse me, I must go. The Lord bless you and your little boy.'

'Vincent is a friend of mine,' Eleanor said. 'He's generous and brilliant and – '

'You don't have to make excuses,' Ethel said.

For a while Eleanor lived in fear that Rick would strike again.

She installed a steel-plated front door to her studio and changed all the locks, but still she was not reassured, and at night she would lie awake and imagine Rick on the rampage with a knive in his hand ready to mutilate Orlando. The night-mares became so bad that she began to think of moving. And then one afternoon Rosie said to her, 'He's dead.'

'Who?'

'Rick. Drove his bike into a wall. His mum's ever so upset.'

Dominic held an exhibition of Eleanor's watercolours of Dyne, and they sold out, and at long last new commissions trickled on to Dominic's red leather order book, family portraits against a country background (in order to capitalize on Eleanor's newly discovered talent as a landscape artist). Old commissions which had been postponed were rescheduled by an exultant Dominic who said, 'I told you so . . . the bad patch would not last. You're too good, Eleanor.'

Eleanor kept thinking of Vincent's warning: 'Not too many portraits . . . go forward, always go forward . . . promise me!' That winter almost every weekend she went to stay with her mother, where she spent part of each day outside, in the thin afternoon light, wrapped in sweaters, waiting for the rain to drive her inside, painting by the edge of a ploughed field: black furrows rock-hard and glistening with frost. The mood was bleak and compelling. Dominic liked these stark compositions and talked of an exhibition in spring. The spring! To Eleanor that meant only one thing: another child.

It would come to pass, just as Orlando had come into this world and was now the light and joy of her life. The little boy needed a brother or a sister, it was obvious! In the daytime he played with Rosie and Dolly, but at nighttime he went to bed alone, and Eleanor imagined the years ahead, a solitary child plotting his mischief alone. He would miss the whisperings in the dark and the pillow fights and the games of poker beneath the sheets. A little brother or sister would make all the differ-ence! But an inner voice protested, 'Have you thought of the cost? It's hard enough to bring up one child on your own . . . how can you manage two? You've just come out of a bad patch . . . no work . . . now things are better, but for how long? You have no security . . .'

'I have love,' Eleanor thought to herself, 'and somehow I

will manage. I can always go to New York and work for Ethel Wingate. She will give me work, I'm sure. I will manage, somehow.'

On Armistice Day, 11 November, Dominic burst into Eleanor's studio with momentous news: 'We've done it! I knew we would. The silly old fart – you remember, the ageing fossil they chose to paint the Queen – well, he's dead. After lots of headscratching the Royal advisors – whoever they are – have come up with the most enlightened decision: that unorthodox yet brilliant artist, Miss Eleanor Wynn! We've done it, Eleanor! This will make you world famous – commissions will come pouring in. I shall have to get an assistant.'

'That settles it,' Eleanor thought. 'The money's there . . . I can go ahead and have another baby.'

26 Stephen Budd, the gynaecologist, leant back in his chair and said, 'I'm sorry, Eleanor, but I don't follow you. What exactly do you want to know?'

'I want to know if I can be impregnated with sperm from a sperm bank.'

'Just like that?'

'What do you mean, "Just like that?" '

'Well, you are still unmarried?'

'That has nothing to do with it. I want to know if women in Britain have the same opportunity as women in the United States, for example, who can go to a sperm bank, chose sperm according to the man's colour and IQ, be impregnated and have a child. Is this service available to me as a British woman?'

'No, Eleanor, it is not. In Britain we do not have sperm banks. Of course we help married couples who cannot have children, and we are world leaders in extracting the female egg, fertilizing it with the husband's sperm outside the womb and replacing it back in the womb, but no, the service – as you call it – of a sperm bank does not exist.'

'I think it should. You wouldn't like to launch a campaign, on behalf of women?'

'No, Eleanor, I would not.'

'You're so old-fashioned, Stephen.'

'No, I am not old-fashioned. Look, Eleanor, why don't you just get married. It's so much simpler!'

'Get married and be unhappy like everyone else, is that what you mean?'

'It doesn't have to be like that.'

'It's not an option. There is no one in my life.'

'There will be . . . in time.'

'And that is just what I don't have, time! Stephen, I am nearly forty. If I want another child, I must go ahead, now!'

Stephen shook his head.

'I don't know . . . I really don't know what to say!' he told her.

'Wish me luck.'

Stephen laughed.

'Good luck!' he said.

It was New Year's Eve. Snow fell softly on the skylight and the studio was absolutely silent. Eleanor had spent Christmas at her mother's house in Dyne, and she would always remember Orlando standing in front of the Christmas tree, gasping in childish wonder, hiding his face in his grandmother's lap when the excitement became too much for him; and Anne smiling down at her grandson with her blind eyes, stroking his head and whispering, 'There, there.'

Eleanor watched the snowflakes melt against the cold panes of glass. Vincent said he would come back, after Christmas. 'He won't,' she told herself. 'I am nothing to him any more.'

The telephone rang. Eleanor stared at it for a moment, imagining the sound of his voice, controlling her longing to hear his voice. She picked up the receiver. It was her brother-in-law, Ralph.

'Hello, old bean. How are you? I've had a terrible Christmas. All alone, at Kirkenny. In the past we always had such jolly family Christmases with masses of children and cousins – you know. But this year I was by myself. I was pretty grim, I can tell you. And now it's New Year's Eve. I was wondering if I could come by for a drink. Of course I understand if it's difficult. You're probably going out to some glamorous party . . .'

'I'm not going anywhere. Orlando is asleep in his cot and I am reading a book.'

'Really? Gosh, well, could I come by?'

'Of course.'

'I promise not to stay too long. I have to have dinner with my father. That won't be much fun. He think's England's had it – too many immigrants, too much crime, all of that . . . Well, if it's really all right I'll come now.'

'Come whenever you like.'

'Eleanor, you're a brick.'

Eleanor hardly knew her brother-in-law. In all the years he had been married to Marcia they had talked in generalities; no confidences had been exchanged. It did not help that he was immensely polite. That evening Ralph looked drawn, as if he had not been sleeping. He brought with him a magnum of Dom Pérignon, which Eleanor opened.

Ralph said, 'I say, this is a stroke of luck, finding you on your own like this! Let's drink the whole bloody bottle.'

'So you thought we could get drunk together,' Eleanor laughed.

'It would take more than that to get me drunk! We'll just be merry, that's all. I need a bit of merriment. I haven't lived alone for years. I'm trying to keep everything exactly as it was, in Scotland and in London, I mean, so that if Marcia comes back she'll find everything just as she left it. She was a marvellous housekeeper. Everything was always perfect. Anyway, I mustn't let things go, I must think of the children.'

He paused, in case Eleanor had something to say. She did not, so he went on, 'Marcia telephones every week to tell me how the children are, and she sends them to me for the week-end once a month. It's very considerate of her. Other women wouldn't do that.'

'You are amazing, Ralph! There is no venom in you, no bitterness.'

Startled by her remark, he said, 'But I love her!'

'Yes, but other men would – '

'I'm not other men!' he interrupted. 'Do you remember our wedding? Do you remember the Shakespeare sonnet that my brother read out? – "Love is not love which alters when it alteration finds" – That's how I feel! That's how I shall always feel.'

'I think Marcia is a fool,' Eleanor said.

'I won't hear a word against her. Not a word!'

'You are too nice, Ralph. Too vulnerable. You will always get hurt.'

'I'm not amusing. I know that.'

'That's not what I said.'

'No, but it's what you meant. I know that I'm not amusing . . . I don't know how to be. I can never remember jokes and I don't laugh enough.' He sighed deeply. 'I don't find life very funny. Do you?'

'Now and then. But on the whole – no. I'm rather serious too. But I've grown used to myself. I'm no longer trying to be different.'

Ralph was not listening. 'I know I'm boring,' he went on resignedly. 'Marcia told me I was boring, in bed and out. Yes! That's what she said, "What a bore you are – in bed and out." '

'That's wasn't kind.'

'She was being honest.'

'She was being cruel.'

'No. I let her down. She was disappointed. I understand! In the last few years we hardly made love at all.'

Eleanor put her hand on Ralph's arm.

'I really hope you and Marcia get back together, you love her so much.'

'I was never unfaithful to her. Not once!'

'Ralph,' Eleanor said gently, 'have some more of your delicious champagne and tell me about Scotland. Tell me about the the forests and the trees.'

Ralph was not an urban animal; in cities he felt suffocated by fumes and people, and his spirit felt as if in chains, but when he got back to his homeland and the unending purple moors of Aberdeenshire, then he felt free, then he felt a man! He spoke of the raw red heather with its rough texture and the sharp wind and driving rain which stung your skin; and the clouds scudding across the Scottish skies as if driven by the zephyrs. Whenever there was an outburst of nature – a storm, or a shaft of brilliant sunlight – Ralph (who had read classics at Oxford) thought the Zeus commanding the elements; it made him believe in God.

'I worry for this world of ours,' Ralph said. 'Men are destroying the planet. My trees are sick! All over Scotland – all over Europe – the trees are sick from acid rain because we're poisoning the air. I do what I can – I plant new trees – but it's no use until people stop polluting the atmosphere with these poisonous gases. I must sound like one of those left-wingers, talking like this!'

'You sound to me like a man who know's what's going on.'

Suddenly Ralph raised his glass and said, 'Here's to Marcia, God bless her!'

There was anguish in his voice; for a moment they sat in silence and then Ralph continued, 'What is right? Tell me, Eleanor, what is right for Marcia? If she is in love with this man, really happy with him, fulfilled and all of that, then she would stay with him. Don't you think?'

'I don't know.'

'She was never in love with me, but we built a life together. And we have children. I think it would hurt the children. Don't you?'

'Very much.'

'It's so difficult, isn't it?'

'Yes.'

He drank hastily, in large gulps, and went on, 'You will put in a good word for me, if you get the chance?'

'Of course I will, but she doesn't ring me, except to wish us Happy Christmas. We're not close, Ralph. You must know that.'

'She admires you. So many times she's said – '

'Ralph,' Eleanor said, interrupting, 'what time is your dinner? Hadn't you better be going?'

'My God, you're right, I'm late already. Thanks so much for the chat, Eleanor. You've been a real tonic. The children are coming to stay with me for part of the holidays. Will you come over . . . give me a hand?'

'Of course I will. And any time you feel low, ring me. I guarantee to cheer you up.'

'You're a brick, Eleanor.'

Ralph took several large, dejected strides towards the door and left. There was more champagne in the bottle. Eleanor filled her glass and in the silence of her studio she lay back on her bed and listened to the steady rain on the skylight window waiting for the last few hours to slip by and the chimes of midnight to herald the New Year. Outside a car drew up. Her doorbell rang.

Over the intercom she said, 'Who is it?'

'*Sono io* . . .'

Moments later Vincent walked into the studio, arms outstretched.

'*Eccomi!*'

'What are you doing here?' she said, her whole face lit by her smile.

'I told you I would come – New Year's Eve, don't you remember? I leave for Moscow tomorrow night – I'm doing *Boris Godunov*, did I tell you? Quite a fantastic production. My *Fidelio* at Covent Garden was a huge success. I hope you saw it? No? But that's terrible, I should have sent you a ticket. My fault. I'm so sorry. Look, have you eaten? Here is some caviare. And Russian vodka. Ice cold.'

Vincent looked around the room and smiled.

'You know, I thought I might find you in bed with a lover. That would have been embarrassing, wouldn't it?' he said.

'I don't have a lover.'

'Yes you do.'

He moved towards her, but she stepped back to the window and looked out into the street. It was snowing lightly and she could see the shiny black roof of Vincent's limousine disappearing down the street.

'You've sent the car away,' she said.

Vincent took her face in his hands and smiled again.

'I told you, Schmetterling, I've come to stay. You're not going to send me away, not tonight?'

'No, not tonight.'

That night she loved him unconditionally, body and soul, obliterating from her mind the past and all its pain. Vincent made love in his usual frenzied way, and as he was inside her thrusting furiously, Eleanor prayed, 'Dear God, please let me conceive his child.'

Vincent stayed with Eleanor all the next day, a public holiday, 1 January, and they walked in St James's Park and Vincent talked about himself. It was the same familiar story: Marina was still dancing, Dasha was still sad; the mistress in Rome struggled on with her drug-addicted daughter; Alexei was fighting the Soviets, in Afghanistan, over the radio waves. Ethel Wingate was the only defector. She had removed herself and her money from the inner circle. Vincent would not go into detail.

'We are no longer friends, but then nothing lasts for ever, does it, Schmetterling?'

A frail and melting carpet of snow covered the park, and their feet crushed the glinting flakes.

'Once upon a time our love was very strong,' Vincent said. 'Do you remember Paris, and your hat blowing into the Seine?'

In the afternoon they went back to the studio and made love, and Vincent held her close for a long time; then the limousine arrived and he left.

Ralph had a magnificent body. There was no fat on his lean,

manly frame, and the pelvic line was as pronounced as in a Greek statue.

'For God's sake, Eleanor, hurry up. I feel an awful ninny standing here starkers. If anyone came in, what would they think?'

'Don't be so bourgeois. I'm an artist. I've painted a hundred nudes . . . but I am very grateful to you, Ralph. I can't paint from memory, and this painting has been in a cupboard since last summer. One day we had a picnic at Stowe and these two boys were bathing in the lake. They looked so beautiful in the first flush of youth.'

'That's hardly me.'

'They were with their father. He stood there for a while, wondering if the water was too cold. Then he got ready to dive. That's you – about to plunge in! Don't lower your arm, please! I'm sorry it's such an awkward pose. Ralph, you have a superb physique, have I told you?'

'Yes, yes you have. But I'm freezing. My balls are going to drop off if you don't hurry.'

'There! Finished! Thank you very much, Mr Penrose.'

Hurriedly Ralph dressed.

'I don't know how I let you persuade me to strip, I really don't. For God's sake don't say a word to Marcia. She'd have a fit.'

'I can't see why.'

Ralph's children came to London and Eleanor took them ice-skating, and to the Safari Park at Windsor, and to see *The Wizard of Oz*. One evening Marcia rang.

'I've heard all about the weekend – the cinema and the circus. The children had a great time,' she said.

'They're terrific children. We always have fun.'

'I just wanted to thank you for . . . taking my place.'

'Are you all right?' There was a silence. 'Ralph misses you terribly.'

'You are trying to make me feel guilty.'

'He really loves you, Marcia. He's absolutely miserable.'

'I can't go back to him. I can't!'

Meanwhile the portrait of Lord Tilbury, Knight of the Garter, was overdue. The taciturn but charming octogenarian stood straight-backed and solemn, leaning only slightly on his ivory-handled cane, as Eleanor painted in silence. Now and then she would say, 'Wouldn't you like a chair? Please sit down and rest. This must be very tiring.'

The old gentleman shook his head.

'At my age you are always sitting down. I like to stand. It makes a change.'

How did Rembrandt paint the texture of old skin, so accurately and yet so lovingly? How did Frans Hals create the invisible divides of light and shades? Eleanor was not happy with her painting. Something was wrong. What was it?

'Opaque,' she called out. 'It's too opaque.'

Of course, it was obvious! For the background she had used raw umber and ultramarine, and the result was oppressive. Frans Hals in all his genius could make ivory black look the coolest blue. Eleanor took her palette knife and began to scrape away the wet paint.

A telephone rang. It was Ralph. He said, 'That most amazing thing has happened. It's so amazing that I don't know how to tell you. Marcia has come back! She's here at Kirkenny with the children. At first I thought she was just paying a visit. But then I saw her suitcases. And I said, "Are you staying long?" and she said, "This is my home!" Oh, Eleanor, I'm so happy. So incredibly happy!'

'I'm delighted for you, Ralph. This is wonderful, wonderful news.'

'I want to thank you, Eleanor. You were so kind to me.'

'I didn't do anything.'

'Eleanor, you were a brick.'

27 Eleanor was pregnant and once again a great tranquillity descended. Already she felt an immense love for the unborn babe in her womb, and she greeted the first stirrings of life with intense joy. She decided to say nothing to anyone. Eventually from her expanding shape, people would guess.

Stephen Budd, the gynaecologist, was cool.

'Eleanor, is this child by the same father?' he asked.

'No.'

'Does this father know?'

'No.'

'Are you planning to marry the father?'

'He is married.'

Stephen Budd leant back in his chair, took off his spectacles and wiped them with a clean white handkerchief.

'I can't say I am exactly surprised, considering our last conversation . . . but I wonder if you have thought this through . . . You may well live to regret all of this . . .'

'No, Stephen, no! I have loved Orlando from the moment he was conceived. I have loved carrying him inside of me, I loved bringing him into this world, and every hour and every moment of his life I have loved that child. And so it will go on all of my life. I shall care for Orlando, and I shall care for this second child. They shall not want for love.'

'Whatever you say, Eleanor, fathers are important. A child is the product of a man and a woman. Even you cannot get away from this fact. A father has a role. I am speaking to you not only as a doctor, but as a father.'

'Of course the father has a role, but later on. And later on I shall find a father.'

'Eleanor, you said that to me when you were expecting Orlando, but if I understand correctly, you are still living alone?'

'Yes.'

'You do not live with the father of this . . . this second child?'

'No.'

'In other words there is no stability in your life.'

'But there is! *I* am stable! I'm here to love these children at their waking and at their sleeping and all the hours in between!'

'I don't want to argue with you, Eleanor, but I warn you now, it may be all right for the first few years but later, when Orlando is six or seven, when this child is five . . . those children will ask to meet their fathers. And you will have problems.'

'Of course I will have problems. I am expecting them! You see, there are problems in every family, however happy it seems from the outside. I had a wonderful mother and a wonderful father, and a sister, and from the outside everything seemed perfect, but half of the time I was miserable, especially as I grew older. My sister didn't like me. I don't know why, but she taunted me, and told me that I was ugly and useless, and what is so stupid is that I believed her. I allowed her to destroy my self-confidence, and I came back for more, again and again. I couldn't tear myself away from her even though I knew she was bad for me, and all the while I felt I *had* to love her and look after her because she was my sister. Finally, some time in my mid-twenties, I stood up and said, "I don't have to love Marcia." And once I said this she no longer had the power to hurt me, and my life changed. The odd part is I do love Marcia, despite everything. I am only telling you this because you must understand that I know about problems . . . I am not afraid of them!'

Eleanor was agitated; the words had tumbled forth in a torrent of pent-up feeling and she was surprised by her own fervour.

'Don't upset yourself,' Stephen said.

'You will look after me, won't you?'

'Of course I will.'

The Penrose family moved back to London, and almost immediately Marcia came to see Eleanor.

'The Prodigal Wife has returned,' she said as she walked

brusquely into the studio, holding her fur coat close to her throat. 'How can you paint in this arctic temperature?'

'I don't feel cold.'

'It's so bad for Orlando.'

'He hasn't had a cold all winter. He's so sweet, Marcia. I can't wait for you to see him. He waddles about on his tiny legs – it's so sweet to watch.'

'How long can this cold weather last?' Marcia said, sitting down on the chaise-longue. 'I hate the winter! It seems to go on for ever . . . Well, I am waiting.'

'Waiting for what?' Eleanor said, her mouth going dry.

'Waiting for you to say, "I told you so." '

'What did I tell you? I can't remember.'

'You told me Ralph was a saint and I was mad to leave him.'

'He missed you terribly.'

'Yes . . . yes . . .' Marcia said impatiently. 'He said that you were his greatest support. "Eleanor was a brick" – that's how he put it. Well, I want to thank you for being so good to Ralph and the children. They love you.'

'And I love them.'

'It's funny, but I never thought you liked Ralph.'

'I didn't know him. For the first time we became friends . . . He's a most sensitive and interesting man. He knows all about acid rain . . . talk to him about it!'

'I don't want to . . . but that's neither here nor there. The die is cast. I fled the nest only to return, my tail between my legs. Were you surprised that I came back to Ralph?'

'A little.'

'So was I . . . I mean, if there had been any other way I would never have come back. It's not only Ralph . . . it's the whole life. I don't want to live like this any more, but there's no way out. At least not any way that I can see. For a moment I was free, and I would do it all again just to feel as I did in those first few months. We were all so happy, the children, Matthew, me, the baby . . . we were all so carefree . . . The children climbed the Welsh hills and rode ponies. Matthew doted on Clare – he would put her on his shoulders and walk across the fields. He even talked about having another baby. And then things changed. I don't know why. At first I didn't even notice. Clare was teething and cried all night, the nanny got exhausted and grumbled about the weather, and the children wanted to come to London to be with their father. Matthew went on longer and longer walks by himself. I found him poring over the *National Geographic*, staring at photographs of Mexico. His eyes had that peculiar expression of a man who is trapped. We were suffocating him. In one horrible moment I realized it would never work. So . . . so I made things easy. I told him that I had to go back to Ralph for the sake of the children. He was very sweet, he pretended to be heartbroken.'

Her voice trailed off. She looked so wretched that Eleanor put her arm around her sister and said, 'You've had a difficult time.'

'Of course I hoped right to the last minute that Ralph wouldn't take me back. I had this feeling he was seeing someone. I don't know why. I hoped so much that there *was* a new woman in his life, and he would turn around and say, "I'm sorry, Marcia, but I've found someone else." But no. When I said I would like to come back he burst into tears. And when we met he took me in his arms and hugged me until I couldn't breathe. As a last resort I told him that Clare was not his daughter.'

'Was that necessary?'

'I felt he ought to know. I suppose in my heart of hearts I hoped it would put him off. But all he said was that as far as he was concerned Clare was his daughter, and he loved her with all his heart. So, that was that. There was nothing more to say. The Prodigal Wife was home, welcomed with open arms by her adoring husband. Oh, I do wish you would stop looking at me like that! I know what you're thinking. I don't deserve Ralph. He's too good for me.'

'Yes. That is what I'm thinking.'

'You're wrong. I've given Ralph a great deal: a son and heir and a daughter – and I run his shooting perfectly. You're jealous – you have no one in your life. You may have a child, but what's that? Anyone can have a baby. It's more difficult to find a husband, and you . . . you never will. You're an old maid and you always will be!'

'You've said that before.'

Eleanor waited for the rage to pass. Marcia stammered, 'I shouldn't have said all that. I'm sorry. Forgive me, Eleanor, forgive me! But at times you look at me with such hatred!'

'I do hate you . . . sometimes. Not very often any more,

now that I have Orlando, but there was a time when I envied you your doting children and your doting husband. It didn't seem fair that you should have such a perfect life while I was . . . well, so hopeless.'

'You . . . hopeless? But that's ridiculous! You were making a name for yourself. Becoming a woman in your own right. I've only ever been a wife!'

'I never looked at things that way. All I know is that I felt a failure. And to me you were dazzling in your success, until that day when you told me that you were unhappy . . . that you were in love with another man . . . Then I realized that you didn't have the perfect life. You were just like everyone else. It came as a relief. That may not sound very nice, but that's how it felt. Anyway, that's all in the past. I've got my son Orlando and you've got your husband and your children and your lover. I don't imagine the affair is over?'

'Of course it's not over,' Marcia said irritably. 'Matthew is part of my life. I'll never give him up.'

She turned away from her sister and, moving nervously about the studio, she said, 'I'm sure it won't be long before you find someone.'

'I'm not looking.'

Suddenly Marcia laughed.

'For God's sake, why do we always quarrel? Let's have a drink. Have you any wine in your fridge? Let's open a bottle and you can show me your latest work. Everyone is talking about you. I went to a party the other day and someone said you were the best portrait-painter in England. I felt very proud.'

Eleanor opened a bottle of wine and Marcia began to inspect the canvases stacked against the wall.

'Here, have a glass of wine,' Eleanor said.

Marcia was crouched beside a painting of men bathing.

'But this is Ralph!' she said.

'Yes, it is.'

'How did he get there – stark naked, in your painting?'

'How do you think he got there? He came and posed for me one afternoon. You know, I think you're very lucky to be married to a man with such a magnificent body.'

'He posed *nude* for you, his sister-in-law?'

'I'm a painter, or have you forgotten? Oh, Marcia, you're

not going to make a song and dance about this, are you? You're not going to imagine we had an affair or something insane?'

'Did you?'

'Don't be so idiotic.'

They drank the wine and all the while Marcia stared at the painting.

'I suppose he is a good-looking man,' she said.

'He's magnificent.'

'If only he weren't so boring!'

'Give him a chance, Marcia. He loves you so much. I hate to see him suffer. He's like a wounded animal dragging himself about.'

Marcia waved her hand in the air. 'No lectures, please. I've come back, haven't I? Here I am, once again, by his side, ready to do my bit.'

28 The secret was out: Eleanor was having another child. Anne Wynn had known all along, or so she said. Dominic was astounded, and had to sit down and have a drink of neat vodka. Marcia was incredulous; she had to see for herself.

'No wonder I didn't notice! You hardly show at all!' she said.

'I'm five months pregnant.'

'It's your painting smock. It hides everything. Is this another mystery baby, or are you going to tell us who the father is?'

'I'll tell you one thing. It isn't Ralph.'

'That wasn't funny.'

From New York Regina Bruce telephoned.

'Is it true? Another baby? Is this for real, Eleanor, or is it one of Dominic's perverted jokes? I rang up to buy one of your paintings – by the way, the catalogue of the watercolour exhibition was perfectly beautiful – and Dominic told me. I want confirmation from the mother herself.'

'Yes, it's true.'

'Father undisclosed?'

'That's right . . . father undisclosed.'

'Is this a piece of one-upmanship, a sneaky plan to outdo the friend that got you thinking along these lines in the first place? I feel cheated! Yes I do. And incredibly jealous. God, Eleanor, how I envy you, and I'm so happy for you. My dear, dear friend.'

'When are you coming to see us? You have never seen your godson.'

'And you have never seen yours!'

'But this is ridiculous! You're not having a christening?'

'Certainly not! Test tube P.897 was Jewish. I'm staying clear of all religion. What about you?'

'I don't know . . . I haven't decided.'

'Come and stay with me this summer. I've got a house in Maine.'

'I'm going to Italy. I must go to Italy.'

'Then stay there and wait for me. I am singing *Tosca* at La Scala in November. I shall drive down and see you. And in the meantime you kiss that little boy for me, and take care of yourself. Remember, I love you very much.'

'And I love you too, Regina.'

Vincent sent a postcard from Russia with a scribbled message that *Boris Godunov* had a new Arab backer, a pliant prince, as Vincent called him, and filming was underway once again. A few weeks later he sent a photograph of himself in a Russian hat in front of a domed church in Leningrad, and Eleanor pinned the photograph to her easel so she could look at it while she painted.

Just before Easter there was a telephone call from a secretary in Paris with a message from Mr Buonarotti. He would like to take Miss Wynn to dinner next Wednesday. Would that be convenient? Very convenient, Eleanor replied, and for a moment she imagined that Vincent had changed. Then, on Wednesday morning he rang.

'Schmetterling.'

'Where are you?'

'Thirty-five thousand feet above the Atlantic. In a Gulf Stream jet.'

'Don't be late for dinner. I'm so looking forward to seeing you.'

'That's why I'm ringing, Schmetterling. I have to go straight to Salzburg – there's a memorial concert for Karajan and Karl Henkel is conducting. I must be there . . . I'm so sorry.'

'Never mind.'

'I've been so busy with the film – I'm sorry I haven't been in touch . . . This line is terrible . . . can you hear me?'

'Yes, I can hear you.'

'It's going to be a beautiful film . . . I've just seen the rough cut . . . Giuseppe – do you remember him? – well, he has produced these extraordinary shots of Leningrad in the snow . . . And you, Schmetterling, tell me your news.'

'No news. I am well. So is Orlando.'

'Say that again, I can't year you!'

'I am well, so is Orlando.'

'I kiss you, Schmetterling . . . We see each other soon, soon!'

Italy! The longing to be in that country, to hear church bells chime in the warm evening air, to smell the garlic and the mint, to walk through olive groves and fields of sunflowers, this longing to be in Italy had grown overwhelming, and at last Eleanor made her decision: she would give birth to her second child in the land of the painters. She made preparations, and started to clear the studio floor, piling her books into boxes. She did not hear Dominic as he moved with the stealth of a cat across the wooden floorboards. He wore a black tie and his long red hair was tied back with a black velvet ribbon.

'What's wrong?' Eleanor asked.

'Hugo is dead. The cremation was this morning.'

'Oh, Dominic, Dominic.'

Carefully Eleanor put Orlando down, and she enfolded Dominic in her arms. He began to cry; she had never seen him cry. Softly she said, 'My dear, dear friend.'

Orlando stared up at the weeping man and suddenly he too began to cry, loudly and fearfully. Dominic smiled through his tears and said to the child, 'Don't you cry, little boy. You're too young for sorrow. Don't you cry! Here, I'll wipe my eyes. There! See? I'm not crying any more. Where's the champagne, Eleanor? I want to toast my friend, my lovely Hugo. He was a man of taste, and that is rare – taste in all things, music, literature, shoes, ties, everything! And I loved him.'

Eleanor opened a bottle of champagne and sat and drank with Dominic, and Orlando stood at his knee and Dominic let him dip his finger into the glass.

'Have you seen the *Sun*?' Dominic asked.

'I don't take the *Sun*.'

'That reptilian journalist – do you remember the creature? A woman of unforgettable ugliness and her bulbous cohort, the photographer – do you remember him? Both of them loathsome! Anyway, the reporter has excelled herself. You, it seems, confessed. Don't look so surprised. In the strictest confidence you named the father of your child. Nay, of both children. And guess who drew the lucky number? Me!'

'You?'

225

'Quite ridiculous, I agree, but there we are. I shall of course sue. It's terribly damaging to my reputation as the most interesting homosexual in London.'

They both began to laugh. Dominic said, 'If only Hugo were alive. He'd laugh himself sick.'

'Come to Italy for the summer. Let's be together!'

'Are you really going?'

'It's all arranged. An Italian painter and his wife and small child are coming here to live – here in my studio – and Rosie will help to look after the little girl. And I'm going to live in their farmhouse in Umbria. We'll live very cheaply – oh, I can't wait to go to Italy. I'm going to drive out – with Orlando and my mother. There's room for you. Come with us! Please! Let's be together!'

'You're such a bad driver, I shall have to come.'

Orlando began to laugh and clap his hands.

'Infant,' Dominic said to the child, 'if you are sick down my neck there will be trouble.'

'Of course he's not going to be sick.'

'I am not taking any chances. We'll put the baby chair behind the passenger seat. Then he can be sick all over his grandmother.'

It was the eve of their departure for Italy. Anne Wynn had settled on the chaise-longue with Orlando on her knee and they were both laughing and blowing kisses; and it was so good to hear her mother laugh, so good to see the infinite love in her blind eyes as she held her grandson. To Eleanor it seemed that children are born to rekindle our faith in the human race.

'Tomorrow we leave! I'm so excited. I feel like a child. I am so glad we shall all be together,' she said, and she went over to her mother and knelt beside the chaise-longue. 'I wish I could thank you.'

'For what?'

'For loving me. All my life. No matter what.'

'You don't have to thank me, my darling. It is a mother's privilege, as you will discover with your children.'

'I am so glad you will be with me when I have this baby.'

Anne Wynn smiled and stretched out her hand, her fingers fluttering, and Eleanor took her hand and kissed it.

Rosie was there to see them off, Dolly in her arms. Beside her stood her new boyfriend, a chartered accountant called Jeff, dressed in his city suit and wearing glasses. 'They go well together,' Eleanor thought.

29 Eleanor gave birth to her second child in Siena, but Anne Wynn did not live to see her granddaughter. She died a month before the child was born, in her sleep and with no pain.

Death came suddenly: there was no lingering illness. Right up to the moment of death, they were all together – Anne, Eleanor, Orlando and Dominic. It was an idyllic time, each day more beautiful than the last and for the rest of her life Eleanor would remember this time with intense happiness.

All day the sun beat down and the fields of sunflowers and tobacco shimmered in the heat haze that gripped the plain until the early evening, Eleanor's favourite time of day, when a breeze blew and the contours of the Mediterranean pines and the cypress trees and the tobacco factory and the fields of sunflowers became sharper; and the sky filled itself with violent shades of orange and red and purple; and the air was warm and filled with the sound of crickets, and the wine tasted cool.

Eleanor had rented a small farmhouse on a steep slope outside Cortona, surrounded by small farms, woods and Mediterranean pines. To the west lay Tuscany and the glorious towns of the Renaissance: Siena and Florence and Montepulciano and Volterra; and spacious villas and miles of impeccable vineyards on white ground. To the east lay Umbria, a wilder, less developed terrain, with ruined castles on hilltops, and Gubbio and Spello, small towns of breathtaking beauty. A small, dark-haired woman from Calabria called Andrina came in each day to clean the house. She fell in love with Orlando and asked if she could take him home to play with her two-year-old daughter. And so, each afternoon, Orlando ran riot on Andrina's small farm in the valley, chasing chickens and talking to the goats, and being spoilt by any number of Andrina's relations. He was allowed to stand on the seat of a tractor and hold the steering wheel, and to toot the horn of a motor bike, and he learnt to say 'Ciao' and to open and shut his hand in the Italian manner. Each evening, when Eleanor came to take him away, he blew kisses to Andrina and her family.

That summer every painting, every church, every view seemed more beautiful than ever. Eleanor stood on a small hill covered in ripe corn and gazed across the Tuscan fields towards San Giminiano, at the skyline of towers, thirteen in all, built seven hundred years ago. In the cathedral museum in Cortona, she marvelled at the power and beauty and blazing colour of one of the great paintings of the Renaissance, Fra Angelico's *Annunciation*. But the painter who dominated all others that summer was Piero della Francesca. Time and time again Eleanor returned to Arezzo to the basilica of San Francesco to see the great frescoes depicting the Story of the True Cross. And three times she journeyed to the Arezzo museum to see Christ stepping out of the tomb, while at his feet the Roman soldiers slept; and twice she went to the chapel at Monterchi to see the *Pregnant Madonna*. What was it about this painter that set him apart? For Eleanor it was his sense of drama which made each painting so extraordinarily powerful (and she marvelled at the sleeping soldiers in their abandoned positions, and all the complicated foreshortening that was involved), but it was the beauty of each and every face which stayed in her mind: the heavy-lidded eyes set far apart, the full mouths and the high foreheads, the strong build of the men and the full bosoms of the women – these people were of the soil, not frail and floating creatures of so many Renaissance paintings; they were fierce, confident and absolutely beautiful.

Eleanor took her mother on all her excursions and described to her everything she saw and felt. At first Anne was reluctant to come: what was the point of taking a blind woman to look at paintings? She had brought a tape recorder and would stay at home and listen to cassettes, but Eleanor would not hear of it.

'You don't understand. I need you! You're a great help to me,' she insisted. 'With you by my side I really look. I notice everything. As I describe a fresco or a picture I concentrate hard and see all sorts of things that I didn't see before!'

Eleanor always felt that Karl Henkel and her mother were

destined to meet once more, and it happened in Italy that summer. Eleanor was sitting in a café in the Piazzo del Campo in Siena, admiring the Palazzo Pubblico, the medieval town hall, and watching the children chase pigeons across the sloping cobblestones of this extraordinary square, laid out in the shape of a shell, when she noticed the man at the table next to hers. He sat with his back to her, smoking; Eleanor recognized the yellow fingers.

'Alexei!'

Alexei turned and a slow smile spread across his face and the smoke seeped through his discoloured teeth as he slowly rose to his feet.

Eleanor said, 'I never expected to meet you, of all people, here, in the most beautiful square in the world!'

Alexei joined Eleanor at her table and told her that he was staying with Karl Henkel and every night he was taken to hear Mozart in the Palazzo Chigi Saracini as part of the summer music festival which Karl was conducting.

'Karl has a flat here, in this piazza, over there,' and Alexei pointed to a small, yellow ochre palazzo next to the Torre del Mangia.

'I sit here every day and drink Italian beer – look how fat I am! I have become lazy, soft . . . just as you wanted!' and he heaved his shoulders and laughed.

'It's called having a holiday, Alexei. And don't tell me you are not moved by Mozart, and don't tell me Siena is not beautiful!'

Alexei inhaled deeply on his cigarette.

'Italy is very corrupt, you know. Government does not really matter. It is all big business. Gianni Agnelli controls twenty-five per cent of Italian stock exchange. Incredible! One man owns the quarter of the nation! And then there is the Mafia. Into everything. Extorting bribes. Corrupting politicians. The usual.'

'Now don't be depressing, Alexei. The point of Italy is its beauty, not its morals. Look around you – don't tell me you are not moved by this!'

'I am moved! I am moved! I come here every day. This is another world, and I need a rest. I am tired.'

'I'm not surprised. You can't live in a state of war all the time. No one can.'

'Tell that to the Mujahedin!' Alexei said, laughing, and he told Eleanor about the long months he had spent on the border between Afghanistan and Pakistan, transmitting radio broadcasts on the army frequencies to Russian soldiers. Seventeen soldiers had defected.

'Seventeen. It sounds little,' he explained, 'but each defection was of enormous consequence to morale of those regiments. You have to remember that defection is unheard of in Soviet army. And then was major operation to get soldiers into Switzerland away from Russian court martial.'

'That was a great achievement, Alexei.'

'Not great. Small. Nothing compared to sacrifice of Mujahedin. They defeated Soviet army! They pushed them back, back into Soviet Union. Now, Soviet army has left Afghanistan, and now, as I told you, unrest is beginning to spread, in Georgia, Azerbaijan, the Baltic states, Poland, Hungary. This is real test for Gorbachev!'

'And what are you going to do?'

'I go back to school! My student years I spent in prison. Now, in middle age, I go back to study! I have grant to study psychiatry at King's College Medical School, in London. And Dasha has raised money from refugee foundation for flat in Bloomsbury Square!'

They were interrupted by a soft German voice.

'*Meine liebe, liebe Eleonora, dass ist aber schön!*' Karl Henkel cried out, and embraced Eleanor, and they ordered more wine and talked and laughed, and Karl agreed at once to come to lunch the following day, once he knew that Anne would be there. Eleanor got up to leave, and only then did Alexei notice her pregnant stomach.

'What is this?' he said.

'It's a baby, Alexei!'

'And husband?'

'No husband.'

'Two babies and no husband?'

'Yes, that's right.'

Alexei threw back his head and laughed; Karl raised his glass.

Anne was nervous; she could not decide what to wear and she asked Eleanor to help her with her lipstick.

'I wish you hadn't asked him,' she said, as she sat in front of the mirror and Eleanor adjusted her hair. 'I would like him to remember me as I was, not as I am now.'

'You are beautiful.'

'I am old and blind.'

'I'm not going to argue with you.'

Anne and Eleanor sat in the cool white room with its simple wooden furniture, and Anne stared with her unseeing eyes at the door and said, 'Karl is bound to be disappointed. I used to be so pretty. It's a lovely thing for a woman, to have beauty. It is a gift from Heaven, it really is. After all, you do nothing for it, you certainly don't deserve it, but it gives such pleasure! When I was twenty I sat next to a man of around seventy at a dinner and I could not think of anything to say, and he said to me, "Please smile. That's all I ask. You don't know what pleasure the smile of a pretty girl gives an old man like me!" '

As she was telling her story a car drew up on the uneven dirt track and Dominic shouted, 'They're here!'

Almost under her breath Anne said, 'I'm so nervous. Isn't it ridiculous?'

Moments later Karl Henkel was embracing his old love, telling her in his gentlest of tones, 'You are still the same beautiful Anna!'

'And you are still the same irresistible charmer! Do you look well, Karl? Does he, Eleanor? I'm blind, my friend. Old and blind.'

Gently Karl took Anne by the arm and said, 'Eleanor will tell you my hair is white, and so is my beard, and I too am old, but how well we have aged, you and I! Your eyes are just as bright even if they cannot see, and look at these lovely hands! Come, Anne, we are going for a walk, you and I. We shall be away for a long time, *meine Kinder*, so don't be alarmed!'

Dominic played his guitar while Alexei chased Orlando about the house, and rolled on the floor with him, and hid his face under the table cloth, and made noises of animals, and the child shrieked with delight. Eleanor watched Alexei and thought, 'He has so much love to give. Look how he plays with Orlando!'

'You're going to be a psychiatrist, really?' Dominic said to Alexei later that afternoon. 'Well, my dear fellow, I can send hundreds of people your way. Yes I can! All my friends need professional help. They are up the wall, most of them. By the way, Alexei, I read your book. It depressed the hell out of me.'

'And me!' Alexei said, heaving his shoulders and laughing, 'and me!'

'Well, Dr Kinski, the best of British luck to you,' Dominic cried.

Alexei smiled and went on, 'Sometimes I wonder if this is not a crazy plan . . . there are so many years of study in front of me. But I want to understand workings of the mind. How is it possible for men to see truth around them, and to speak lies? How do they justify this to themselves? Is this not madness? In Soviet Union there is mass delusion – a form of collective madness.'

Anne, who had been listening intently, asked, 'And Gorbachev? What are his chances to change it all?'

'He is one man . . . against him is the KGB. Over five million people work in KGB. They do not want to lose jobs. But if glasnost and perestroika happen, then there is no job for enormous KGB. So, KGB will fight Gorbachev. Old party officials will fight Gorbachev. Army will fight Gorbachev, but mass of people will support him. I have hope. I must have hope. And those who believe in God, let them pray!'

Before dinner Eleanor and Karl walked beneath the Mediterranean pines and Eleanor said, 'Did you ever think of divorcing your wife and marrying my mother?'

'Never. I was young, ambitious and poor, and my wife was young, ambitious and rich. She was also kind and intelligent and she loved me very much. I could never leave her. She died three years ago, after forty-seven years of marriage. Imagine! I think I was a good husband – I hope so. I tried hard, until I met your mother, then I did not try at all. I was in love! I walked on air! For nearly a year I was the happiest man in the world. Oh, she was so pretty. I wish I could make you understand how pretty your mother was! And you, you have inherited her looks and her charm!'

Karl kissed Eleanor on the forehead. *'Du bist mir sehr lieb.'*

'I love you too, Karl. You've been a wonderful friend to me. And my mother is so pleased to see you after so long.'

'She prays for death.'

'Yes, I know.'

'I would too. No one wants to live in blackness.'

'It's grey,' Eleanor said. 'Like a television screen that doesn't work.'

Later that evening they cooked spaghetti *alle vongole* and sat outside beneath the vine drinking Chianti and telling stories.

'If only I had known you were here!' Karl said, throwing out his long, beautiful hands, 'you could have come to my concert last week, the *Prague* symphony. The orchestra played in the Palazzo Chigi Saracini. Imagine, Mozart in a medieval setting! It was sublime! Buonarotti was there, and he cheered us to the rafters!'

Eleanor looked up sharply.

'Is Vincent here?' she asked.

'He has a house in Lucca, didn't you know? It's a lovely seventeenth-century villa. I went to lunch there last week. The house was full of people staying, and many women, of course.' Karl smiled at Eleanor. 'But it's not the same any more. He seems disorientated. He doesn't know what to do now that he's alone.'

'What do you mean?' Eleanor said.

'Dasha has left him. You didn't know? I thought everyone knew. They're getting a divorce.'

Eleanor stared in disbelief, first at Karl and then at Alexei and said, 'I am amazed. I never thought Dasha would leave. I thought she was the sort of woman who put up with anything. What happened?'

'Alexei knows better than I do,' Karl said. 'He is Dasha's friend. You tell us, Alexei.'

'What you say in English? Last straw breaking camel's back!'

'What was this straw?' Eleanor asked. 'Another woman?'

Alexei nodded. 'Another woman. No one important. Just another woman. But for Dasha it was the end. Finish. Marriage was dead. Vincent thought she must be joking. But she moved to Paris and asked for divorce, and now she uses her Russian name – and she has new life. And Marina and Nicholas see her all the time. And she is happy.'

'A free woman,' Eleanor said.

'Vincent is so angry!' Karl said. '*Ganz böse, wie ein Kind, der blöde Kerl!*'

'*Vincent* is angry!' Eleanor burst out.

'His pride is hurt,' Karl chuckled. 'He goes around telling

everyone that Dasha was a bad wife, that she was never interested in his art, and we all laugh and say she was too good for him. He is furious with the children too – they have taken their mother's side. He told me something I shall never forget, he told me, "My children must renegotiate their relationship with me." I said to him, "You're wrong, Vincent. Your children don't need you. It is *you* who needs your children. Be careful," I said, "or you'll find yourself alone." He was so angry! He said, "I don't care! I don't care! They have betrayed me, all of them." I have never seen him so agitated. I felt sorry for him.'

'I always thought Vincent could do anything and not pay the price,' Eleanor said.

'I used to think so too,' Karl agreed, 'but now I'm not so sure. These last few months have been very hard for him, der armer Kerl. Ethel Wingate pulled out of *Boris Godunov*, quite suddenly, with no warning. Vincent had started shooting and he had to stop – it was very embarrassing. It was also incomprehensible – after all, Ethel had backed all of Vincent's last films. I found the whole thing astonishing, so, on behalf of my good friend, I went to see Ethel in New York, and she told me that God had spoken to her and warned her that Vincent was some sort of devil!'

'Oh my God,' Eleanor said.

'Ethel is eccentric, we all know that, but this was absurd. Anyway, Vincent came to London over the New Year to be alone and think things through, at least that's what he told me. Who knows, perhaps he was seeing some girl,' and again it seemed to Eleanor that Karl was directing this remark especially at her. 'Anyway, he met an Arab with the same passion for opera as the Mactoum brothers have for horses.' Here Karl paused and sipped his wine, and his eyes were mischievous as he concluded, 'I am beginning to think Ethel is right, and our dear friend is indeed Mephistopheles. When you think of it he does have the luck of the devil!'

Later Eleanor asked Karl for Vincent's number in Lucca.

'He has many guests,' Karl warned.

'Of course.'

Karl paused for a moment and then said, 'Does he know you are having another child?'

'No, he doesn't.'

'Do you want him to know?'

'Not especially.'

Eleanor looked straight at Karl, fending off his inquisitive look.

'Schmetterling, how nice to hear you! I called you in London but they said you had gone to Italy. Listen . . . I've been lent a yacht in Izmir. Come with me! Let's go down the Turkish coast together!'

'Vincent, be serious! Karl Henkel has been telling us all your woes and I was worried. He says you've had a difficult time.'

'Terrible! Terrible! My Italian mistress, and the Hungarian girl, they are *both* talking about marriage! I had forgotten all about these intolerable pressures of bachelorhood.'

'I didn't know that you and Dasha had got a divorce. I only just heard.'

'*Che posso fare?* She will be sorry . . .'

'What about *you*? Are you sorry?'

'Sorry for *what*? I live life on my terms . . . I do not want to change! Schmetterling, thank you for ringing, I am very touched, *da vero!*'

'As long as you're all right.'

'And you, Schmetterling? How are you? And the little boy? We should have a child, you and I!'

'You had your chance.'

'Yes . . . yes I did. And now *purtroppo* the moment is passed. You and I, we move on. I read that you are going to paint the Queen. Brava! You will be famous! And you will forget your old love.'

'I won't.'

'Come to Izmir and we can make love in the Aegean.'

'Why don't you come to Cortona, it's closer.'

'Wait for me! I am coming! *Aspettami!*'

Vincent never came. He was spotted by the paparazzi in Florence with an Austrian contralto, and in Siena with an Italian woman (the mistress perhaps, Eleanor thought). And one day Karl reported that Vincent had left for Turkey.

Each day the friends journeyed through Tuscany, moving from one splendour to another, from the Greek statue of the Three Graces in the cathedral at Siena to the Giotto frescoes of Assisi, from the Palazzo Ducale in Gubbio to the Etruscan museum of Volterra. On the days that Karl was rehearsing and could not be with them, Alexei took over the role of companion and guide to Anne, and led her gently by the arm, and described to her the landscape and the buildings.

'But what date is it, Alexei?' she would ask.

'It's old, old, everything in Italy is old!'

In the evenings they would sit in the garden and talk, and Anne would always face the sun, to feel the last rays warm her face; and once again Eleanor was touched by the gentleness of the Russian.

One evening Anne said, 'Alexei, are you there?'

'I am here.'

'I don't know why. I thought you had gone inside.'

'I am here.'

'I want to talk to you. You are too solitary. Why don't you find a nice girl and get married?'

Alexei threw up his hands in horror and said, 'But I've done my term of hard labour!'

The sunflowers drooped their heads and summer drew to a close. Karl left for Munich while Dominic and Alexei went to London. Eleanor got ready for the birth of her child.

Now that Karl Henkel had gone away Anne no longer went out. She sat in the garden listening to the chatter of her grandson and the gentle cooing of Andrina, the farmer's wife. In the distance she could hear the drone of tractors as the sunflowers were cut down.

Anne died without warning. One evening she felt tired and went to bed early. In the morning she did not come down for breakfast. Eleanor went upstairs and knocked at her door, but there was no answer. Gently she pushed open the door. Anne lay against the pillows, and Eleanor knew at once she was dead. For a long while she stood quite still staring at the corpse. In death her mother seemed so small and still, whereas in life she had seemed tall and vibrant, always moving, always smiling. The pain at the centre of her soul grew until she could stand it no longer, and she ran into the garden and threw herself on to the grass and cried out in anguish, 'Why have you left me in this world alone? Why?'

All she could hear was the shudder of a tractor in a nearby field and the barking of a dog. She lay on her back and stared up at the heat haze of an August sky, the round yellow sun of a child's painting, and she repeated over and over to herself, 'Where are you now, my darling mother?'

All day Eleanor sat by her mother's bed holding the hand that was still warm, feeling the warmness leaving the body, letting her tears fall steadily on the unfeeling skin. The child in her womb moved and Eleanor thought to herself, 'I am not alone, I have my children, the born and the unborn . . . Without these children I should feel a blast of loneliness so cold that I should die . . . but I shall not die . . . I shall live and I shall carry you in my heart and in my mind all the days of my life. Oh, my mother, my darling mother, I shall miss you and mourn you for ever.'

The funeral was in Florence. Marcia came alone without Ralph, who sent a thousand apologies, but there had been a terrible forest fire, and he could not leave Kirkenny. Karl Henkel came from Munich and played Bach on the organ, and after the service he gave Eleanor and Marcia lunch at Harry's Bar. Karl held his glass high and drank to the memory of his friend, and to her daughters, and there were tears in his eyes.

In the afternoon the sisters climbed the hill to the church of San Miniano with its breathtaking view of Florence and then walked in the cool of the cypress trees.

'I'm so glad you came,' Eleanor said.

'I had to come . . . she was my mother too, you know. I wasn't as close as you, but I loved her very much and I shall miss her. I wasn't a very good daughter. I took from her but I didn't give back. I wish I'd made more effort, taken her on a few nice holidays, given her some fun, you know, but I kept pretending there was no time, and now it's too late. She was a wonderful mother to me. That's why I'm here, to thank her.'

Eleanor looked into her sister's beautiful face and wondered, 'Is she happy? Is she all right?'

Suddenly Marcia said, 'I'm having another child. Oh, don't look like that! This time it's Ralph's.'

'I'm so pleased for you,' Eleanor said quietly. 'So very very pleased.'

At Florence station Eleanor saw Marcia on to a train bound for Pisa airport.

'Give my love to Ralph and tell him that a Brazilian woman paid a lot of money to look at his beautiful body!'

'I won't tell him anything of the sort.'

Anne Wynn had carefully divided her estate between her two daughters. To Marcia she left her house, to Eleanor her possessions. Eleanor, who had decided to stay on in Italy now that her mother was dead, came to England and spent several days at Dyne sorting through Anne's belongings, and only then did she appreciate the variety of her inheritance. There were boxes of letters from her father to her mother (she would take these to Italy and read them later), and there were trunkloads of artefacts and curios from tribes all over the world which her father had so carefully collected in his lifetime of exploration. Eleanor delved into the trunks and pulled out wooden carvings, feather headdresses, shells and horns and twisted tusks, and leather pouches and ivory carvings and even a dried head from Borneo.

She decided to keep almost everything, and build some glass cases and put these strange objects on show, and gradually find out what they were. (In this way she would find out more about her father.) But one large terracotta figure, a fertility goddess, was too ugly to look at, even behind glass, and Eleanor gave it to Sotheby's to auction. Two months later back in Italy she opened a letter to discover that it had fetched £68,000 as a masterpiece of pre-Columbian art.

With this, her father's money (she always thought of it as such), Eleanor decided to make Italy her home. She bought a small house on the outskirts of Cortona and engaged a farmer's wife, to help her with the children. She would have to keep her studio in London until she had completed the painting of the Queen; then she would sell it and buy a studio in Rome, and move between the city and the country, from portraits of fashionable Italians in Valentino dresses to landscapes of the wild hills of Umbria. In Italy she could educate her children for free, and the huge sums of money she would have needed in England to send them to private schools would go on holidays and travel. 'We shall have a lovely life!' she told herself. To her surprise Dominic was won over by the idea too, and he talked of opening an office in Rome, and cultivating the *società Romana*. The only casualty would be Rosie, who was still living in Eleanor's studio in London, waiting for her return.

'I'm not coming back,' Eleanor told her over the telephone.

'What's up then? Have you found a fella?'

'No. It's nothing like that. I've found a new home. But it

means that I'll have to sell the studio. Not for six months or so, mind you. First I have to paint the Queen.'

'I beg your pardon?'

'I'll tell you about that when I see you. I just wanted to let you know so that you and Dolly had plenty of time to make plans.'

'I've made other plans already. I'm getting married. Me and Jeff. But you've got to be there. If you like you can bring the Queen!'

Eleanor had Lucy, her baby daughter, in the Ospedale degli Innocenti in Siena. From her window she could see a cluster of farmhouses, an old convent surrounded by a small vineyard, neat rows of vines stretching across white soil. She could hear the distant rumble of a tractor and the shouts of farm labourers in the fields, and she could smell the dampness of autumn.

Lucy was dark with blue eyes and wonderfully grave, and Orlando kissed the tiny face again and again and would not sleep unless his sister slept in his room. In the morning he would stand in his cot and look down at the sleeping baby and shout, 'Baby, wake up! Wake up!'

Once again Eleanor was absorbed in every detail of this new being. She would hold the little girl in her arms and stare down at the puckered face, and all the questions of human existence seemed answered in these moments of total love. When Lucy was asleep Eleanor missed her, and waited eagerly for the child to wake; and as she sucked at her bottle (this time she did not even try to breast-feed) Eleanor whispered, 'I shall be at your waking and at your sleeping, and my love for you is infinite.'

30 There were no birds in the Italian winter sky, not even in spring so the local people said; the Italians had shot them all. Eleanor stared into the birdless cerulean blue sky and felt the heat of past summers stored in the infinite blueness above; there was a clarity and a warmth even on the coldest days and a promise of the heat to come. As she painted outside, wrapped in sweaters, Eleanor could feel the history of Italy rising from the land itself. Beyond the ridge of wooded hills lay Lake Trasimene, where Hannibal defeated the Romans. Eleanor imagined the screams of elephants and the bloodcurdling battle cries of Hannibal's soldiers as they plunged their spears into Roman stomachs. In the age of Rubens she might have been commissioned to paint a thirty-foot epic of the Battle of Trasimene; instead, she painted a cypress tree alongside a crumbling church. Inside her house, stacked against a wall, were seventeen finished canvases, and Dominic had fixed the date for the summer exhibition: 'Eleanor Wynn in Italy'.

Eleanor marvelled at the way Italians behaved with children, especially the men, who would pick up Orlando and kiss his round face, and call him sweet names, while the women would cluster round Lucy and smile and chatter to the bewildered baby. Eleanor felt comfortable in this land of uninhibited love, and she knew that Italy would always be her home.

It was the Communist grocer in the local shop at Pergo, a small man called Pietro with a fine moustache, who asked the question, 'Are the children baptized?'

Eleanor shook her head, and Pietro threw up his hands and said, *'Bisogna! Bisogna!'*

'Indeed,' Eleanor thought, 'the time has come.'

It was to be a joint affair, Orlando and Lucy to be christened at the same time, and the godparents would act for both children. After much telephoning and a visit to the English church in Florence Eleanor arranged the date for mid-December.

The excitement of Christmas was in the air; shops were decorated in gold and silver tinsel, and children pressed their faces to the panes of glass and stared with longing at the bright new toys in shop windows. 'This is a time of joy,' Eleanor thought.

Regina Bruce was the first godparent to arrive. She came on the train from Milan, and there were photographers waiting at Cortona station, and autographs to be signed. (Her *Tosca* at La Scala had been a triumph.) She brought with her Augusta, her Portuguese maid, and her son Harry, a beautiful child with blond hair and large brown eyes.

'Not bad for pot luck,' Regina said, stroking his head.

At last Eleanor and Regina met as mothers. Each one found the other more beautiful, more calm and infinitely happier. To Eleanor, Regina seemed like a woman reborn, she was confident and carefree, on the crest of life's wave. Her skin was that of a young woman, and Eleanor told her so.

Regina laughed and said, 'It's the hormones. When you have a baby they're renewed! We all look ten years younger – and that includes you. My God, what a transformation! When I think of you in New York, wandering around my apartment like some sort of sheet-white zombie, with that cadaverous expression and bloodshot eyes – '

'I did not have bloodshot eyes.'

'Did you ever! And that sort of deeply unhealthy pallor, like some consumptive about to kick the bucket. Look at you now – superb! And always smiling. Have you ever smiled so much since you had the children? I'd forgotten how to smile, I swear to God. The muscles were unused, and all of a sudden there I was, grinning from ear to ear, all day long, and by God, in the middle of the night I'd sit up, think of Harry and off I'd go again, smiling! You know, Eleanor, I can't think what I did before Harry. How did I spend my day?' Regina took Eleanor's hand and said, 'Isn't everything great? Just great!'

'Yes.'

'You know, so many people – people I thought were my friends – tried to persuade me to have an abortion. I swear it! They said, "At your age you will ruin your voice. You'll never adjust." So I said to them, "OK, then I'll ruin my voice." But it didn't happen. In fact, the amazing thing is, my voice is better than ever. Even the critics have noticed. They're talking about Regina Bruce's new maturity. I felt like saying to them, "Hey, you guys, it's the new baby, that's the secret!" '

In the sharp December light they walked along the ridge of hills, through woods with tangled trees; sunlight filtered through the naked black branches and old, dead leaves crackled beneath their feet; and later they drank the red wine of the region and talked and laughed, and felt so well in each other's company. Eleanor thought to herself, 'I treasure the friendship of this woman.'

At one point in the evening Regina said, 'You've heard about Vincent? He's having a rough ride – Dasha's left, the children have taken her side, whatever that means, and now Ethel Wingate thinks he's the devil and won't lend him any more money, and he's deep into debt over *Boris Godunov*. Although the latest rumour is that he's found an Arab to foot the bill.'

'Vincent is indestructible,' Eleanor said. 'And he's brilliant. Did you see *Bohème*? It was beautiful. He's got something to offer the world, a sort of genius. No one person is indispensable to Vincent, and as far as money goes he'll always find a backer.'

'My God, you still love him.'

'I'll never go back to him.'

'Dangerous word, "never".'

'I shall never go back to that state of submission. I'm a free woman, Regina, and I would not change my state with kings!'

'Just promise me one thing – you won't pine.'

'I won't pine.'

They laughed and drank and ate spaghetti and the evening slipped into night; and by candlelight they drank more wine while the children slept and Augusta watched an old American film dubbed into Italian, and the log fire crackled and spluttered.

'You made me feel guilty, you know that? I haven't told you, but Larry wants to get married. Do you remember Larry Stern – my agent? He's very sweet and he loves Harry. I've been telling myself it's not such a bad idea. Until now. You make me feel I shouldn't do it.'

'Of course you should marry him if you want to.'

'We work together, and now we sleep together . . .'

'Marry him!'

'You make me feel guilty.'

'That's your problem.'

Both women laughed and Regina said, 'It's good to see you like this, so sure of your ground.'

Dominic and Alexei arrived together on the same aeroplane and took the train from Pisa to Florence and went directly to the English church of San Marco in Via Maggio where Eleanor stood by the font holding Lucy, who was wrapped in blankets. Orlando stood impatiently, longing to run up and down the pews and pinch his new friend Harry, who was pulling on his mother's arm and making faces at the sombre paintings on the wall. The shopkeeper Pietro was there with his large, pink-faced wife and his two daughters, all smiling. It was a short and simple service, during which Eleanor prayed to her dead father and to her dead mother, thanking them for her life, and reassuring them, 'I'm all right; I've got two beautiful children and wonderful, wonderful friends, and the example of your love and devotion will shine in my heart for as long as I live,' and as she thought this the tears came to her eyes.

They drove back to Cortona in the late afternoon, and the children were taken off to the *gelateria* by Augusta and Andrina, while the others went into a local café and drank capuccino. Alexei chain-smoked and asked about the responsibilities of a godparent for a man who did not believe in God.

'What can I do? I cannot give religious instruction.'

'Love,' Eleanor said firmly, 'that's what Orlando needs from you, Dr Kinski!'

Dominic leaned across the table and said, 'And lots of presents, Alexei! That's what children like. Large, exciting packages to open!'

That evening the four friends had dinner together in Cortona. They told stories late into the night; no one wanted the evening to end. It occurred to Eleanor as she looked around the table that they were all free beings, and all single. No one was trapped by an unhappy marriage nor jaded by the disappointments of everyday life. Suddenly she was on her feet, holding a glass of wine.

'I want to thank you all for coming. And I want to tell you that I love you very much.'

'Oh my God,' Dominic said, 'Eleanor is having one of her sentimental spasms. We're all meant to turn on the taps and have a good boo-hoo.'

'That was a lovely speech,' Regina said, laying her hand on Eleanor's arm. Alexei blew more smoke into the air and stared at Eleanor with bloodshot eyes.

It was a mild night, and after dinner they wandered in front of the magnificent steps of the fourteenth-century town hall into the main square, where men were sitting drinking in the few late-night bars, and somewhere music was playing.

Eleanor took Alexei by the arm and said, 'Come live with me, and be my love.'

'Impossible!'

'You needn't look so frightened, Alexei. I'm only reciting poetry.'

Alexei looked at Eleanor, his eyes bright with amusement. Then he threw back his head and laughed loudly, and the laugh echoed against the walls of the great town hall and rose up to the red-ochre rooftops of Cortona and lost itself in the December sky, among the winter stars.